NAME MAKER

A SAM POPE NOVEL

ROBERT ENRIGHT

In memory of Liam Seager,

CHAPTER ONE

As always, the gun felt comfortable in his hand.

Sam Pope crouched beside the parked lorry, shielded from the few streetlights that were still working, as well as the full moon, which illuminated the night sky with a beautiful glow. The cool spring evening had only just dipped into darkness, and a gentle breeze coasted across the street, tickling his muscular forearm as he held the weapon.

After nearly two decades as one of the UK's most dangerous ever snipers, and a few years as the country's most wanted vigilante, the Glock 17 that he held in his grip felt as much a part of him as the hand that clasped it tightly. It had been a long road to this moment, one which Sam had never expected to travel again, especially after walking away from his war against crime under the false pretence of his death. Despite his staged demise, helped by a notorious Motorcycle Gang in South Carolina, The Death Riders, nearly two years ago, Sam had found his way back once again. When he had first taken a stand against the criminal underworld, it was an outlet for him. A way to deal with the devastating death of his son, Jamie, who had been killed nearly six years ago by an errant drunk driver who had escaped the full penalty of the law. From that moment on, with the remaining fragments of his heart still beating, Sam had channelled his deadly skills into bringing justice to those outside the law, for those who couldn't fight back.

Jamie's death had ripped a hole through Sam's life, costing him his marriage to Lucy and shutting him off from the world. While she had managed to move on and find happiness in a new marriage, Sam had never been able to forgive himself for failing to protect his son.

For failing to do what a father should do.

In the years since, some of the most dangerous and powerful criminals the UK had ever seen had fallen by his trigger finger.

Frank Jackson.

Andrei Kovalenko.

Harry Chapman.

General Ervin Wallace.

And most recently, Slaven Kovac, a brutal ex-mercenary who had staked a claim to the throne that Sam had left vacant when he slit Harry Chapman's throat. But that wasn't the reason Sam had returned to the fight.

It had been personal.

A good friend of his, Sean Wiseman, a man who Sam had pulled out of the criminal lifestyle and thrust into the mentorship of Adrian Pearce, found himself in the wrong place at the wrong time. Beaten to near death in a vile act of intimidation, Wiseman had done nothing but fall in love with a reporter who was on the cusp of the dangerous breakthrough.

A story that people were willing to shed blood over.

Sam just made sure the rest of the blood that was shed was their own.

Since then, with the rumours of his return escalating within the press and multiple police forces, Sam had all but confirmed them when he took down Slaven Kovac's gun and drug operation by destroying one of his shipments before gunning down him and his entire crew in Kovac's remote cabin in the Suffolk woodland. An undercover police officer, Jack Townsend, received the plaudits and was hailed a hero. Townsend was a good man and had saved Sam's life by hauling him out of the blazing building Sam had burnt to the ground.

Kovac's entire operation was nothing but ash, and despite Townsend doing his best to deflect away any notion that Sam Pope was involved, the police and media soon started to piece it together. After Sam's vengeance for Wiseman's attack, the police found the slaughtered body of Daniel Bowker and his crew, jumpstarting the idea that Sam Pope was alive and well. A few weeks later, Kovac and his entire operation were put in the ground, cementing their theory.

Sam Pope was back.

The Metropolitan Police had already released a statement claiming they were to coordinate a nationwide operation to bring him to justice, and that the sins of the men that Sam killed didn't wash away his own. The press had jumped all over it like a breaking celebrity scandal, each one throwing their own spin on what Sam Pope truly stood for.

To some, he was a murderous psychopath who needed to be stopped.

To others, mirroring the take of the sadly deceased Helal Miah, Sam was the hero the country needed.

Either or, as Sam crouched against the side of the lorry, he knew that now he had returned to the fight, there was no way back off the road he had chosen. His one and only chance to walk away and disappear had been thrown away, and now he knew that eventually, despite everything he did to stay a step ahead, there were only two ways his journey ended.

Prison.

Or death.

There would be no riding off into the sunset, and as a soldier who had faced the barrel of many a gun, he didn't fear death. There would come the time where he would see his life flash before his eyes, and he would cling tightly to the images of his son and hope that Jamie was there to welcome him on the other side. But until that moment came, Sam knew he had to keep fighting.

To fight back.

That was what had brought him to the abandoned industrial estate just outside of Draycott in Derbyshire. Less than ten miles out of the city centre, the industrial park had once housed a number of major UK businesses, providing a perfect central location for their manufacturing needs. But over time, as businesses cut costs and sought cheaper alternatives overseas, the large factories soon found themselves emptied and abandoned. Although not an impoverished area of the country, as had happened with numerous factory towns, hard times had fallen across the majority of the midlands, meaning there were count-less vacant buildings such as the one Sam found himself watching.

Hard times also meant opportunities, many of which were snapped up by ambitious criminals, looking to prey on the desperate or the terrified.

Hard times also meant desperation, which saw many good, law-abiding citizens turn to drugs or worse, a life of crime, just to get through.

Headlights illuminated the street and Sam shuffled back into the shadow afforded to him by the van, and he watched as a grey minivan approached the abandoned factory on the other side of the street. As if by clockwork, as the van swung round to reverse, the shutter that adorned the factory wall began to rise, welcoming the vehicle into its dark mouth. Within a matter of seconds, the van had been expertly guided into the darkness, and the shutter slammed shut.

That was Sam's signal to move.

Keeping low to the ground, Sam swept the street with his expert eye and tucked his Glock into the waistband of his jeans before scurrying across the empty road, through the chain-link gate and pressed himself against the factory wall. With his ear close to the shutter, he listened to the commotion within.

Two doors slammed shut, indicating two people getting out of the van. Two voices could be heard, swiftly followed by another.

A minimum of three men.

Minimum.

Sam had already scoped the site before, watching the operation unfold from a different vantage point, just so he could mentally document the process. The last two times he'd taken on criminal outfits, he had gone in blind, which had proven a near fatal mistake on both occasions. Bowker's men had cornered him in an abandoned factory, only for Sam to just about survive. Without the help of Jack Townsend, Sam would have been incinerated alive in a burning mansion.

A Sam Pope that went in unprepared was dangerous.

A Sam Pope that had done his homework was deadly.

Once a week, Sam had watched as the grey minivan entered the factory before exiting less than thirty minutes later. Having followed the van before, Sam had ascertained that it belonged to Hakan Sanli, a Turkish drug-dealer who had stepped up to run the drug imports formerly under the control of one of Slaven Kovac's men. Transporting drugs from the Port of Felixstowe, Sanli and his henchman had carved out a nice payday from the embers of Kovac's broken empire. Driving them one hundred and seventy miles across the country, Sanli would then drop them to his benefactor, George Murphy, who had become a prominent drug dealer in the Derbyshire area. Despite his illegal operation, Murphy wasn't a hard man to track down, and Sam had spent a few days following the criminal as he flashed his ill-gotten wealth in bars and casinos, all while under the watchful eye of his bodyguard, Terence. Murphy was dangerous, and Sam had the testimony of a number of local businesses about the man's violent temper and more worryingly, his undeserved sense of importance.

Terence, however, was a mystery to Sam.

But judging from the man's size, his flattened knuckles and permanently crooked nose, Sam could at least logically estimate that the man enjoyed a scrap or two.

Murphy's distinctive Irish accent echoed behind the shutter, and Sam pushed away from the wall and followed the building round to the far side. Earlier that evening, before the incumbents had arrived, Sam had driven his elbow through the glass pane of the emergency exit, meaning gaining entry to the building was simple. As quietly as he could manage, Sam slid his arm into the opening, thankful for the protection of his leather jacket, and he slowly pressed down on the release bar that ran the length of the door.

The secure lock flicked open with a gentle clang, quiet enough to be absorbed by Murphy's ego, and Sam entered the abandoned factory and pulled the door gently behind him. The emergency corridor was pitch-black, with only the far end illuminated by the dim lighting of the main factory floor, which Sam used to guide himself forward. With each careful step, Murphy's voice boomed louder, the man making thinly veiled threats to his Turkish business partners, all while maintaining they were going to be rich men.

With the economy taking one of its most severe hits in decades, unemployment and poverty had washed over so much of the country that people had become easy targets. As desperation kicked in, those affected looked for any escape, and by undercutting the drug market, along with cutting the cocaine with laundry detergent didn't just mean they could sell more, it also meant they could sell cheaper than any other rival drug dealers in the area. It had pulled in a number of "employees", all of whom had begged Murphy for a slice of the action. With an ego in constant need of satisfying, Murphy had been more than happy to expand his product's reach, which was now the most notable strain of cocaine in the entire county.

But it was also the deadliest.

By cutting the already potent and dangerous drug with detergent it had caused an increase in overdoses within his customer base. Sam knew, from the time he spent working inside the Met over three years ago, that a drug overdose didn't register highly on the police's list of priorities. Ironically, his own fight against such criminals had pulled the police's attention away from them.

To the police, men like Sam were more of a danger to the public than those who preyed on them.

There was no way of knowing how many deaths Murphy was responsible for, but Sam knew, without intervention, there would be countless more.

As he took considered steps towards the doorway to the factory floor, Murphy's booming laugh echoed through the building, with the wild claims that he ran things now. Moments later, a gunshot rang out, followed by the unmistakable sound of a dead body hitting the ground.

Sanli yelled something angrily in Turkish, his words

laced with venom, before they were instantly shut off by another gunshot.

Sam backed up against the corridor wall, his shoulder in line with the door frame, and ever so slightly, he arched his head around the corner.

Murphy was in the midst of taking a deep breath, the gun loosely hanging by his side. Before him, on the large table, were piles of white blocks, wrapped in clingfilm. Stacks of money and a few guns were also visible. Sam noted the weapons, confident they were loaded, and then looked at the two bodies on the floor. Sanli and his associate were dead, their prone bodies quickly being surrounded by their own blood as it pooled around them. Terence, Murphy's loyal attack dog, hauled Sanli's feet up and carelessly dragged his body across the factory floor, leaving a smear of blood behind him like an injured slug.

Two other men were present, both seemingly unmoved by the unceremonious ending of a partnership. To Murphy and his crew, it was a hostile takeover, and as Sam moved back into the corridor, he knew he was responsible for some of the chaos.

He had removed Harry Chapman from the criminal machine, and from the moment he had slit the man's throat with a box cutter inside a maximum-security prison, he had set off a chain of events that had undoubtedly led to moments like this. Men like Murphy, and before him, Slaven Kovac, who saw an empty throne atop a pile of drugs and money and fancied themselves as the rightful heir.

Murphy had got a taste, and clearly, it had only whetted his appetite.

'Clean this fuckin' shite up and then let's get this movin'.' Murphy ordered, placing a cigarette between his lips and lighting it. His crew went to work moving Sanli's associate from the room as he blew a victorious plume of smoke into the air.

Sam took a moment, drawing his shoulders back and cracking his neck slightly. Now into his forties, his body, despite the peak physical condition he kept himself in, had been through the wringer one time too many.

The scars of war adorned his body, and he needed to work out any stiffness from it. It had been nearly a month since he'd taken down Kovac, and since then, he'd tried to lie low.

Tried to finally keep his promise to his son.

A promise not to kill anymore.

He took a breath, patted the Glock that was pressed against the base of his spine and hoped he wouldn't have to use it. Given what had just transpired, he doubted it.

But he would give them a chance at least. He owed it to Jamie to try.

'Here we go,' he uttered to himself, and then stepped out of the corridor and into the dim light of the factory.

CHAPTER TWO

George Murphy loved being a criminal.

After years spent working in construction in Dublin, Murphy had eventually found himself unemployed, as the recession hit his home country like the plague. With a rocky marriage that was undercut constantly by his adulterous ways, his wife left him as soon as his employment did. Desperate, he had taken stock of what he could do to get ahead, and with little to no education, he turned to the one thing he knew he could rely on.

His penchant for violence.

Murphy had gained a reputation throughout the bars and pubs in the city as a man who didn't just know how to handle himself in a fight, but as a man who actively enjoyed it. Growing up with two older brothers and a father who drank, Murphy could take a beating.

He quickly learnt how to dish one out as well.

But it was two months after his wife had left him that Murphy had his awakening. Stepping outside of a local pub for a cigarette, he stumbled straight into an awkward drug deal. As the punter ran away in panic, the dealer, foolishly trying to save face, squared up to Murphy with fake aggression. Reasonably wasted and with months of pent-up fury coursing through his body, Murphy unloaded on the man with reckless abandon. Once the man had stopped moving and the gasps from the onlooking crowd quickly turned to emergency calls, Murphy took off and within hours, he was hiding away on a boat across the Irish Sea. Once he arrived in England, he took up a job as a bouncer, found his way into the drug game and in the three years since, he'd been biding his time.

A year after Murphy arrived back in the country, Sam Pope eliminated Harry Chapman, declaring it open season for any perspective drug lord. When news of Sam's demise filtered through the country, it was as if a starting pistol was fired into the sky. The criminal underworld began to eat itself, with every ambitious criminal slithering over each other, trying their best to get a stranglehold on the country.

Some came close.

But the landscape had changed with the recent murder of Slaven Kovac and the destruction of his empire. While others were running scared, Murphy had stepped up, grabbing the opportunity and now, as he lowered his gun on the table before him, he knew he'd made the right choice.

As the bodies of Hakan Sanli and his associate were being carted away to be disposed of, Murphy drew a long, victorious pull on his cigarette. With Sanli out of the way, he would take over the importing of the drugs at the Port of Felixstowe, filling the gap Kovac had vacated. Without Sanli taking his cut, Murphy's grip on the cocaine supply in the Midlands was ironclad, and with his adoration of the lifestyle, he was already making plans to expand.

To take everything.

Taking another puff of his cigarette, he tipped his head back and blew the smoke upwards, allowing the rush of killing two men to filter through his body like a good meal.

Out of sight, Terence was dragging the bodies to the

van, where they would be taken to a local scrapyard. Tommy, one of Murphy's crew, had family who worked there, and they'd be more than happy to stuff the bodies in the next car headed to the crusher.

Job done.

Murphy heard the footsteps before he opened his eyes and smiled.

'I think that went well, Terence. What do you think?'

'I think you're done here.'

The unfamiliar voice sliced through Murphy's victory like a bone saw, and his eyes flared with rage. He turned to the muscular man who was approaching from the far corridor. With the dim lighting offering a modicum of visibility, Murphy snarled as the man approached. He was over six feet tall, with broad shoulders that impressively filled his leather jacket. His short, brown hair was parted slightly at the side, with flecks of grey at the temple. A similar shade had begun to dominate the thick stubble that adorned his powerful jaw.

As the man approached with his hands raised slightly, as if in surrender, Murphy felt a cocktail of excitement and fear rattle around in his stomach.

The man stepped into the brighter light, roughly ten feet from the table, and confirmed what Murphy had ascertained.

Sam Pope.

'Well, fuck me.' Murphy chuckled, taking a final puff of his cigarette. 'The pigs weren't lying for once. You're Sam Pope.'

'And, like I said, you're done here.'

'Is that so?' Murphy dropped the butt on the concrete and stamped it out, allowing the smoke to filter through his nostrils. His eyes flicked to the gun on the table.

Sam saw it.

'Don't,' Sam warned. 'There's a much easier way to do this.'

'Is this the speech?' Murphy mockingly trembled. 'Is this what everyone gets to hear before the great Sam Pope puts them down? Let me tell you something, things have changed, son. You, you had some input in that. When you put some of those big hitters in the ground, you opened up the playing field for guys like me. And…for guys like him.'

Murphy pointed to behind Sam, and out of the corner of his eye, Sam could see the figure of a man emerge a few feet behind him. He couldn't tell if the man was armed or not, but judging by his stance, he was like a coiled spring ready to launch.

'And the others?' Sam raised an eyebrow at Murphy, who seemed to be enjoying himself.

'Well, Shane is the gentleman behind you.' Two more men appeared from the shadows of the factory, this time behind Murphy. One of them was unmistakably Terence, whose hulking frame was maximised by the tight T-shirt that clung to his body. His blood-stained hands held a cigarette, which he lifted casually to his crooked mouth. The other, a scrawnier, unruly looking man, completed Murphy's crew. 'This is Terence, and this ugly cunt is Michael. He might look small, but just like his mother, he never knows when he's had enough. Isn't that right, Mikey?'

'The woman's a saint.'

Murphy chuckled and then swept his hands out.

'Like I said, Sam. Is this how it goes? Because by the looks of things, we have you outnumbered and surrounded. And we also have guns. I'd say that puts us at an advantage and puts you up shit creek.'

'Actually, what you have done is give me time. Time I didn't think I was going to have.'

'What the fuck are you talking about?' Murphy spat.

'Did he call the police?' Shane piped up from behind Sam.

'Don't be stupid, you twat,' Murphy angrily replied. 'This man doesn't work with the police. He's alone. Alone and right now, he looks like he's pretty fucked.'

Sam rolled his eyes.

'When I heard you kill both Sanli and his friend, I only thought it was you and Terence in here. But you've just introduced me to your team and given me enough time to reasonably size up how quickly I can take them out. Now Shane, despite not seeing him' – Sam jabbed a thumb over his shoulder – 'he needs to take a few paces to get to me, which means I know when he's coming. Judging by your disposition, George, you're probably going to go for the gun. Terence, you'll be the problem I have to handle, and thankfully, George here has given me enough time to put together a loose plan on how I can do that. And Mikey, is it? You're the furthest away right now, so you'll probably watch it unfold, panic slightly, and then go for the gun as well when George doesn't quite make it. However, I doubt you've used a gun before and therefore, by the time you even register how deceptively heavy it is, it will just be me left standing. In which case, you'll have two options, one of which ends with you still alive.'

A silence greeted Sam's bold statement, accompanied by a nervous shuffling from a few of the men before him. Sam had hoped to rattle them, knowing that despite their ambition, they were still small time. George Murphy clearly had no problem using a gun, and Terence was a slab of violence. The other two were lackeys, and when push came to shove, there was no chance Murphy was paying them enough to put their life on the line.

Not when the man who was claiming it was a man with Sam's reputation.

'Boss?' Shane called out again, trying, and failing, to keep the nerves from his voice.

'Now, there is another option.' Sam said, taking a few steps towards Murphy and the table. 'You can think twice about going for that gun. Tell your boys to step down, and you guys wait patiently for the police to arrive and shut this operation down.'

Murphy burst into laughter, exaggerating it by holding his stomach. Mikey smirked nervously while Terence remained stoic. After a few belly laughs, Murphy pretended to wipe his eyes.

'Oh boy, that's a good one. The great Sam Pope. Killer of criminals, asking us to play nicely. What's the matter, Sam? You lost your bottle?'

Sam gritted his teeth and pulled his lips into a thin line as he contemplated the promise he'd made to his late son.

A promise he had broken time and again.

No more killing.

'I'm just trying to do things a little different this time round.'

'Well, fuck me.' Murphy clapped sarcastically. 'Sam Pope, turning over a new leaf. Unfortunately for you, you dozy cunt, I have no intention of doing that. In fact, being the bastard who put a bullet in Sam Pope's skull will make me. So, if anything, I should probably thank you for what's coming next.'

'Last chance, George,' Sam offered, holding his hands up slightly.

'I'm bored now…'

Murphy stepped towards the table, his hand reaching for the gun. As he did, Sam leapt forward, covering the space he'd reduced while talking, and he planted his left foot firmly on the ground. Using the momentum, Sam launched his right leg forward, driving the sole of his boot into the edge of the table and pushing it with all his might.

The table shunted violently forward; the edge driving painfully into Terence's stomach. As the big man hunched over in pain, Murphy wildly clamoured at the gun, which slid off the table and rattled onto the concrete, along with a stack of unmarked notes. Murphy turned in fury but was immediately met with a vicious right hook from Sam, sending him sprawling across the table and into the stacks of pre-packed cocaine. Footsteps echoed behind Sam as Shane rushed forward, but Sam threw all his body weight backwards, driving an elbow into the man's gut, and then in one swift movement, hooked an arm under the man's shoulder and lifted him off the ground. Shane flipped over, and his spine collided sickeningly with the solid edge of the table before he crumpled onto his neck on the hard ground below.

Murphy pulled a knife from his pocket and slashed wildly at Sam, who dodged a few swipes before blocking with his forearm, and then driving his elbow with trained precision into Murphy's jaw. Murphy dropped the knife, which Sam caught with his other hand, and as the leader flopped onto the table, his head rattled from the blow. Sam pinned Murphy's hand onto the table and then drove the knife through the centre of it.

Murphy let out a blood-curdling scream as the blade ripped through his bone and tendons, burst through his palm and embedded itself in the wood of the table, pinning him in place.

Terence.

Sam ducked a sledgehammer of a right hook, and as he swivelled away, he slid his hand to the back of his jeans and retrieved his Glock 17. Dropping to one knee, Sam lifted the gun, gripped it expertly, drew the sight to his eyeline, and squeezed the trigger.

The bullet flew from the barrel and obliterated Terence's shinbone, and the previously mute monster howled in agony as he dropped to the ground. His meaty hands slapped over the devastating bullet wound. With the behemoth grounded and groaning in agony as the blood pumped through his fingers, Sam stood and surveyed the situation.

Terence was down.

Shane was motionless.

Murphy was pinned to the table and roaring in agony.

As predicted, Mikey was the last one standing, his eyes wide in shock and his body shaking slightly. Having witnessed the entire crew be systematically taken apart, he watched in shock as Sam slid the gun into the back of his jeans, turned and faced him. Straightening the lapels of his leather jacket, Sam raised his eyebrows at Mikey, as if to say *I told you so.'*

Murphy's pain-stricken voice cut through the silence.

'Fuckin' kill him, Mikey.'

Predictably, Mikey's eyes shot to the gun on the ground, and he darted towards it, trying his best to make up the ground as Sam also approached the weapon. Mikey whipped it off the ground with one hand, and as Sam had predicted, was caught off-guard by the weight of the weapon. He'd never held a loaded gun before, and as he swung his arm up to aim it at their attacker, Sam cut him off with a clubbing forearm. Sam's power rocked Mikey's arm, causing him to relinquish the weapon. Terrified, Mikey swung his left arm in a wild attempt to land a blow. Sam ducked, driving his knee into the young man's gut, drilling the air from his body and causing him to hunch over. In one fluid motion, Sam then drove his elbow down into the back of the man's skull, shutting his lights out and leaving him stretched across the floor.

Everyone was down.

The only sounds were the agonised grunts from Murphy and Terence, and Sam leant down, lifted Mikey's gun and then turned back to Murphy. As he approached the table, he looked at Terence, who had turned a sickly pale. He was losing a lot of blood, and Sam knew they didn't have long.

'Keep pressure on it.' Sam offered to the big man, who now seemed completely vulnerable. Terence reapplied his grip, grit his teeth and rocked onto his side in a puddle of his own blood.

'Just take what you fuckin' want, okay?' Murphy begged, his entire attitude crumbling under the realisation of defeat.

'Phone.' Sam lifted the gun and pressed it against Murphy's skull. 'Now.'

'Back pocket. It's in my back pocket,' Murphy stammered. 'Please don't kill me.'

Sam stuffed his hand into the back of the man's jeans and retrieved the phone.

'Pin.'

'Eight, eight, three, four,' Murphy responded, his eyes locked on the blade that had nailed him to the table. 'Just please, don't kill me.'

'I told you, I'm doing things differently now,' Sam said calmly, as he tapped the screen three times and lifted the phone to his ear. 'Police, please. Thank you.'

'Look, just take the money. Take what you want and just let us go.'

'I don't want your money.' Sam spat through gritted teeth, and then returned his attention to the phone. 'Hi, I'd like to report a gunshot, a man with a bullet wound, a man with a stab wound, two further dead bodies and a lot of cocaine. Location is the Herman Factory in Draycott Business Park. My name? It's Sam Pope. And I'd hurry up, as one of these guys is losing a lot of blood.'

Sam hung up the phone, dropped it onto the ground, and crushed it under his boot. He knew giving his name would drastically reduce the response time, and he had no plans to greet the boys in blue at the door. Sam stepped closer to Murphy, who had given up the fight and was now kneeling against the table, his hand stuck and his head planted on the wood.

'I told you there was an easier option.'

Murphy turned his head and looked Sam dead in the eye.

'When I get out…'

'I'll be waiting.' Sam slammed his hand down on the handle of the knife, driving it another inch into the table and crushing it through Murphy's hand, drawing a blood-curdling scream. Sam turned and marched towards the emergency exit of the building, ignoring the faint groans from Terence. As he emerged out of the damaged door at the side of the factory, he straightened his leather jacket, put his head down and walked briskly towards the labyrinth of alleyways that would lead to his car. A grin threatened to break out across Sam's jaw as he headed into the dark cover of the alley, knowing that another criminal operation had been reduced to dust. He could already hear the piercing squeals of the sirens as they rippled through the night sky, trying their best to get to him.

They could keep trying.

One day, they might actually catch him.

But not tonight.

CHAPTER THREE

The entire conference room was alive with activity as journalists and cameramen jostled for position. Every seat in the room was filled by an eager reporter with their recorders and pads at the ready. Around the edges of the room, stoic, grim-faced police officers watched on disapprovingly, their hands clasped behind their backs and their shoulders straight. There was a sense of pride for all of them to be standing in a room that was adorned with the Metropolitan Police badge, and their duty was to control a room full of evasive people who were looking for blood.

Sam Pope was back.

The rumour mill had been in full flow for the past few months, ever since a London-based security operation, Stonewall Security, had been ruthlessly murdered. Although there was no hard evidence that Sam Pope had risen from the grave, the sensationalists within the journalism game had poured gasoline on the rumour.

Police Commissioner Bruce McEwan had quickly vanquished those flames, but less than a month later, Slaven Kovac, one of the most dangerous men in the country, was found dead in his remote woodland home near Norwich, along with his entire crew and the remnants of his drug and gun trade.

Someone had taken them out.

The press had a field day.

The conference room within the New Scotland Yard building was usually fairly spacious, but with so many people desperate for the scoop, the walls seemed closer together. The roof a little lower.

That was the feeling that hit Commissioner McEwan as he barged through the double doors at the back of the room and headed towards the risen stage, where a table and several microphones were waiting. His entrance caused a rise in the volume of the room, and he turned and uttered something to his Public Relations Officer, who followed behind him, her arms wrapped around a myriad of manila folders. She plonked them on the desk, and then carefully poured two glasses of water from the jug, trying her best to keep her arm from shaking.

The country was watching.

They wanted the confirmation.

Commissioner McEwan stopped as he approached his chair and removed his hat, freeing his surprisingly thick grey hair, and he ran a hand through it, re-establishing the neat parting. For a man in his mid-fifties, he was in tremendous physical shape, taking his health as seriously as he took his position as the leader of one of the world's greatest police forces. He stood over six feet tall, with his broad shoulders neatly filling the navy jumper that proudly bore the emblem emblazoned on the wall behind him. In the near two years he'd been in post, the public had rallied behind him, and his strong jaw and authoritative voice deepened with the ferocity of his Glaswegian accent, both powerful weapons at his disposal.

Commanding the respect and silence of the room just

by looking out at them, he politely nodded and then took his seat, ignoring the flashes of the cameras.

'Good morning, ladies and gentlemen,' his PR Officer began. 'In light of yesterday's arrests in Derbyshire, I'm sure you all have questions. Please, can you remain respectful while your police commissioner gives his statement and there will be time for questions afterwards.'

A few murmurs rippled through the seats.

'Unless I fancy an early lunch that is.' McEwan smiled at the crowd, who politely chuckled back at his, at times, forced charm. 'Ladies and gentlemen, thank you for your presence and your time. As I'm sure you're aware, the Metropolitan Police have been working with countless police services across the country to align our efforts to ascertain if Sam Pope is still alive. With the recent murders of prominent criminals, these rumours had gathered pace, not without some considerable work by some of the people in this room. With that being said, last night, at approximately twenty-three hundred hours, a call was made to the Derbyshire Police Department, with the caller claiming to be Sam Pope.'

An immediate outpouring of gasps and hands shot into the air.

'Is it him?'

'Is Sam Pope alive?'

'Will you catch him this time?'

The PR Officer leant towards her microphone, cutting through the noise.

'Please hold all your questions until the end.'

'Thank you, Julie. But yes, if it is him, we will catch him. Upon arriving at the scene less than six minutes after the call was made, in a sterling effort by the local officers, they arrested George Murphy, a wanted drug dealer, and his entire crew, who had been attacked. Since no money or drugs were taken from the scene, and the confirmation from George and his crew, we believe that, yes, Sam Pope carried out this attack and is now operational once again within this great country.'

'How come he didn't kill them?' A voice emanated from somewhere within the room.

'Of that, we can't be sure. It certainly doesn't fit his usual MO, however witnesses at the scene made claims that Sam himself claimed he was trying to do things differently. Let me make this very clear to everyone in this room and those who will hear this through whatever medium. Sam Pope, *if* he is in operation again, is a very dangerous man. While he may target criminals, the man is responsible for over forty deaths that we know about, as well as escaping not once, but twice from prison. As a highly trained and highly skilled army veteran, he has severe PTSD not just from his time served, but also from the tragic loss of his son. Noble as some may see him, he is without a doubt the most dangerous criminal this country has seen in a long time. Which is why as of this morning, with full parliamentary backing and funding, we are re-launching Project Watchdog, which was originally launched three years ago to bring Sam Pope to justice. This will be a nationwide task force, with the best minds and best officers from across the country pooling their efforts and intel, not just to locate Sam Pope, but to stop him before anyone else gets hurt.' McEwan took a brief pause as the journalists frantically scribbled on their pads. As he took a sip of water from his glass, he knew he'd struck the right tone of authority and he afforded himself a brief smile. 'And as for Sam Pope. If you are out there and have returned to your crusade, then I implore you to do the right thing. As a man of apparent integrity, you must know the fear you strike, not just into the hearts of the criminals you target, but of the civilians who do not follow your example. Of the good people of this country who rely on the police to keep them safe, not a broken man with a gun and a penchant for violence. You once served this country with pride and distinction, and I call upon you to keep your duty to this country and hand yourself in. Or mark my words, when we find you, and we will find you, I will bring the full force of the law down on you like the hammer of Thor himself. Thank you, ladies and gentleman.'

The room did their best to catch up with McEwan's words, all in a desperate attempt to get their question in first. Almost in unison, to the delight of Commissioner McEwan, dozens of hands shot into the sky, as his threat to Sam Pope and his promise to the public was about to spread like wildfire.

————

'*Stern words from the Commissioner of the Metropolitan Police, who not only confirmed that Sam Pope is alive and active once more, but that Project Watchdog had been resuscitated and would now work in conjunction with every police force across the country. With public safety very much the top priority, it appears that Commissioner McEwan is driven to bringing Sam Pope to justice. This has been Lynsey Beckett, for BBC News.*'

Sam hit mute on the remote control and afforded himself a smile. It was nice to hear Lynsey's Northern Irish accent once again, and it filled him with an odd sense of pride to see her anchoring such an important story. Having saved her life a few months before, he'd given her permission to tell the world that he was back, to break the story of the decade and reap the rewards.

But she hadn't.

She had appreciated just how hard he had fought to avenge the brutal beating of her boyfriend, Sean Wiseman, who'd been left in a coma by Daniel Bowker and the rest of the Stonewall Security crew. Instead, she hid Sam's involvement, giving him enough time to disappear before he ignited the manhunt himself.

Now, it would seem, he was once again public enemy number one. The new commissioner had a reputation as a bulldog, and Sam was under no illusions that the man would throw every resource at bringing him in. The same obsession had engulfed the former Deputy Commissioner Ruth Ashton, whose tunnel vision of bringing Sam down had ultimately led to her dismissal.

Sam switched the television off as he stood, stretching out his back before surveying the room. Finding temporary accommodation had never been easier, and with the fake identity that had been built for him by an old friend, he was able to book long stays at multiple Airbnbs at a time. With a small fortune left to him by the same friend, he was capable of paying for a whole month up front, which usually went down very well with the homeowners. The one-bedroom ground-floor flat he currently occupied was at the beginning of a quiet street in a small village called Spondon, situated only a few miles from the centre of Derby. The quiet streets, narrow and cobbled, offered Sam a peaceful resting place as he plotted his next move. The village was tight-knit, with most people of an age where retirement was fast approaching, and the rat race of life could be left far behind them. A few quaint shops, along with a pub, a school, and a coffee shop more or less completed the itinerary, allowing Sam to hide in plain sight. There were a number of streets with vast, expensive houses set back from the road, which told Sam that most of the people who resided in the village didn't concern themselves with the usual problems of the less fortunate, and most wouldn't even be aware of who he was. While the tabloids liked to vilify or sensationalise his war on crime, the broadsheets were less inclined.

Sam filled the kettle with water and set it to boil and then turned to the fold-out kitchen table that was bolted to the wall of the modest kitchen. He had removed all the trinkets that had adorned it and replaced them with what remained of his arsenal. Having lost some of the weapons in the brutal fight at the Kovac estate, he still had an impressive selection of guns for his mission.

Two SA80 Assault Rifles.

Two Glock 17s.

Three grenades and enough ammo to last multiple assaults.

Sam lifted the carrier bag from the floor and began to remove the cleaning products he'd brought from the large supermarket on the outskirts of the village. Having spent so long in the army, Sam lived by the code that his weapons deserved the same amount of respect as he did, and as he pulled out the fresh cloths and placed them on the table, he knew that it would take a few hours to dissemble and clean each weapon.

It would be a laborious task.

But one that he relished.

The kettle clicked, and steam bellowed from the spout and Sam turned backed to the kitchen counter. The mugs were in the top cupboard, and as he reached up for one, a stabbing pain rumbled from his shoulder. It had been a month since he had crudely treated the stab wound in his shoulder, and while he had done a decent job of cleaning and stitching it, the echoes of the attack still remained. Adrenaline had kept it quiet during his fight with Murphy and his crew, but now, having overexcited his shoulder, he gritted his teeth as his body reminded him that Commissioner McEwan wasn't the only possible way that his war on crime ended.

His body had taken a beating.

Three years ago, one of Frank Jackson's blood thirsty henchman had stabbed him.

A bullet had ripped through his thigh at the Port of Tilbury.

He still bore the burn scars from the time he was blasted down the cliff face in Afghanistan.

His broad chest, chiselled from the hours of exercise that Sam put himself through, was still tattooed with the scars of the two bullets that General Ervin Wallace had sent through him.

His ribs, while no longer broken, were as fragile as they had ever been, and Sam winced throughout the day if he moved too quickly.

Sam was born to survive.

But that survival meant suffering.

With a grimace, Sam retrieved the mug, made himself a welcome cup of tea, and then lowered himself onto the cheap wooden chair that was slotted under the table. He took a calming sip, let the taste wash away the nagging discomfort, and then he placed the tea carefully away from the weapons. He thumbed through his phone, found the BBC app and switched on *Radio One*, and set the phone beside the hot cup.

To the backdrop of the latest songs and the idle chit-chat of the presenters, Sam began to dissemble an assault rifle, hoping the white noise would replace the words of Commissioner McEwan that were racing around inside his head.

Sam knew he was being hunted once more.

Little did he know, Commissioner McEwan wasn't the only one.

CHAPTER FOUR

The violent tension in the room was palpable.

From the moment the first knuckle rapped against the metal door, Uri Zubov had been on high alert. It had taken them over a month to put all the pieces into motion, but now that the ball was rolling, they'd made their way to the United Kingdom for this exact moment. There had been loose ends to tie up in Kyiv, with the arduous process of liquifying enough assets to pull the money together, but somehow, Dana Kovalenko had been able to do it.

Once again, he had underestimated the women, which he knew was foolish on his part.

Having spent years of loyally working for her uncle Sergei, as head of security, he knew just how dangerous that name was. While he manned the front door of *Ешелон*, a nightclub that Sergei used as a base of operations which translated as 'Echelon', Uri had witnessed the empire grow. The cold, cynical grip of the Kovalenko family as they choked the country into submission. The right people in the right places were on Sergei's payroll, meaning the further he branched, the stronger his grip.

Drugs.

Guns.

Women.

A long-standing relationship with the notorious Harry Chapman opened up opportunities for the Kovalenkos to expand into the United Kingdom, and at the behest of his nephew, Andrei, Sergei soon saw a new marketplace open up.

The transfer of young English virgin girls into the European sex trade.

They came at a premium, but Sergei, who had groomed his two nephews and niece into his operation after Andrei had murdered his own father, knew they could handle it.

In fact, he'd been proud of them all, and Uri sensed it whenever Sergei gloated about how the Kovalenko name wasn't just feared, it was envied.

Then, over two years ago, one man brought it all to its knees.

Sam Pope.

Killing both Andrei and his brother, Oleg, in a violent shootout in the UK, Sam Pope even made his way to their front door, thanks to a snivelling politician who was rotting in hell.

Sergei was killed.

The Kovalenko empire was ash.

It shouldn't have surprised Uri when Dana Kovalenko returned, having laid low for a few months. As the sole heir to the fortune, she managed to claim it before the government did, and with it, she began to rebuild.

Brick by brick.

Gun by gun.

Body by body.

While not as physically imposing as her male relatives, her mind was sharper; hardened and reshaped by the loss of her family. Behind the striking looks and crystal-clear blue eyes was a violent force of nature that had given Uri more than enough to keep him busy.

But now, as Uri cast his eyes over the four men who were sitting around the table, he realised how personal things had become.

The moment Dana Kovalenko discovered that Sam Pope was alive, everything changed. Uri was the one who'd told her, and immediately, she gave the order for Uri to put the word out.

'Five million alive. Three million dead.'

Despite how the media portrayed the world as a safe haven for its inhabitants with opportunity and wealth aplenty, there was a dark, sadistic under-belly that ran through it. A global acceptance that the world was a dark and dangerous place, and while ninety-nine per cent lived in an oblivious bubble above the precipice, it was the one per cent who thrived.

Who truly understood what it took to succeed.

It hadn't taken Uri long to find the appropriate channels to spread word of the contract Dana had put out on Sam Pope's life. Once it had filtered onto the dark web, it soon gathered pace.

Uri had been through the process countless times at the behest of Sergei, but never for such a rich bounty.

But then again, never had a target been so renowned.

So feared.

While there were usually hundreds of wannabe thugs or contract killers nipping at whatever offer was tossed into the ocean, this one landed differently.

This one took a while.

In their line of work, death always a possibility, and most hitmen or women would balance that out with the high probability that they were more skilled than the target. That any retaliation could be handled instinctively.

This was different.

This was Sam Pope.

Eventually, once Dana had confirmed the movement of assets and the freeing of funds, they got their first offer.

Mendoza was the only name that was given, but the roll call of hits the man had performed was impressive. Born and raised in Havana, the man presented a laundry list of credentials, from years spent as a soldier within the paramilitary regiment of the Cuban Revolutionary Armed Forces, to more bespoke work as an agent for the government. Considering the blood-thirsty regimes that had led the country to the brink of war, Uri immediately green lit the application.

Sat on the far right of the room, Mendoza hadn't spoken a word, just presenting his application at the door and his refusal to remove his sunglasses spoke of the man's secrecy. His navy checked suit clung to a well-toned frame, and the tattoos that clearly covered his body peeked out from under his open collar and over his wrists, covering the backs of his hands and his fingers.

Hands that had, by the man's own admission on his response to the contract, shed the blood of over seventy political and personal targets who'd been unfortunate enough to cross his path. His hair was cropped close to the scalp, and his thin, sharp face was framed with an immaculately shaped goatee. When Uri had demanded the relinquishing of any weapons, all Mendoza handed over was a flick knife and a set of sharpened knuckle dusters. Considering the skills the man clearly had when it came to eliminating targets, he was justified in travelling light.

He also worked alone.

Which was the opposite of the burly man who was sitting across from Mendoza. His dark hair was cut in a short, neat crop that screamed military, and a thick, ginger-tinged beard covered his powerful jaw. The man was a brute, with his powerful arms folded across his barrel-like chest and resting on a gut that had started to sag. Roland Brandt was a highly decorated soldier, having served in the *Kommando Spezialkräfte*, an elite German special forces squadron, organised under the Rapid Forces Division, for twelve years. His deadly skills and unwavering efficiency had seen him recruited by General Ervin Wallace as part of Blackridge, and since its dissolution at the hands of Sam Pope, Brandt had moved into contract killing.

A man had to make a living.

Brandt had made it clear when he responded to the hit that he now led a four-man crew, including himself, which had been nicknamed the *Endwache*, which translated as the End Watch.

They were a ruthless, independent military outfit that had been running countless kill missions across Europe for the past two years. Without Wallace's power to open doors, Brandt had been able to forge a few contacts from the ashes of Blackridge, including a technical expert called Kyle Dallow, who had proven very effective in tracking down targets and lucrative contracts. When Blackridge was operational, Dallow had implemented a clever system of communication within a gaming server to hide any dispatches or requests through the *Ghosts*.

Dallow, despite Brandt's constant belittling, was the most important part of the crew. He just didn't know it.

When the name Sam Pope appeared on the kill list, Brandt was adamant on taking it.

For him, it was personal.

A few days before Ervin Wallace was killed when he plummeted from the derelict remains of the High Rise, Brandt had been tasked with bringing Sam in during an undercover operation within London Liverpool Street Station. Using a young detective as bait, Sam had lured Brandt and two other operatives into a trap, and he had handily dispatched them.

The broken bones Sam had given them, including the crooked nose in the centre of Brandt's face, weren't all he had destroyed.

Their pride and their careers had never recovered.

Will Cook and Sarah Masters, the two other Blackridge operatives who had been incapacitated that day, made up the other members of *Endwache*, and were more hesitant in taking on the job.

Brandt insisted, and although he made it clear to Uri that the crew would be taking on the job, his lone presence was enough to show that he was the one calling the shots.

Then there were the Americans.

The final name thrown into the ring to try to take down Sam Pope, but it didn't come from them personally. An elite organisation, known as The Foundation, accepted the contract and assigned two of their best assets to the job. Dana didn't care. The higher the calibre of killer, the more likely Sam Pope would be extinguished. And while both men who arrived were clearly ex-military, the only similarity was their expensive clothes.

Elias Defoe was every bit as arrogant as Uri had anticipated, with the 'jock' energy he had dismissed as a terrible stereotype in pathetic television shows. However, Defoe stank of arrogance, chewing his gum loudly and checking every so often for a reflection, to ensure that his slick hair was still intact. The Foundation had sent across the resumes for both hitmen, and Defoe, despite the deplorable attitude and punchable face, certainly had the record to back it up.

Over thirty successful contracts.

All of them kills.

However, it was the man beside him who interested Uri the most.

Jacob Nash.

Older than Defoe, and clearly more world-weary, Nash

33

was the embodiment of the strong, silent type. While Defoe mouthed off a few times about the run-down state of the meeting venue, Nash hadn't batted an eyelid. His tanned skin, clearly from an Asian heritage, was slightly wrinkled and having entered his mid-forties, his hair had long since left him.

Like Mendoza, there were glimpses of tattoos between the buttons of his shirt and poking out over the backs of his hands. Nash was big. Uri, who was no slouch himself, estimated he was about six feet four inches, and weighed at least nineteen stone of pure muscle. Along with his impressive physique, the man had over eighty confirmed kills for the Foundation alone, and Uri was sure, if he went digging deep enough into Nash's records as a Marine, he would find countless more.

The man hadn't uttered a word, yet Uri had already made a personal bet with himself that if any of the men in the room were likely to bring Sam down, then it was Jacob Nash who would do it.

Never, in his entire lifetime, working for some of Ukraine's most dangerous people, had he ever been scared of another man.

But Jacob Nash, who was sitting, disinterested, and waiting patiently as he sipped on his Starbucks coffee, had changed that.

A few glances were shot between Mendoza and Brandt, both men eyeing up the competition, and Defoe, with a toothpick arrogantly hanging out of the side of his mouth, smirked.

'If you boys are gonna fuck, why don't you get a room?'

'What you say, *vato*?' Mendoza spat back, drawing another smirk from Defoe. As Mendoza made to stand up, Defoe nonchalantly leant back in his chair, goading the man with another smirk across his classically handsome face.

'Sit down,' Brandt commanded, with his thick, emotionless German accent.

'Fucking hell, we got ourselves a German.' Defoe turned his attention to Brandt. 'Hey, Adolf, why don't you sit this one out, eh?'

'Enough.' Nash finally spoke. His soft voice carried more threat than all three men combined. Uri stood, the only one of them who was allowed to carry a weapon in the room, and he made a point of showing it. Mendoza, with his eyes glued on Defoe, straightened his blazer and then sat back down, muttering in Spanish under his breath. Brandt turned back, but not before offering a nod of respect to Nash, who didn't acknowledge it. Defoe chuckled as he sat forward and rested his hands on the table.

'Tough crowd.' He set his eyes on Uri. 'Hey, big guy, how much longer do we have to wait?'

Right on cue, the metal door at the back of the room wrenched open, the hinges screaming for attention, and the sound of high-heel shoes echoed from the shadows, signalling the meeting was ready to begin.

CHAPTER FIVE

TWO AND A HALF YEARS AGO...

Grief wasn't something Dana Kovalenko had ever experienced.

As the youngest of the three kids, Dana had never experienced life with their mother before she'd left their abusive father and after that, the terrifying grip he held on the family was something she'd grown accustomed to. While it was never explicitly laid out to her, they all knew that the reason their father, Igor, had left her alone was due to her being a girl. To him, they were useless, and the stories she'd heard of her mother's abuse only backed that up.

But the boys, Andrei and Oleg, they were to be men.

Act like men.

Be tough, like men.

It was pitiful. For as strong as Igor Kovalenko was physically, his mental state was a minefield of inadequacies. His brother Sergei was a rich and powerful crime lord, whereas Igor's only use was to watch the door at Sergei's night club and dish out a beating like an obedient attack dog. It put food on their table, but his own brother's lack of respect and reward had caused Igor to turn to the drink and turn his frustrations on those beneath him.

Andrei had taken the brunt of it.

As the oldest, Andrei was fearless in his contempt for their father, and when their old man lashed the poor teenager with his leather belt, Andrei gritted his teeth and took it. Oleg was equally silent in his punishment, and physically resembled their father in both looks and stockiness. Unlike Andrei, however, Oleg had serious learning difficulties, and he accepted the beatings as part of his upbringing.

Andrei didn't. He remembered every single one of them and with every laceration he added more fuel to a fire that would one day combust.

Dana idolised Andrei. With her father's domineering control over her life, she found herself without friends or any hope of romance. It's why she found herself falling in love with her own brother. Something she knew was gut-wrenchingly wrong but was the only conclusion to how he protected her.

Then, as she approached her mid-teens, her body changed, and she began to resemble the beautiful woman that her mother had been.

Her father took notice.

One fateful, snowy night, Igor had burst into her room, the fumes of alcohol pouring from every inch of his body. His eyes were wild with lust and as he marched towards her bed, Dana knew she would never be able to fight back. As he clawed at her bedding, his mouth salivating, he had mumbled something about always taking care of her.

That it was time to repay him.

Those would be the last words he ever spoke as without hesitation, Andrei yanked the remaining strands of their father's hair, pulling his head back.

Then he slit his throat.

Without looking back as their father gasped for life, Andrei had led her and their brother outside, where they sat in the snow and waited for Uncle Sergei to fix things. He did, and a decade later, the three of them were running a wildly lucrative sex trafficking business in England.

All because of Andrei.

Her sweet, handsome saviour.

Then Sam Pope killed him.

After laying siege to the Port of Tilbury to find a missing girl, Pope had eliminated most of the Kovalenko crew. Dana hadn't been there, but she read the reports and she knew what happened.

Andrei was surrounded by the police, on the verge of arrest, when Sam Pope removed his arm with a pinpoint shot from his sniper rifle. The blood loss from the injury sent Andrei into shock and he died on his way to hospital.

Her sweet, handsome Andrei.

Murdered.

The police sweep of the area soon found Oleg strung up from the ceiling of a nearby tower, with a rusty metal hook embedded in his jaw.

Both her brothers, dead.

Murdered.

By Sam Pope.

In her immediate panic, Dana went into hiding, avoiding Andrei's penthouse, which was soon under the guard of the authorities, and his good name was plastered across the media like a monster. After a week in a state of shock, she reached out to Sergei, hoping for some comfort, only to find that the same man responsible for her brother's deaths had finished the job.

Sam Pope had gone to her home and murdered her uncle.

Only Uri, her uncle's trusted right-hand man, had survived the onslaught, and with his help, Dana was able to return to Kyiv and lay claim to the remains of her uncle's fortune. For six months, she plotted and dreamt of her revenge, of being able to end Sam Pope's life, but not before finding those who he held dearest, and making him watch as she put them through what he had enacted on her siblings.

The pain he had caused.

But then, nearly six months after her brother had been killed, word came through that the man was dead.

Sam Pope had been killed in South Carolina and his body identified through DNA.

Dana Kovalenko felt empty. All the pain and rage that had taken hold of her every movement instantly left her, and for comfort and purpose, she turned to Uri. She knew their relationship meant more to him than to her, but she found comfort in his muscular arms and soon, she went about rebuilding the Kovalenko empire. With his ex-military background, Uri guided her into the gun traf-ficking game and silently, she funded a Croatian mercenary called Slaven Kovac who had already infested the UK with illegal weapons and drugs.

The power was returning, if not the purpose.

For the first time in two and a half years, Dana Kovalenko felt the inklings of a life returning to her.

She had money.

Power.

A dedicated partner who worshipped her how she had worshipped her brother.

It was enough to sustain her.

Then rumours began to spread through the grotesque city of London that Sam Pope was alive. As her hope built, Sam Pope's execution of Kovac and their business confirmed it.

He was alive.

And in returning from the dead, he resuscitated Dana without knowing it. From the very moment Uri uttered his name into her ears, she made a solemn promise that she would use whatever resources necessary to repay him for the pain he'd caused her.

Dana Kovalenko had finally experienced grief. But quite quickly she found that vengeance was a lot more to her liking.

———

With every click of her heel on the concrete floor, Dana felt a step closer to her revenge. As she emerged from the shadows that engulfed the edges of the room, she knew she'd drawn the attention of every male gaze awaiting her. Her pencil skirt was clasped tightly to her frame, and her open-collar shirt offered just enough to get their minds racing.

Dana smirked to herself.

All these killers in one room, yet there was nothing more dangerous than a woman.

'Gentleman,' she said warmly, offering her million-dollar smile. Her Ukrainian accent was soft and sultry. 'Thank you for your participation in this contract.'

Uri leant forward and pulled out her chair for her. Dana nodded her thanks as she sat, tossing her blond hair gently over her shoulder.

'You wanna come tuck me in, big boy?' Defoe chuckled, looking round the room for a smile. He didn't get one.

'You. Funny boy.' Dana pointed her manicured finger at Defoe. 'Now is the time for you to listen.'

'Anything for you, sweet cheeks.' Defoe winked. Nash rolled his eyes. Dana stared at the man, her cold, blue eyes drilling holes through him until he frowned with annoyance.

'Let me make clear to you all that by accepting this contract, you work for me. If you do not show me the required respect, then I will have Uri here take your balls and feed them to you. Is this understood?'

'Kinky,' Defoe uttered. Dana shot a murderous look to Defoe, who after a few moments of trying to hold her stare, eventually looked away.

'Let's get down to business.' Dana laid her hands out on the table before her. 'Three million dead. Five million alive. By accepting this contract, you are in it until one of those conditions is met. This man killed the only two people I ever loved, and I will have his soul for this. If you have to take it from him, then I will still pay you handsomely. If you offer me the opportunity to do it myself, then you get everything.'

'Who's the mark?' Nash asked politely, even going as far to raise his hand.

'Sam Pope,' Brandt said without looking back. 'Didn't you read the contract?'

'Hey, asshole. Our bosses don't give us the details, they just send us here with a name and that's it,' Defoe spat. 'Unlike you, we ain't some two-bit operation.'

'If you have his name, then you have what you need,' Dana interjected, putting out the potential fire in the room.

'I mean, who is this guy?' Nash shrugged. 'Why did he kill your brother?'

'What is this shit?' Defoe turned to his partner. 'We don't ask questions.'

'You don't shut up, either.' Mendoza finally spoke.

'Hey, Enrique Iglesias, why don't you stick your head up your fucking ass and bailamos your way outta here, eh?'

For the second time, Mendoza stood, his rage causing his fist to clench, and Defoe grinned like a Cheshire cat. As he took two steps forward from his seat, the room fell silent as Jacob Nash stood. Although he looked reluctant to do so, he stood between Mendoza and Defoe, and the weary look on his face told the hot-headed Cuban than if he needed to, he would interject. Mendoza looked Nash up and down, clearly analysing the situation before he uttered something under his breath and returned to his seat.

Uri and Dana watched on with excitement.

In that moment, they both knew that Sam Pope was no match for this man.

As Nash lowered himself into his seat, Defoe sarcastically patted him on the back, drawing a murderous look from the man. Defoe, despite trying to shrug it off, diverted his gaze and in an instant, the cocky persona disappeared.

'Are you boys done playing?' Dana asked coldly. 'To answer your question, I have five million reasons why I don't need to tell you anything more than his name is Sam

Pope and I want him alive. Dead if you have no other choice. Is that clear?'

The men nodded. Dana scowled at them before continuing.

'He is a very dangerous man. He will be armed and, according to the press, he was active in Derbyshire two days ago.'

'The press?' Defoe cut in. 'What is this guy, a celebrity?'

'He is a murderer.' Dana slammed her fist on the table. 'You have everything you need. I'd suggest not killing each other, but again, I have five million reasons why I don't care whether you live or die.'

Dana stood, and Uri followed suit, standing loyally to attention.

'Right, well, let's go kill this motherfucker,' Defoe said as he also stood. 'You boys may as well stay here. Let the pros handle it.'

Brandt turned to Defoe, who cockily winked at the bruising German.

Dana shook her head and strode back towards the shadows, disappearing behind the metal door that clunked loudly behind her. Uri marched to the other door, hauling it open for the dangerous attendees to leave, while making a show of the gun he had strapped to his waist. Mendoza was the first to leave, eyeballing Defoe as he did, who returned the gaze with an arrogant kiss. As the members of The Foundation headed to the door, Brandt cut them off, drawing a sneer from Defoe and a calculated step to the side by Nash.

Whatever Brandt was threatening to do, Nash would handle it. Uri was certain of it. However, part of him hoped he'd let the German get at least one shot in before he intervened.

'You have no idea what you're getting yourselves into.' Brandt spoke as if he was at a funeral.

'It's called a three-thousand-dollar suit.' Defoe looked at Brandt's leather jacket and then reached out and straightened the collar of it. 'You should look into it.'

Shaking his head, Brandt turned to Nash.

'You get to this guy first. Otherwise he will kill your friend.'

'He's not my friend,' Nash replied coldly.

'Ouch, Jacob. How could you?'

Brandt ignored Defoe and kept his eyes on Nash. The two behemoths were a few inches apart, and neither one would ever back down.

'You find this guy before I do. You better kill him.'

'Hey, dumbass, we get more money for him alive.' Defoe buzzed around the stare down like an unwanted fly at the picnic. Nash's eyebrow arched slightly; his interest piqued.

'You'll make more than money if you are the one to kill Sam Pope.'

Nash nodded, understanding the warning that Brandt was offering them. This wasn't a macho play by the burly German.

This was professional courtesy. Something that was clearly lost on Defoe, who screwed his face up in confusion and shrugged.

'What else will we make if we kill him?' he finally asked.

Brandt kept his eyes locked on Nash, knowing he was the one who needed to know.

'You'll make your name.'

CHAPTER SIX

Brandt had returned from his trip to London on a train straight from London St Pancras to Derby. The recently renovated train station looked like the architect had lifted its design straight from a catalogue, and as he descended the staircase to the ticket barrier, he noticed a few eyes on him.

He stood out.

As a six foot three, burly man with a thick beard, he drew attention, but there was a danger that emanated from his every movement. Brandt was a highly efficient killing machine, and although he didn't blend in, he knew that should he return any of the gazes that were on him, those responsible would quickly turn away. He readjusted the rucksack on his shoulder which housed his weapon and shimmied through the barrier when it opened.

Masters was waiting directly outside the automatic door, sitting behind the wheel of a sleek, black Mercedes which she had rented under a fake name. Brandt placed his rucksack in the boot of the car, then dropped into the passenger seat.

'Sir.' Masters was a proud soldier, and her hands were

already bringing the car to life. The sleeves of her checked shirt were rolled to the elbow, exposing a plethora of tattoos. 'Good trip?'

'I need a drink,' Brandt replied before resting his head against the leather seat. Masters understood the request for silence, and pulled away, weaving through the one-way system that engulfed Derby city centre before heading towards the Holiday Inn they'd claimed as their base for the operation. Brandt turned his head to the window. The large Derbion shopping centre was lit up spectacularly, promising its patrons the best restaurants and the latest movies.

Secretly, Brandt had hoped nobody else would have been foolish enough to accept the contract. Having experienced Sam Pope's expertise first hand, with a permanent reminder in the centre of his face, he had hoped that Pope's legacy would have been enough to give them a clear run at him. There had been enough testosterone in that room to power a space station, but it wasn't the lurid machismo of Defoe that had made him anxious.

In fact, it had been the calm, almost uncaring nature of his partner that had given him the most food for thought.

Jacob Nash.

On the train ride back from the capital, Brandt had requested Dallow find any information he could on the other hitmen, and although there wasn't much, the man had once again pulled a rabbit out of the hat. Defoe, for all his bravado, actually had the skills to back it up. In fact, according to his CIA record, which abruptly ended six years ago, the man had a proclivity for reckless violence. Brandt assumed, logically, that was why he was recruited for whatever organisation he now worked for.

Nash, however, had an extensive record with the US Marines, buried behind firewalls and dummy folders.

Dallow had found it, and it underlined exactly what Brandt had known when he had stared into the man's eyes.

That he was one of the most dangerous men the US government had ever been able to call upon.

Again, the trail went cold, which meant Nash had been handpicked to disappear and become a contract killer but judging by the questions the man asked and his clear disdain for his partner, Brandt speculated that there was more to Nash than just money.

That somewhere deep within him, he was still a soldier, and should it come down to it, Brandt knew that was possibly the man's only weakness.

Apart from one police report about how Mendoza had systematically tortured a paedophile by skinning him alive from the feet up, there was nothing else about him. The man was effectively a spectre that haunted the underworld, offering his services to the highest bidder and ensuring a violent end to whoever he was directed at.

But Brandt knew he had one thing that they didn't. Beyond having his team, working ferociously to give them a head start, there was one trait that existed within him that they couldn't possibly equalise.

For him, it was personal.

Masters pulled into the Holiday Inn car park and expertly reversed into a parking spot. Her short, jet-black hair was pulled tightly into a loose ponytail, exposing the shaved head that undercut it and numerous piercings that ran the curve of her ear. Without a word, she killed the engine, exited the car, and then retrieved Brandt's bag from the boot.

Brandt stepped out, cracked his back, and then took the bag.

'Thank you.'

'We're already checked in, sir.' Masters motioned to the front door. Brandt nodded, and then the two of them headed to the entrance. 'Kyle's already working on locating the mark.'

'Hopefully, Cook has let him get on with it,' Brandt muttered as they stomped across the foyer and waited patiently for a lift. A young couple were at the check-in desk, and both of them diverted their looks as soon as Masters shot them one of her own. As they looked anywhere but at her, she smirked, blew a bubble with her chewing gum and followed her boss into the lift. As they rode up to the sixth floor, Brandt prepared himself for the two remaining members of his crew to greet him with a bickering match. Dallow wasn't a soldier like they were, and Will Cook, the final member of his team, was aware of it. Harnessing the same energy as the deplorable Defoe, Cook had a habit of intimidating Dallow whenever he had the chance. While he put it down to a gentle ribbing, it was the sort of American arrogance that didn't sit well with Brandt's stern German principles.

He had emasculated Cook multiple times, usually to the enjoyment of Masters.

As the doors opened, Masters led the way to the four rooms she'd booked. She knocked on one of the doors.

'This one's yours, sir,' she said as she continued walking.

'This is me. This is Cook.' She stopped at the final one and knocked again. 'This is Dallow's.'

As Brandt approached the door, it was pulled open and a scowling Cook quickly stood to attention.

'Welcome back, sir.'

Brandt stepped into Dallow's room, followed by Masters, who glared at Cook as he glanced at her chest. Two years ago, in the ashes of Blackridge, she had been weak enough to sleep with the man. It was a mistake at the time, but she knew the man pined for another opportunity.

'I trust we're making progress,' Brandt said firmly,

looking around the room. Dallow was sitting at the tiny desk that was against the far wall, where he'd set up three separate monitors. To the side, there was a hazardous number of cables, each looped round and feeding into the portable modem that powered his operation. The young man turned, and as always, his face looked gaunt and terrified.

'It's been…interesting,' Dallow said, before guiding Brandt to the plethora of scrunched up paper balls that surrounded his desk, clearly thrown at him by Cook. Brandt turned to Cook, who meekly shrugged before setting about clearing up the mess.

'So, we got the contract?' Masters asked, leaning against the back wall, her arms folded.

'It's an open contract and we aren't the only ones hunting.' Brandt opened the small fridge under Dallow's desk and helped himself to a beer. Without even flinching, he twisted the jagged metal lid clean off and took a sip. 'But nothing we can't handle.'

'Well, that's good,' Cook said, tipping the remaining paper into the bin. 'Because last time, that motherfucker was enough to handle on his own.'

Silence filled the room as the three ex-soldiers remembered their humiliation at the hands of Sam Pope. Cook rubbed a hand across his surgically repaired jaw, remembering the beating he had taken. Masters also zoned out. The pain of being beaten had hurt her pride more than her physical self. Brandt took a swig of beer and looked out of the window, surveying the vista that offered him a great view of Derby and the surrounding fields. The evening was slowly starting to take hold of the sky, sending the sun into retreat and bathing the skyline in a brilliant deep pink.

Brandt took it in, helped himself to another swig of beer and decided to take control of the evening ahead.

'Put it all to one side. I want to kill this man as much as you do, but he is worth a lot more alive. Understood?'

'Yes, sir.' The other two agreed.

'Kyle, what's the update?' Brandt turned to his analyst, offering him a warmer tone.

'I'm just cross-checking CCTV, money withdrawals and any other potential fingerprints he may have left. The man pays cash, clearly has a fake identity and knows how to disappear.'

'Can you find him?'

Dallow tapped a few keys on the keyboard, and his face lit up. One of his monitors had a topographical map of Derby, and as he hit the final key, a red circle appeared around the small village of Spondon on the outskirts of the city. The screen zoomed in, putting the streets within a one-mile radius clear as day. He turned to the three dangerous soldiers, and with a confidence he'd never felt before, gave them a beaming smile.

'I just did.'

———

'Hey, ladies, this guy here is a real-life hero.'

Detective Constable James Saddler blushed as his friend and fellow detective, Liam Anderson, accosted the two ladies at the bar. It had been a whirlwind few days, as ever. Since the call had come through from Sam Pope himself, Saddler's world had been turned upside down. He had been with the Derbyshire Police for nearly a decade, joining them as a fresh-faced boy who'd studied a useless degree at university, and had since blossomed into a man. One whom his superiors had taken a liking to, and after eight years on the beat, had made sure his application to become a detective went through with little interruption.

Now, happily engaged and working hard to pay off his

first mortgage, Saddler felt embarrassed as his good friend leered over the two, obviously uncomfortable women.

'Ignore him,' Saddler cut in, his words only slightly slurred from the alcohol. They both smiled and then one of them leant in towards him.

'Why are you a hero?' she asked, her eyebrow raised inquisitively.

'I'm not.'

'He's shy,' Anderson said, clearly inebriated. 'This man is responsible for four dangerous criminals being off the streets and ladies…' Four shots were placed in front of Anderson and he handed them out. '…I believe that's worth celebrating.'

The two ladies shrugged and joined them for the drink, the four of them clinked their glasses and knocked back the burning Sambuca. All of them gasped afterwards, pushing through the general distaste of the drink.

'God, I hate Sambuca,' Saddler uttered, drawing a smile from the woman next to him. He shuffled uncomfortably.

'So what are you, a police officer?' she asked, leaning in so her voice could be heard over the thundering base of the speakers.

'A detective, actually.'

'Fancy.' The woman smiled. 'I'm Gemma.'

'James.' Saddler looked at his friend who raised his eyebrow. 'This is my mate, Liam.'

'Detective Liam.' Anderson extended his hand, and she took it before he turned his attention back to the other woman.

'So, you guys really are celebrating, eh? I mean, it's barely even seven o'clock.'

'What?' Saddler yelled, pointing to his ear to indicate he couldn't hear. It worked, and Kylie stepped close to him, her mouth a few centimetres from his ear.

She smelt great.

He immediately felt guilty.

'I said, you boys are really celebrating, aren't you?'

'I guess.' Saddler shrugged, and then rolled his eyes as another four shot glasses were laid out before them, promising another disgusting experience. 'I'm not sure I deserve it, though.'

'Oh, stop being such a little bitch about it.' Anderson rudely interrupted as he handed out the shot glasses again. 'He's just mad that someone gave him a little help, is all.'

Saddler shook his head in frustration as Anderson and the two women knocked back their shots. Noticing his friend's reluctance, Anderson sighed.

'Look, James, just take the fucking win, buddy.' He then nodded towards Kylie and her friend, who were obviously discussing the two of them and the potential for the rest of the night. 'Now, let's *really* celebrate.'

'Not for me, thanks.'

'I won't tell Hannah, if that's the problem?'

'No, it's the fact that I love Hannah.' Saddler pushed his undrunk shot into Anderson's hand. 'Have a good night.'

'James…come on…'

'Everything okay?' Kylie asked, her eyes offering Saddler a hopeful look.

'Sorry, darling, but I have to go. Nice to have met you.'

Kylie shrugged and turned back to her friend, who immediately guided her towards the dancefloor. Anderson watched them leave, then turned back to his friend with a scowl.

'You fucking pussy.'

'What, because I don't want to shag random women?'

'No, you're just too fucking sensitive about everything. So what if Sam fucking Pope got to Murphy first? You still brought him in. Eight months and bang, you nicked him. Like I said, take the fucking win.'

'Maybe that's not enough for me, Liam? Maybe I wanted to actually see it through properly.' Saddler shook his head again and zipped up his gilet. 'Besides, I thought you'd be pissed off with Sam Pope pissing on your doorstep.'

'Look, I didn't ask to be the fucking liaison for us and whatever Commissioner Dick Head from the Met is setting up.'

'Then why do it?' Saddler shrugged. 'Why not turn it down?'

'Are you serious? I have an advantage over every other poor fucker who's been roped into this manhunt. He's on our doorstep and we've already narrowed down his where-abouts to a few streets.' Anderson motioned for another drink. 'Give me a week, and I'll have Sam Pope in cuffs and then those girls will be dragging me onto a very different dance floor, if you know what I mean.'

Saddler patted his drunken friend on the arm.

'Have a good night, Liam. Don't be stupid.'

Anderson gave a mocking salute as his friend ventured towards the door, before he turned sloppily back to the bar. The barman put a beer in front of him, followed by a warning that it was his last one. Anderson scoffed and turned to the man stood next to him.

'Can you believe this guy? Telling me I've had enough.' Anderson took a big swig of his beer. 'Nice tattoos.'

The man lifted his drink as a show of thanks, and Anderson necked the rest of the beer, belching grotesquely before sticking a middle finger up at the bartender. This immediately drew the ire of the bouncer, who within seconds, snatched Anderson by the back of the neck.

'Hey, what the fuck?'

'Right, time to go.'

52

'I am a fucking detective…'

'I'll take him home.' The man next to Anderson turned and calmly defused the situation. His strong accent caught everyone off guard, and by the way his unnerving stare bore through the bouncer, the large man eventually loosened his grip.

'Settle your tabs and get out.'

'Will do. Gracias.'

The bouncer nodded to the kind stranger, and Anderson patted aimlessly for his wallet, before his new friend tapped his own bank card on the reader and paid the bill.

'Wow, thanks mate. You're too kind.'

'Kindness makes the world go round.'

'Bingo.' Anderson shot him a finger gun before nearly stumbling over, only for the kind stranger to catch him and drape Anderson's arm over his shoulder. Once steady, the man slowly walked them towards the door, where the doorman watched carefully as they left. As soon as they were outside, Anderson pulled a cigarette from his pocket and offered one to his new friend, who politely accepted.

'Gracias.'

'Kindness makes the world go round.' Anderson started laughing. 'You taught me that.'

The man chuckled alongside him, the open button of his shirt exposing a tapestry of ink. The man pulled out his own lighter and lit his cigarette.

'We need to get you home, eh?'

'Whoa, buddy. I ain't up for any funny business. Not my cup of tea.'

'You misunderstand me, *vato*. I am ordering a cab. We will drop you off on the way home. Maybe you can tell me more about Sam Pope?'

'Oh right. But…shhh…' Anderson drunkenly swayed

and lifted a finger to his lips. '…it's on a need-to-know basis.'

'Don't worry, no one will ever know what you say to me.'

As the Uber appeared around the corner, Anderson patted his new friend on the shoulder and went about finishing his cigarette. By the time the taxi pulled up at the curb, Mendoza took his own final puff, stamped it out on the pavement and then guided a tiring Anderson into the back.

Then, he went about changing the destination to somewhere a little more remote.

CHAPTER SEVEN

With a thunderous roar of anguish, Jacob Nash completed his final curl with the barbell, before dropping the weight to the ground. The metal hit the padded floor with a velocity that shook the gym, with the only other guest, a young lady on a treadmill, glancing over with concern. Nash held up an apologetic hand, then turned and leant against the nearest apparatus.

As he had entered his late forties, he certainly felt the aches and groans of his body growing with every workout, but it had been drilled into him since his days as a fresh-faced marine. Despite being a ruthless killer with any weapon in his hand, Nash's most deadly weapon available was himself. At just under six foot four, he was an intimidating specimen, with a muscular physique that was covered in tattoos. His entire chest, both arms and his back, were riddled with ink, each telling their own story and all of them acquired from his travels around the world.

Two decades as one of his country's greatest hitmen had led to a lonely existence, and Nash had found peace and meaning in the words and images scribed across his body.

Most of the people he interacted with were through the end of a scope or killed by his hands.

Those he had grown close to had been lost along the way.

The solitude had never really bothered him. Having grown up as an immigrant orphan, he was moved through the system, until he eventually discovered some semblance of family in a foster home, run by Ruth and Albert Manning. For the two years he spent under their roof, he felt the fingertips of family and while Albert had long since lost a battle with kidney failure, Ruth was still very much alive and very much putting other people first.

That was where most of his money went. The eye watering amount he was paid by the Foundation certainly allowed him to live comfortably, but as he grew older, and the allure of materialistic living lost its shine, he found a modicum of peace in giving that money to something good.

Nash took a deep breath and pushed himself off the apparatus and caught a glimpse of himself in the mirror. His muscles throbbed after the strenuous workout, and a huge vein slithered down his arm like a venomous snake. It took him a few moments, but eventually he forced himself towards the door that led back to the plush, five-star hotel the Foundation had paid for.

His lack of enthusiasm concerned him.

Traipsing through the hallway towards the grand foyer, Nash scouted a few of the rooms he passed. Besides the modestly stocked gym, there was an indoor swimming pool, a sauna and a litany of well-decorated meeting rooms which he was sure were available at extortionate prices.

Prices that companies would needlessly pay in an attempt to appear successful.

As he passed a window, he took an appreciative glance

at the immaculate grounds, and he understood why the Smithson House Hotel was a popular wedding venue. For him, the notion of tying himself to one person for his entire life was moot, as he knew that they would either be caught in the crossfire or walk away when he didn't return the affection.

Nash made his way to the lift and was pleased when it was immediately available. For a man of his size, sharing a lift was always an awkward moment, but luckily, he rode up to the penthouse suite with no visitors.

Reaching the door to the suite, he lifted his key card and then stopped.

Something was wrong about this contract.

It had been nagging him since the moment it had arrived, and when he contacted their handler, Callaghan, he knew his misgivings would be dismissed. As a former assassin himself, Callaghan carried a lot of credibility and respect throughout the Foundation, a lot of it coming from Nash himself. Having grown up with no parents, Callaghan had put an arm around Nash as his commanding officer in the Marines, and when he left to join the off-the-books operation, Callaghan soon came calling for him.

He had offered Nash everything he thought he wanted.
Travel.
Money.
Immunity.
The chance to disappear.

For the first decade and a half, it had been everything Nash had wanted, and successful kill after successful kill had cemented him not only as a legend within the Foundation, but as the most dangerous man working for Uncle Sam.

But it had long felt like he didn't work for Uncle Sam anymore.

Somewhere along the way, the higher ups began taking on contracts that didn't have political meaning, and Nash found himself putting down people for nothing more than cold hard cash.

The Foundation was named so aptly because it held up the United States of America. Off the books, they were the ones who put America first when the country needed them to. There had been numerous regime changes in allied and enemy countries based on the work of Nash and the rest of the Foundation. Operating from the shadows, they had helped America shape the world on the basis of freedom.

Their definition of freedom.

But now, the more the contracts rolled in, the more Nash saw the game had changed. Callaghan waved away his concerns, telling him to stay out of the politics of it all. Funding had to come from somewhere, and if the US government could only give them so much, then those in charge had to earn it from elsewhere.

Nash wasn't a killer.

He was a soldier.

One of the best.

But as he tapped his key card and stepped into the grandiose suite that consumed the top floor of the expensive hotel, he felt like nothing more than a mercenary. One who knew what he was doing but kept looking the other way.

'Took you long enough.'

Defoe greeted him with the usual swagger, and Nash grimaced internally. With a smug grin on his face, Defoe opened the mini bar in the kitchen area of the magnificent room and took out a mineral water. Still dressed in his sportswear, Defoe had joined Nash in the gym. But his session was over in less than forty five minutes, and while he was certainly no slouch, he was considerably leaner than his veteran partner.

'This is why I usually work alone,' Nash said, taking the water from his colleague. 'Less chit-chat.'

'You're so sensitive.' Defoe shook his head as he marched to a table, where three high spec laptops were set up, all of them running lines of code that ran searches across multiple UK databases. 'Just waiting on them to move.'

'Who?'

'Old Adolf and his band of merry men.' Defoe sat down at the laptop and picked up the open can of Coke Zero and took a sip. 'I stuck a tracer on that big German bastard. He's made his way to the town centre, but he hasn't moved from the hotel for a while.'

'You stuck a tracer on him? Why?'

'The big fuck was running his mouth about having a crew already working on locating this Sam Pope guy, so I figured I'd keep tabs on him.'

Nash took a sip and raised his eyebrows with approval.

'Smart.'

'Don't sound so shocked.'

'Any more information on Sam Pope?' Nash said, taking a seat opposite.

'Shit loads. The man is basically a one-man army. Last few years, he's taken down multiple criminals and their empires. This country fucking hates him, judging from the press.'

'Don't believe everything you read in the paper,' Nash said wisely, screwing the lid back on his bottle. 'If he only kills criminals, do you think that's what he did to her brother?'

'What is it with you? What's with all these questions about why we are doing this?' Defoe slammed his hand on the table in a poor attempt of intimidation. 'We never ask. That's the point. We get given a name and we fucking kill em. There's nothing more to it.'

Nash shook his head and stood.

'There used to be.'

Turning on his heel, Nash stomped out of the room towards the bathroom. His body was slick with sweat, and he needed the warm water to cool him off and wash away the nagging doubts that insisted on staying. His stomach grumbled too, and Nash knew he needed a hearty meal to satisfy the body he had just put through the wringer. As he left, Defoe sighed and shook his head, wondering how Callaghan would react to the revered Jacob Nash suddenly growing a conscience.

Defoe's computer screen bleeped.

A smile spread across his face.

'Hurry up with that shower, big guy. Ze Germans are on the move!'

———

The small village of Spondon was picturesque when the sun started to set, and Sam had enjoyed his evening walks since he had located there. With access to the generous fortune his good friend Paul Etheridge had left for him, Sam was able to pay upfront for his Airbnb, and book it for as long as he needed. His falsified documents, also courtesy of his now unfindable friend, meant his identity was never questioned.

Recently, with his name and clean-shaven army photos making the national news, Sam had worried about being spotted, but he hoped the shorter hair and the thick, greying stubble that clung to his strong jaw was enough of a disguise.

But he had since noticed something else that made him feel more secure in public.

Numerous times, whether it was sitting in the local cemetery garden or just buying a coffee, he had clocked a civilian giving him a careful eye, as if rushing through their own internal archives to place his face. On the rare occasion one of them had made the obvious connection, Sam didn't feel any slight of panic as they reached for their phone.

Instead, they just gave him an almost approving nod.

Derby was a working-class city, and the various villages that spawned around the main city centre weren't ripe with prosperity. To the locals, Sam was doing what the country needed, what the rich and powerful had failed to do and that was to protect them.

It not only gave him a sense of calm, but a sense of pride, one he hadn't felt since he wore the uniform that was being splashed across the news.

As he wandered down the cobbled path, and past an immaculately kept row of flower beds, three youths with their hoods up came into view. One of them, slowly riding his bike in the inner curb of the street, motioned to Sam, and the other boys seemed to change their stance. Gone was the relaxed gait of a teenager; replaced with a fake intimidation, as they pumped their chests up and tried to widen themselves across the pavement.

It would have worked on an old-aged pensioner, who would no doubt be trembling as they walked by, giving the youngsters a false sense of power.

But Sam didn't bat an eyelid.

On a pleasant evening such as the one he was enjoying; Sam even left the house without his trusty Glock 17 tucked into the back of his jeans.

He wouldn't need it.

The three of them approached and Sam continued his pace, his hands stuffed in his pockets and his shoulders broad. A foot or so away, one of them opened his mouth to say something, but Sam paid no mind, storming through the centre of the two walking lads and knocking them both to the side with his considerable power.

'What the fuck?'

'Oi, the fuck is wrong with you?'

Sam turned and glared back at them, watching as their scowls quickly faded, along with their complexion. Quickly realising they were in over their heads, the boys held their hands up apologetically, not even trying to retrieve any sort of dignity. Sam gave them a stern nod, hammering home his lack of fear and then continued his walk, as the lone cyclist heckled his friends for being pussies.

The sleepy village was calm, and as dusk fell about, Sam counted only one car that had passed him during his stroll. A few dog walkers were returning from the fields that backed onto the village, their canine companions excitedly bounding towards the cars in the local car park. They smiled at Sam, who returned in kind, and he turned onto the quaint strip of shops that comprised the village's high street. A hairdressers, a bank, a charity shop and a local supermarket took up the most space but tucked among them was Mama's Café. A typical greasy spoon that took pride in their traditional menu, it was a family run business that was open every day of the week.

The working-class village in action.

As Sam checked the road before walking over it, he once again spotted the black Range Rover ever so slightly edging its way up the road.

It was the third time he'd spotted it, and he was under no illusion the driver, and potentially the passengers, were watching him. As he approached the café door, he sighed, not because of fear of who was in the car, but of the inconvenience that he was likely going to have to relocate once again. Noticing her new customer's forlorn face, Maggie, the 'Mama' of Mama's Café greeted him with a grin.

'Evening, love. Why the long face?'

'Long day.'

'Ah, we all have them from time to time. Makes us who we are. Coffee?'

'You bet.' Sam smiled, sliding his muscular arms from his bomber jacket and lowering himself into a chair in the far corner. The café was modest, with eight tables, four of which could accommodate four chairs. Sam took a seat at the smallest table by the window and dumped his jacket on the large windowsill that was decorated with fake plants and a few candle holders.

A few minutes later, he watched with interest as the Range Rover rolled past, before its indicator signalled, and the driver took it down the first left turn that led to the alleyway behind the café. Maggie, who despite her spritely personality, looked and moved like a woman approaching seventy, ambled out from behind the counter with Sam's coffee in her hand.

'Here you go, love.'

'Thanks. Hey, Maggie, you expecting anyone else here tonight?'

'Not tonight. To be fair, and I don't want you to think yourself a burden, but I only stay open this late because I know you'll be after a good meal.'

'Oh, you never had to do that on my account.'

Maggie reached down and squeezed Sam's hand.

'I don't. But good men like you deserve good things.'

In that instance, Sam realised Maggie knew exactly who he was. He had introduced himself as his alias, Johnathan Cooper, but she hadn't bought it. But just like her community, she saw the good in what Sam was doing, and had welcomed him in with open arms. As he returned her smile, he noticed a man striding up the street, from the direction where he'd first seen the Range Rover. The man was muscular, with longish dark hair and a stubbled jaw.

63

Wearing a high-vis jacket, he looked like he had walked off a construction site, and as he crossed the road towards the café, Sam could see that his build suggested he'd been doing it for a long time.

The man walked with purpose. And as he approached the parade of shops, Sam noticed how clean cut the man was.

Sam turned back to Maggie, who hadn't noticed the approaching.

'Maggie, do you trust me?'

'Of course.'

'Then I need you to take yourself downstairs to your stock room and lock the door.'

'Oh lord, what's the matter?'

'Might be nothing. Might be something. But don't open that door for anyone other than myself or the police, do you hear me?'

Without hesitation, Maggie nodded and quickly scrambled back behind the counter, disappearing behind the plastic curtain that led to the kitchen, which was generating enough heat for Sam to know she had kept it going for his proposed supper. Just as he heard Maggie ascending the staircase, the door pushed open, accompanied by a small shrill of a bell, and the man entered, blowing out his lips in disappointment at the venue. Sam kept his eyes on the man as he wandered into the room, the man casually eyeing up the chalk menu displayed above the till. After a few moments, the man arched his neck towards the curtain of the kitchen, looking for service.

'She's just stepped out,' Sam offered from across the room. 'Cigarette break, I think.'

'Ah, I see,' the man responded, his American accent hard to disguise. He helped himself to a seat at the table nearest to the till and returned his gaze to the menu. 'Food good here?'

'I like it.' Sam shrugged and took the final sip of his coffee. As the man continued to look around the room, Sam took a final glance at the street outside. The Range Rover was nowhere to be seen, and the streets were clear of any civilians.

Any witnesses.

'She usually take this long?' the man asked, his thumb motioning to the till.

'You've grown your hair out,' Sam said, before calmly sipping his coffee. 'And they fixed your jaw, I see?'

'Excuse me?' the man spat angrily, turning on his seat as if ready to pounce.

'Liverpool Street. Two years ago. I believe I had the displeasure of meeting you then.' Sam finished his coffee and set the mug down. 'I'm assuming you're not really here for the food?'

'Listen up, motherfucker.' Exposed, Will Cook dispensed with the niceties and the fake accent. 'There's a lot of money on your head, more if we bring you in alive. So why don't we do this the easy way because as much as you got a receipt coming, we want that bigger pay day.'

'We? We got more coming?' Sam cracked his neck and stretched his shoulders back. 'Do me a favour. The woman who runs this place is a nice woman. Let's try to do as little damage as possible.'

Taking a deep breath, Sam pushed his chair back and stood, and then lowered the blind that covered the entire front window of the café, blocking the public from what was about to happen. Then he clenched his fists and turned as Cook's footsteps rushed towards him.

CHAPTER EIGHT

'You really think sending that asshole in first is a good idea?'

Masters raised her eyebrows to the rear-view mirror of the Range Rover, checking to see if her question had registered. The alleyway behind the parade of shops was a tight squeeze for the pristine vehicle, with a number of large, metal bins overflowing with rubbish, pressed against graffiti covered walls. Despite the raw stench of the waste, Masters had rolled the window, and her gloved hand hung over the opening, a half-smoked cigarette clutched between her fingers.

Brandt was in the backseat, his large frame taking up almost the entirety of the leather seat, and his meaty hands were carefully loading a magazine.

'Do you question my judgement?' he asked, without looking up.

'I just think we got a lot riding on this one, and Cook, he's…'

'An asshole, I believe you said.'

Masters shrugged. The calm, cold voice, combined with Brandt's thick German accent always caught her a little off guard. Never had she come across a more dangerous or dedicated killer in her life, but he often spoke as if he was guiding people to a luxury spa.

'I just think I would have been a better bet.'

'You are a better soldier than Cook will ever be.' Brandt sighed, leaning forward. Masters felt a slightly flick of Brandt's beard against her shoulder. 'But this isn't any contract. Since we formed *Endwache*, you have proven that time and time again. But this is Sam Pope. You remember what happened last time?'

'Yup, and that motherfucker's got his coming to him.'

'That was when we had the backing of this country's pathetic government. Still, he took us down.' Brandt sat back, fed the final bullet into the magazine, and then snapped it into his handgun. 'This time, we soften him up before we take him down.'

'And Cook's best placed for that?'

Brandt reached out a hand and patted her shoulder.

'The man may be an asshole, but he is a hell of a fighter. Besides, I don't expect him to win. But I know who I'd rather have beside me when Sam Pope walks out that back door after Cook has given him all he's got.'

Masters lifted her cigarette and took another puff, trying her hardest to temper the smile on her face. Brandt wasn't in the business of handing out compliments. The man was a ruthless mercenary who she had watched beat a man to death with his bare hands. There was a lot of money riding on this mission, with Brandt even intimating it might be enough for them to all walk away from the life. Masters wasn't entirely sure she would but having over a million in the bank would at least allow her to chose her path a little more freely. A few minutes passed and a voice cackled in both their ears.

'He's in.'

Dallow was back at the hotel, monitoring whatever he

could from the comfort of his own chair. Masters pitied the little guy, knowing he lacked any sort of fortitude to throw a single punch, let alone stand up for himself. But the young man was as dangerous as they were, only his weapon wasn't an automatic rifle, it was a keyboard.

'You have visual?' Brandt asked as he scanned the alleyway trying to place the café against the deluge of grey bricks and overflowing bins.

'This place is old as fuck.' Dallow chuckled. 'I doubt they even have Wi-Fi, let alone CCTV—'

'All right, clever dick,' Masters cut in. 'Just tell us what you do know.'

Masters smirked as Dallow's voice trembled in reply.

'The bank at the end of the street has a camera in the ATM. I have eyes on the front of the location. Cook just went in. Also, monitoring all potential emergency calls in case anyone walks by.' Dallow took a breath. 'I'm sorry.'

'Don't apologise for things you haven't done.' Brandt replied, checking the Bowing knife that he usually had strapped to his waist. 'She is just busting your balls.'

'Someone has to.' Masters chuckled.

'Enough.' Brandt held up his hand, before turning back to the earpiece. 'Keep us informed. Any changes, you make it clear.'

'Yes, sir.'

Masters rolled her eyes, took a final drag on her cigarette, and then tossed it into the deluge of trash that comprised the alleyway. As she pulled the window back up in a lame attempt to protect them from the stench, Brandt returned the knife to its pouch.

'How long we giving him?' Masters finally asked, annoyed that she could feel the adrenaline beginning to tremor through her fingers.

'If he's as good as I think he is, a couple of minutes.'

'Cook ain't that good.'

Masters looked into the rear-view mirror once more and was startled at what she saw. For the first time in the almost four years she'd known Brandt, she saw a genuine smile. For someone who was so ruthlessly structured, Brandt very rarely showed anything even close to a raw emotion.

Brandt met her gaze in the reflection and then offered his reasoning.

'I wasn't talking about Cook.'

———

As Cook took his first few steps across the café, Sam immediately regretted his decision not to carry his weapon. Usually, the Glock 17 would be rested neatly against the base of his spine, but he'd been too relaxed.

Sloppy, even.

With a nationwide manhunt and every major criminal looking for him, Sam afforded himself a brief moment of annoyance before his instincts snapped into focus.

Cook was eight steps away, and as he moved forward with intent, Sam noticed the man's hand reach to his belt, his murderous fingers clasping the handle of his own handgun.

Seven steps.

Sam's hand shot down to his table. Cook raised the gun.

Six steps.

The gun rose up. Sam clasped the white, porcelain mug that he'd just drained and then heaved it forward. Just as Cook was about to connect his eyeline with the top of his handgun, the mug shot across the room and connected with his cheek, the velocity of the throw causing it to shatter on impact. The blow caused him a moment's stumble, and just as he tried to re-align his shot, Sam dove forward and drove his elbow into his forearm.

The blow loosened Cook's grip, but he clung on, hoping to end this confrontation as quickly as possible. With his left hand, Cook swung a hard blow into Sam's ribs, but Sam absorbed the blow as he turned his body into Cook, hauling his right arm over his shoulder and with all his might, he pulled Cook forward. The momentum took Cook off his feet, and Sam lifted his shoulder, causing Cook to flip over and crash through one of the old, wooden tables.

The gun rattled loosely somewhere into the room, but Cook quickly scrambled to his feet and raised his fists. Sam stood calmly, gently rolling his shoulder as if working out an ache.

'You want to do this the hard way then, eh?' Cook spat angrily.

'I don't want to do this at all.'

'Tough luck, asshole.'

Cook launched forward again, expertly throwing rights and lefts, which Sam deflected with his forearms, before a sneaky uppercut caught him in the ribs. Rocked slightly, Sam blocked the following knee strike, before he blocked a right hand and drove his own elbow back into Cook's surgically repaired jaw. The mercenary took a couple of steps back, shaking the cobwebs before he roared forward with another barrage.

For all his cockiness, Cook was a skilled and dangerous fighter, and with each clubbing blow that Sam blocked, Sam knew he wouldn't be able to keep it up. Eventually, Cook's strikes would break through. The man was relentless.

Sam had to fight back.

Cook rocked Sam in the side with another right hook, before swinging a vicious left haymaker straight for his jaw.

Sam ducked, then shot back with a right hand that sent Cook back a few steps, giving Sam enough time to rush forward, using his head start to slam his shoulder into Cook's stomach, and then hoist him up by the legs before sending both men crashing down onto another table. The salt and pepper shakers clattered to the floor, along with the fake potted plant, and both men quickly tried to recover the air that had been driven from their bodies. Among the wreckage of the table and chairs, Sam stood, quickly followed by Cook, who brandished a thick, broken table leg. With the heft and accuracy of a pro-baseball player, he swung, and the expert strike caught Sam on the side of the jaw and sent him spiralling into the counter, and a spray of blood across the clear, perplex screen that protected the baked goods.

'Woooo.' Cook celebrated. 'He got a hold of that one.'

As quickly as he could, Sam tried to gather his mind, and he saw Cook lift the weapon once more and threw his arms up to block the impending blow. Cook changed course, and his swing collided viciously with Sam's solid stomach, causing him to double over in pain. In one swift movement, Cook grabbed the back of Sam's head and drove it downwards into his oncoming knee. Sam fell backwards into the counter, and dropped onto the floor, his nose bleeding and his eyes watering.

'You know, the others thought this might be more than a one-man job. That you, the mighty Sam Pope, might be too tough to take down.' Cook drove his solid boots into Sam's rib cage, as he tried to defend himself. 'But last time, you got the jump on me. This time, I saw you coming and look at you now.'

Cook threw another violently kick at Sam but had failed to notice Sam had gotten to one knee. Allowing the blow to connect with his ribs, Sam then locked his arm around Cook's ankle, and locked it under his arm pit.

Panicked, Cook tried to hop out of the hold, but Sam shot upwards, grabbed the front of the man's shirt and then lifted him off the ground and threw him across the counter.

Cook's head hit the solid metal cash register before he crumpled to a heap on the other side with a sickening thud. Sam took a few deep breaths and grimaced at the damage done to his ribs, knowing that the punishment he'd absorbed over his war on crime had made them an easy target. There were only so many times a broken rib could heal properly, and Sam could already feel the bruising on the bone. As Sam shuffled painfully towards the entrance to the counter, he reached down and lifted the table leg that Cook had used as his own personal club, and he stepped through.

Cook was up, and he slashed wildly at Sam with a bread knife that he'd taken from a crumb covered chopping board. Sam dodged the blow, but in the close quarters of the staff area, Cook swung his hand back and the jagged blade slashed across Sam's cheek. The skin split instantly, and Sam felt the sting of a fresh cut and the pouring of blood down his strong jaw. Cook raised his eyebrows, basking in his own glory, and then he flipped the knife round, gripping the handle in his fist with the blade pointing down.

'Last chance, Sam. Like I said, you're worth more to us alive than dead.'

'So you said.' Sam wiped the blood from his cheek with the back of his hand.

'Fine. Have it your way.'

Cook slashed forward with the knife, the serrated blade slicing the air expertly as Sam managed to dodge the fatal swipes. After the third dodge, Sam rammed the table leg upwards, catching Cook on the bridge of the nose. It sent the American stumbling backwards, and Sam spun the make-shift bat in his hand and swung like a pro. The connection with Cook's jaw was sickening, and as the man fell floppy against the counter, Sam knew he'd once again disconnected the bone from his skull. Cook turned onto his back, his eyes filled with rage as his jaw hung slack, and lazily, he launched at Sam with the bread knife again. Only this time, he lacked any of the power he once had, and Sam moved out of the way of the blade, caught Cook with a vicious elbow to the gut and then grabbed his knife wielding hand by the wrist. He dug his fingers deeply into the pressure points either side of the man's veins, loosening the grip, before catching the knife as it fell from his hand.

In the tiny confines of the till area, Sam then drove his boot into Cook's chest, sending him slamming back first into the counter and the impact sent him back towards Sam, who tightened his grip around the knife. A split-second decision raced through Sam's mind, and the trained killer within was telling him to plunge it into his adversary's throat and end the fight then and there.

But Sam thought of Jamie.

This time, he was going to do things differently. He'd killed so many people in the name of justice, but now he would use it only as a last resort.

Only if there was no other option.

As the split second ended and Cook's beaten body rebounded back towards him, Sam tossed the knife to the side, and connected with a right hook that sent the man spinning. Then, with as much power as he could muster, Sam stamped forward into the man's ankle, driving his boot down until he felt the bones and ligaments crack.

Cooked groaned with agony, his jaw flopping uselessly, and Sam sent him to sleep with an elbow to the back of the head. Sprawled on the floor, Cook wasn't moving, and Sam squatted beside the motionless body and checked for a pulse. Relieved, he found one, and knowing the man wouldn't be able to move, even if he woke, Sam stood and took a moment to collect himself. He winced as he touched his cheek, and then spun on his heel at the sound of a door opening.

Maggie.

Stood in the doorway to her storeroom, Maggie's mouth was open, the shock of the scene in front of her causing her to go a faint shade of white. The café was a wreck, and her loyal customer was stood over a lifeless body. Blood was splattered across her cake display; the entire counter area was decimated, and she looked at the bleeding Sam with tears in her eyes.

'Let me get you some ice.'

'Maggie, I told you to stay in there until I told you it was safe.'

'The hell with that. This is my business.' Maggie shuffled behind the curtain to the kitchen and returned with an ice pack that Sam gratefully pressed to his cheek. 'Besides, you need some help with the other two.'

'Other two?'

'There's a window in the store room. Two people sat in a fancy car in the alleyway.'

'A Range Rover?'

Maggie shrugged.

'Could be. I don't know cars, but I do know when someone's face don't fit. They got the same look as this man here.'

'I'm sorry. This had nothing to do with you and…'

'Don't worry about it. Insurance will pay for the damage.' Maggie nodded to the front door. 'You best go round the front. Try to sneak up behind them.'

'I beg your pardon?' Sam looked at the old lady in disbelief.

'Well, I better tidy up if the police will be here soon. So I need to take the bins out.' Maggie nodded to the front door. 'You'd better hurry. I doubt they'll be happy if I see them. What about him?'

Maggie pointed to the prone, beaten body of Cook.

'He's not a problem anymore.'

Sam reached out and put his hand on Maggie's bony shoulder and smiled. It wasn't often he was treated to the kindness of strangers and had spent so long fighting the worst of humanity that he forgot about the rest of it.

Good people.

Doing the right thing.

That's what he'd strived to do, and as he reached down and picked up Cook's Heckler & Koch SFP9. Lifting the semi-automatic handgun, Sam admired the German manufacturing of the weapon but then darted towards the door. He knew he needed to move quickly to make sure Maggie's kindness and bravery wouldn't be for nothing. As she lifted the black bin bag from the kitchen and headed to the back door, Sam slipped out of the front of the café, said a silent thank you that the street was empty, and then quickly raced towards the end of the parade where the Range Rover had disappeared.

He had to move.

And fast.

CHAPTER NINE

'He's taking too long.'

Masters was getting tetchy, and she shuffled uncomfortably in her seat and she pressed the button for the automatic window. Within seconds, another cigarette was lit, and Brandt gave an audible tut at her worsening habit.

'Like I said, let's give him a few minutes. You and I both know Cook will give Pope a hell of a fight, and I'd rather we take in a wounded man than confront one ready to fight back.'

'What if he kills him?'

'Then that's one less cut of the money.'

Brandt's cold response sent a shiver down Masters' spine, and she hated the idea of being worried. She'd spent her whole life fighting back against abusive foster parents, boyfriends and military men, all of whom underestimated just how dangerous she could be. She eventually caught the eye of General Ervin Wallace, who at the time had recently recruited her former commander, Trevor Sims. Soon after, she'd been recruited by Blackridge and put under the tutelage of Brandt, who was the greatest soldier she'd ever met.

Disciplined.

Loyal.

Deadly.

And while over the years she'd earned the man's respect, and in the aftermath of Blackridge's dilution, possibly his friendship, it didn't take much for him to remind her just how dangerous he was. The mission came first.

It always did.

Brandt took great pride in what he called *the service* that *Endwache* provided, and free from the political powers in charge, Brandt was as ruthless as he was fair. He knew Masters was more capable than Cook, and while it would never be spoken, it was the reason she was in the car and Cook wasn't.

He was expendable.

Brandt would never admit it, but Masters was an asset he couldn't afford to lose. As the seconds ticked by, Masters became more agitated, and Brandt sighed audibly.

'Why don't you step outside and calm down?'

'I'm fine,' she snapped back.

'That wasn't a suggestion.'

Masters paused for a brief moment, clearly holding her tongue as she battled with the chain of command. With added aggression she flung the driver's door open and stepped out of the Range Rover, welcomed by the pungent aroma of the alleyway. She slammed the door and then readjusted her shirt, completing a quick check that her pistol was still tucked into the back of her tight, black jeans. Over five minutes had passed, and while Cook had claimed he would handle things with as little incident as possible, the man possessed all the subtlety of a sledge-hammer to the skull. If he'd engaged Pope quickly, then maybe he would have a chance.

If Pope had seen him coming, then it could get messy.

As she lit another cigarette, Masters thought back to their last encounter with the vigilante, in a stairwell in London Liverpool Street Station. With Wallace running the mission, they were following a police detective who Pope was supposed to be meeting. Somehow, Pope got the drop on them, and it only dawned on them after Blackridge had been disbanded that Pope himself had used her as bait to take out Wallace's crew.

To humiliate them all.

During their fight in the stairwell, Pope had managed to systematically break down both her and Cook in the confined space, shattering her colleague's jaw and knocking her out with a clubbing blow to the back of the skull. While their pride took the most damage, Masters had taken some solace that Brandt had suffered a similar fate. Sam Pope was the most dangerous fighter she'd ever witnessed, and as her cigarette burnt smaller and smaller, the length of time that Cook had been gone became a concern.

Brandt shuffled in the back seat of the car and with little update from Dallow, Masters tossed her cigarette.

'Something's not right.'

Before Brandt could once again pull rank, a metal thunk echoed in the alleyway, followed by the loud creaking of a metal door. Masters spun on her heels instantly, whipping her SFP9 from the base of her spine and expertly drawing it in one swift movement. Brandt threw open the door of the car and began to clamber out when an old lady shuffled out through the back of the building. Carrying a black bin bag, it took her a few moments to notice the car, the intimidating man leaning out of the back and then the gun trained on her with deadly intent.

'Goodness.' She dropped the rubbish bag in a panic.

'Who the fuck are you?' Masters demanded, her arms straight and the gun aimed directly at the pensioner.

'Oh my. Please…don't hurt me.'

'Answer the fuckin' question!'

'Calm down,' Brandt said, stepping from the vehicle with his hands out, defusing the situation. 'Unfortunately, we do find ourselves in a situation and…'

BANG!

A gunshot echoed through the alleyway, and Masters span as the bullet hit her flush in the shoulder, sending her to the hard concrete below and her weapon somewhere into the alley. She groaned in pain as she clutched the bullet wound, which had ripped clean through and out the other side, incapacitating her. Brandt sighed grimly, raised his hands and turned slowly on the spot, knowing exactly who he was coming face to face with.

Sam Pope.

Cook had certainly put up a fight, as Pope's mouth and nose were bleeding, along with some light swelling around his left eye. But Brandt was under no illusion that his subordinate wouldn't be joining them, and now with Masters down, Pope had gotten the drop on them. As he approached, Pope turned to the old lady.

'Maggie. Go inside and call the police.'

'But they'll…'

'I'll be long gone by the time they get here. Report the gunshot. I'm pretty sure someone else would have by now.'

Maggie nodded obediently and then headed back through the door, offering Sam one final concerned glance before the metal slammed shut. Brandt watched the elderly women leave, and then turned back to Sam with an impressed nod of the head.

'You looking for a job?' he offered cheekily.

'Toss your weapons.

'What weapons?'

Sam emphasised the gun in his hand and then glared at Brandt.

'Take your jacket off and toss your weapons.' Sam shook his head. 'I won't ask again.'

Reluctantly, and without breaking his stare, Brandt slid the jacket from his hulking frame to reveal the two guns strapped to the holster that wrapped around his colossal back. He unclipped it and tossed the two weapons into the large metal bin that was overpowering the alleyway with its stench.

'Satisfied?'

'Not yet.' Sam then launched forward and caught Brandt in the temple with the butt of the SFP9, driving the consciousness from the burly man in one go. Before he fell completely limp, Brandt wobbled and Sam drove his shoulders into the man's paunch, guiding him to the open door of the Range Rover. Using all his strength, Sam managed to manoeuvre Brandt's unconscious body onto the back seat, and after cramming the German's legs inside the door, slammed it shut. With the key still in the ignition, Sam rushed to the driver's door, stopping only to take aim and blast another bullet at Masters, this time obliterating her left calf muscle.

The woman roared in agony, but Sam knew she could take it. She was made of tough stuff and was a survivor, like he was. But with her inability to move, she would no doubt be having an interesting conversation with the soon to arrive police officers.

But Sam wouldn't be around to see it.

He needed to get out of there and considering his pleasant evening had just been invaded by three vengeful adversaries from his past, he had a few questions.

His passenger had the answers, and unfortunately for the unconscious, bearded mercenary, Sam had ways of getting to them.

———

'I say we go now.'

'Just wait.'

Nash held up his hand, using his seniority to dismiss Defoe's impulsive demand. Their clash of personalities was more of an inconvenience than a hinderance, Nash knew that despite Defoe's rather deplorable disposition, he was a talented and skilled hitman. The sneaky placement of the tracker had been genius, and now, sat in their own rented SUV three streets away from the red dot on their screen, Nash knew the time wasn't right.

Defoe wanted to go in all guns blazing.

They had followed the tracker across Derby to a small village named Spondon, passing through a pleasant part of town called Oakwood. Whereas the city was predominantly working class, with many of the small villages dotted around the city centre in need of repair, Oakwood had seen a cash injection, with roads of newly built, similar-looking houses lining man-made streets and surrounded by well-maintained parks and fields. It had been a rather nice drive, with Defoe even reigning in his incessant talking to allow Nash to take in the scenery before they pulled their SUV into the car park of the small, Spondon town hall. Three streets away, Brandt was waiting, and Nash was certain the man wasn't alone.

Using the wealth of resources funded by The Foundation, Nash had spent some time going through the files of the Brandt and the rest of *Endwache*.

End Watch.

Talented, brutal killers who had forged a profitable outfit that had taken out several high-profile targets across Europe. Their operation wasn't as slick or as pristine as The Foundation, but their catalogue of work was certainly impressive. It was why Defoe's idea of swarming their attempted capture of Sam Pope and engaging them in a gun fight was a bad idea.

They would fight back.

And worse, it could expose The Foundation's existence.

Despite having seemingly lost their moral compass over the past few years by selling themselves out to the highest bidder, the existence of The Foundation had always been strictly need to know. The government called upon them when diplomacy failed, but their work and their legacy was kept strictly to whispers and rumours.

They helped shaped the country. Bullet by bullet.

Body by body.

But they were discreet and while the media often reported of clandestine military outfits operating on behalf of the red, white and blue, every asset on The Foundation's payroll knew they had to keep as low a profile as possible.

Butchering a team of mercenaries and potentially the UK's most wanted man in a sleepy village in the Midlands wasn't exactly under the radar. As they sat patiently, Defoe impatiently drummed his fingers of the dashboard, before checking his Glock 17 once more. The weapon was in immaculate condition, tried and tested by The Foundation's armoury team and offered a promise of efficiency and accuracy.

But Defoe was restless. Impetuous.

Nash knew they were characteristics that one day would see Defoe meet the wrong end of a bullet, but it wasn't his place to bring the man in line. Callaghan, their handler, was responsible for the recruitment of specialist killers into the organisation and Nash recalled the brutal initiation program. Which meant Defoe passed the required level needed, and therefore, he was Callaghan's responsibility.

'They haven't moved for five minutes.' Defoe spat again, looking at the screen of his tablet. 'Either they have him or they're dead. Either way, that sucks for us. Hey, are you even paying attention?'

'I'll listen when you have something interesting to say.' Nash waved Defoe off, his eyes glued on his own tablet as he used his fingers to move the images on his screen.

'The fuck is your problem?' Defoe turned on the passenger seat, puffing his chest out in a redundant show of machismo.

'Look, we were both assigned this job. If I had it my way, I'd work alone. It's what I do best.'

'Yeah, well you ain't exactly a fucking picnic either, pal.'

'Exactly. So, let's just get this job done and get out of this country. Alive. And to do that, I just need you to sit back and shut up. Can you do that?'

Defoe sat back in his chair and shook his head.

'You know, I used to think you were a legend. Like, Jacob Nash...the killer of killers. But I don't know what the fuck has gotten into you. Maybe you found religion or something, because seriously, since we've been here, you've been nothing but a...'

Before Defoe could potentially put his foot further into his own mouth, the silence of the streets was penetrated by the wail of sirens. Instantly, both men slumped back in their seats, with Nash trying, to little avail, to conceal his muscular frame. Three police cars shot past, headed towards the street where Brandt's red dot had been stationary, followed by two ambulances.

'I think we need to go,' Nash said quietly, pressing the ignition button of the SUV and roaring the powerful engine to life.

'I told you. Those guys are fucking dead and our guys in the wind. Either that or he's dumped the tracker.'

'Don't worry about it,' Nash said, pulling the car out of

the gravel covered car park and turning onto the road away from the commotion.

'No? You got a smart fucking plan for finding a needle in a haystack.'

Without answering, Nash snatched the tablet from his lap and tossed it onto Defoe's. With a snarl, the younger assassin began screening the data before him and then looked up at the legendary hitman with a smirk.

'You son of a bitch.'

Nash flashed a grin.

'Yup. We might not have Brandt anymore, but we got his data source.'

Turning onto Brian Clough Way and heading back towards the city, which was now lighting up against the incoming night sky, Nash kept his eyes on the road, knowing full well that Defoe was battling against his own bad attitude. The man was incapable of not having the last word, but Nash had just proven to him why he was the best. Using The Foundation's databases and password decipher software, he'd used a mapping tool to locate any cell phone within a twenty-yard radius of Brandt's position, returning only five.

He had then cross-referenced those numbers with any that had been in their London location that morning.

He had one match.

Brandt had handed his phone to Dana Kovalenko's henchmen at the door and had retrieved it before he had begun his own journey to Derbyshire.

Using the same methodology, it hadn't been difficult to see where the phone had been active for the longest period in the local area, and the screen had swiftly shown them the hotel that Brandt and *Endwache* had taken up as their HQ. Considering there were multiple text messages to Brandt's phone from a number that was still online and based at the hotel, it meant whoever was running their intel was still there.

Better yet, Brandt's phone was on the move, meaning either he or Sam Pope had it.

Nash had a plan, and all he needed was for Defoe to swallow his own ego and let him do what he did best.

As they passed over the flyover that took them past the large, Asda Shopping Centre that was illuminated in a ghastly green, Defoe snorted to himself before muttering something under his breath, claiming the final word and proving to Nash, yet again, that he was his own worst enemy.

CHAPTER TEN

There was nothing worse than not knowing what was going on. It was an issue Kyle Dallow had been battling ever since he was a child, where he'd been ostracised by the "cool" kids at school, and he yearned for their attention as he peered in from the outside. All he'd ever wanted was to be accepted, not just as a person, but as a man.

His father had been one of the toughest men he had ever known and had served as a respected firefighter in Durham in the north of England until smoke damage to his lungs had eventually seen his hero succumb to cancer when Dallow was just thirteen years old. Dallow had always seen it as an unfortunate side effect of his dad rushing into burning buildings, but as he grew a little older and wiser, he had known it was from his father's aggressive smoking habit.

Twenty a day will do that to anyone, and it was why he chastised Masters whenever she lit up a cigarette, only to be reminded of his lack of masculinity.

Dallow had never lived up to his father's machismo, and after the great man's death, his loving mother didn't help matters by mollycoddling him. He loved her dearly, but Dallow had been relieved when his near genius intellect granted him an escape to any of the top universities in the country and he went on to become a star pupil. At that point, his brain became more attractive than many others' brawn, and he soon found himself courted not just by some of the biggest tech companies in the world, but by some of the biggest government agencies to boot. While he would never have the bravery to tackle a raging fire, Dallow wanted to make his father proud, and he soon joined MI5, working extensively to develop a better cloud platform for syncing all confidential files and assigning them auto-change encryptions that only the elite few in the organisation could ever call upon.

It was a success.

It had gotten him noticed.

And soon, he was being recruited for a secret organisation run by General Ervin Wallace, one of the most respected military men the country had ever seen. The hulking man not only oozed intimidation but also charisma, and as the man gave speeches and promises of a better world built on the freedoms they could help achieve, Dallow soon realised he was serving his country in the best way possible.

But Sam Pope put a pin in that, exposing Wallace and Blackridge as the military weapon it was.

With Wallace's death and Blackridge's dissolution, Dallow had found himself hocking his ability to the highest bidder, helping banks double down on their data security while wanting to put a bullet in his own skull.

Being recruited by Roland Brandt had been a godsend. Joining *Endwache* had given Dallow the same sense of excitement that he'd experienced under Wallace's tutelage, but this time, there was no smoke and mirrors.

This was purely for cash.

They dealt in death, and they were paid handsomely for it.

Brandt was a good leader, albeit one who expected everyone to follow the same regimented life he did. Dallow was kept out of the firing line, as his role was squarely behind the computer, but Masters and Cook were both put through the wringer regularly, which caused them to lash out, and being in such proximity, Dallow was the obvious target.

It was like being back at school, where the bigger, tougher kids picked on him, only this time, those who were calling him names were strapped with the best German made firearms money could buy.

Brandt reeled them in. Masters, to her credit, had taken a step back, but it was Cook who enjoyed ribbing him on a daily basis.

But he was part of the team.

He belonged somewhere, and that, ultimately, was what he'd wanted. Sure, they weren't saving the world, but he'd come to realise that the people who usually end up having high paying contracts put out on them aren't usually the nicest people to begin with.

Dallow wasn't sure about Sam Pope. The papers painted a different picture depending on which way they swung politically, and he could see both sides of the story.

Murderous psychopath.

Heroic vigilante.

The people Sam Pope had put in the ground had been some of the worst the country homed, and they were a disease that needed to be eradicated. But eventually, Pope would cross a line, and become the very thing he hunted so expertly.

Maybe *Endwache* would be providing the country a service in bringing him down. It would, at least, save millions in taxpayers money.

But right now, Dallow didn't know.

He'd lost all contact with Brandt, Masters, and Cook. There was no camera feed to the back alley, and the last he saw was Sam Pope emerge from the shop through the grainy camera of the opposite ATM.

Then nothing.

Dallow tapped the padding of his arm rests impatiently and cursed himself for being useless. While he was loath to call any of them his friends, the three other members of the crew were people he depended on. If Pope was as good as his military records and reported crimes suggested, all three of them could have been executed and he could be next.

That thought froze him to his spot.

What if that was the case? What if Sam Pope had taken all three of them out and was on his way to the hotel to rubber stamp the end of *Endwache*?

Suddenly, his laptop speaker crackled as his feed into police radio channel sparked into life.

'Two Americans, both in severe condition. One has been beaten to within an inch of his life, the other has a few gunshot wounds….We're hoping they both pull through…Yes, sir. We think it's him, sir. They're pretty fucked up.'

Dallow felt his hand tremble at the conversation he was eavesdropping on and then he stumbled completely out of his chair as a thunderous fist pounded on the door.

This was it.

Dallow knew he swam in a dangerous ocean, and now it was time for him to swim into the darkest waters. Resigned to his fate, he still lifted the SFP9 from the desk, his fingers fumbling uselessly. He had every intention to use it if needed, but knew he lacked the courage and ability.

'Who is it?' Dallow called out, trying and failing to mask the terror in his voice.

'Open the door, please.'

An American accent caught Dallow offguard, and with his eyebrows raised, he pulled open the door to his hotel room. Two immaculately dressed men were there. The youngest was in the doorway, a grin of perfect white teeth plastered across his handsome face. Behind him, a hulking, more grizzled man stood looking fed up.

'Can I help you?' Dallow shrugged.

'You can lower that thing, for one.' Defoe pointed at the weapon, which Dallow sheepishly lowered. 'We don't want anything to pop off now, do we?'

Just as Dallow was about to respond, Defoe swung a thunderous right hook, connected with the young man's jaw and sent him spinning back into the room. The young man hit the side of his bed and slumped onto the carpet, completely unconscious. Nash sighed and followed Defoe into the room.

'Wow, look at this place,' Defoe said mockingly, shaking the pain from his knuckles. 'It's like a nerd's wanking station.'

'Is he breathing?' Nash asked, closing the door behind them. Defoe squatted down and put the back of his hand to Dallow's lips. He nodded.

'What now, big guy?' Defoe asked as he stood, hands on his hips and a look of disgust on his face.

'We wait,' Nash said, easing himself into Dallow's chair and turning away from Defoe. 'In silence, preferably.'

———

Sam blew out his cheeks and sighed, casting his gaze across the dimly lit industrial park and to the bright lights of Derby city centre beyond the motorways. The police tape was still criss-crossed over every entrance to the abandoned factory, but beyond that, there had been no deterrents. As Sam had cut the lights to the Range Rover and gently steered it into the shadows cast by the factory, he chuckled at the lack of police presence that had been so strong the night before.

Then, after he'd called in and given his name, the boys in blue had flooded the entire area, trying their best to find him but also revel in the capture of George Murphy and his gang. Sam had delivered them on a plate, and with his immediate disappearance there hadn't been much reason for them to stick around after their routine sweep.

They had found the drugs. The dead bodies of Murphy's associates and enough evidence to put the badly beaten criminal and his henchmen behind bars for a long time. The last thing they would have ever suspected was that Sam would return to the scene. As far as they were concerned, he was in the wind, with a nationwide manhunt being put together to bring him in.

That was a lot to process, and Sam stared out of the doorway of the abandoned factory, wishing it was the only thing he had to worry about.

But there was more.

Much more.

After once again delivering a beating to the cocky American, this time at the unfortunate cost of Maggie's café, Sam had thought about what the man had said.

'There's a lot of money on your head.'

'You're worth more to us alive than dead.'

With the American and his female accomplice in the hands of the police, Sam turned in the doorway and looked back at the prone body of Roland Brandt. The man was clearly in charge, had the build and stature of a commander, and considering Sam had already come face to face with him a few years earlier at London Liverpool Street Station, the man swam in the same deadly waters as Sam did.

Sam hadn't even bothered to tie him up, knowing the

only weapon in the room was safely wrapped in his fingers and as he strolled towards the mercenary's hulking body, he let the SFP9 hang casually by his side. Sam had backed the Range Rover into roughly the same spot that Hakan Sanli had parked his van, although that had since been impounded by the police. All that remained of Sanli's memory was the bloodstain on the concrete floor where his dead body had been dragged into the darkness.

After parking the expensive car and then closing the shutter, Sam had hauled Brandt's limp body from the vehicle and left him to sleep on the floor, intermittently checking the man's pulse to ensure he hadn't hit him too hard.

They had been hidden in the factory for over three hours when Sam heard the first grunt of consciousness echo through the room, and he lifted himself from the dusty chair he'd found and then carried it towards the prone man. As Sam approached, he watched as Brandt woozily awoke, his head spinning from the clubbing blow he'd received before he eventually managed to push himself to a seated position, leaning his back against the Range Rover.

'*Scheisse.*' Brandt's vision began to clear and his eyes locked onto Sam. As soon as Sam had the man's attention, he slammed the metal chair down on the ground, the twang amplified by the room and causing Brandt to squint in pain. Sam sat and leant forward; his gun-wielding hand casually draped over his knee.

'What's your name?'

'*Fick dich!*'

'I wouldn't say I'm the one who's fucked here, would you?' Sam gently motioned with the gun. 'So, let's just cut the crap. What's your name?'

'Roland Brandt.' The man finally relented, clearly too proud to play games.

'I know you. You worked for Wallace.'

'Just like you did.'

'Just like I did,' Sam said, with a hint of regret. 'But Blackridge is done. Over. So why the hell are you here after me?'

'It doesn't matter, does it?' Brandt nodded to the gun. 'You have your shot. I suggest you take it before I feel well enough to stand.'

'Answer my question.' Sam ignored the threat. 'If Blackridge is done, then there are no orders. So what the hell is going on?'

'Look, Sam. We are both soldiers.'

'No, we're not. We haven't been for a long time.'

'Fine.' Brandt shrugged, pushing himself up slightly, giving Sam a hint that he was on the mend. 'Then we are both killers. That's what you are, Sam. A cold-blooded killer. You can dress it up as some noble mission, but like you said, there are no orders. Not anymore. Not on this path we have both taken. The only difference between us is that I kill for money, but you kill because deep down, you like it.'

Sam shook his head in defiance, more with himself than with Brandt's words. With them seemingly hitting Sam hard, Brandt took the opportunity of the distraction to shift his weight and slide one of his legs under his bottom. When the moment was right, he would spring forward.

But he would wait.

'I kill because it's the right thing to do. The people who I have put in the ground, they were bad people.'

'Were they killers?' Brandt interrupted. 'Because if not, what right do you have to commit crimes worse than them? The way I see it, you may as well get paid for the talents you have.'

'Your boy, the American, he said that I was worth more alive than dead.'

'Apparently so.'

'Who? Give me a name.'

'So you can kill them?'

Brandt's question rocked Sam once again. Grappling with his own conscience about his mission had been a long and arduous task. It was a battle he was slowly winning, but it didn't take much to let the doubt turn the tide against him. After a couple of moments of contemplation, Sam turned his gaze back to Brandt.

'So I can set things straight.'

'Not with this one. You killed her brother, and now she has put a price on your head so big that some major players have taken the opportunity. You may have stopped *Endwache*, but we are just the start.'

'How much?'

'*Wie bitte?*'

'How much has she put on me?'

'Five million alive. Three, dead.' Brandt smirked. 'That enough for you?'

'I'm a little insulted.' Sam shrugged. 'But was it worth it? For you to lose your crew and be in this situation?'

'Like I said, I get paid for what I do. I know you will probably justify to yourself that killing me is the right thing to do, but here I am. Sat down, unarmed, and offering you nothing but information.'

'Give me her name.'

'Dana Kovalenko.'

Sam raised his eyebrows in surprise. Kovalenko was a name he hadn't heard in nearly three years, ever since he'd taken down Andrei and Oleg in a bloody and brutal shootout in the Port of Tilbury in a successful attempt to save a young girl from a life of sheer horror. Their sex trafficking trade ended with the death of the Kovalenko broth-

94

ers, but it had started with their uncle, Sergei, who Sam had personally visited in Kiev and then eliminated swiftly.

He'd taken down the entire Kovalenko empire.

Brick by brick.

Body by body.

But Sam knew about vengeance. When his son had been taken from him by a drunk driver, Sam had found the man with the intention to kill him. When the moment finally came, and as Sam was halfway through beating the man to death, he stopped and forgave him. That had been the moment Sam knew there were people who needed him to fight for them, people the system and the world had let down, and people who lived in fear of those who did as they pleased.

But vengeance was a crazy drug, and if Sam had removed her entire family, then he understood what Dana Kovalenko was craving. And judging by the amount of money she was willing to spend, her craving was insatiable.

'How can I find…'

Sam's question was cut off by Brandt launching himself forward, trying desperately to cover the ten feet between himself and Sam with his massive frame. Instinctively, Sam lifted his hand and squeezed the trigger, just as Brandt dived forward. The bullet sliced through the thick ginger hair that hung from the man's chin before ripping a brutal hole through his neck. A splatter of blood flicked across the factory and Brandt hit the concrete hard, gasping as the blood began to fill in his throat. Sam stood and with his foot, he rolled Brandt onto his back, helping to speed up the process. Sam stood over his would-be killer with the gun in his deadly grip.

The man was drowning.

His eyes begged Sam for mercy.

Sam obliged.

With Roland Brandt's skull splattered across the

concrete, Sam marched to the table where he'd folded up his jacket, along with the mobile phone he'd taken from Brandt. He pressed the power button, but was greeted with a lock screen.

There was no pin.

Just the request of a fingerprint.

Sam sighed and searched the desk until he lifted a rusty, jagged scrap of metal and then walked back towards the dead body. With the phone in one hand and the implement in the other, Sam squatted down by the body and began testing the motionless fingers against the scanner on the back of the phone until he found the one he would take as a souvenir.

He needed to get access to the phone.

He needed to find Dana Kovalenko before – as Brandt had promised – things became a lot worse.

CHAPTER ELEVEN

DC Anderson couldn't believe how alive the Derbyshire Constabulary Divisional Headquarters were.

At eight o'clock in the morning, he was certain that the early morning shift change would have already happened, and those who were manning the offices would have been too entrenched in their early morning daze to notice him. However, the office was alive with activity, with numerous officers hurrying from briefing to patrol car, while their more senior leaders were busy directing traffic.

Something had happened, and he didn't know what.

The only blessing was, with everyone so focused on whatever had happened, no one could notice the state of him. Still wearing the same shirt as the night before, Anderson limped painfully through the main entrance and used his identity badge to pass through the electronic door. Every step was agony, but to those who did notice him, he looked fine.

Mendoza had made sure the torture had been discreet, and while there were no visible marks on Anderson's arms, hands or face, from the waist down, he had been put through the wringer.

As he shuffled towards his office, he felt an over-whelming rush of pain ride up from his legs to his brain and he felt dizzy, and he felt himself collapse against the wall, struggling to control it. As he wrestled for control, a few footsteps pounded past at the top of the corridor. One of them stopped.

'Liam?'

It was DC James Saddler.

Seeing his friend in peril, Saddler turned from his destination and hurried down the corridor to his friend. Having left the bar early the evening before, Saddler had gone home and spent the evening with his fiancée, Hannah, enjoying a takeaway and a relatively funny movie. By the looks of his good friend and colleague, the man had barely slept. Anderson was prone to a wild night, but rarely had Saddler ever seen him in such a state. For all his bravado, Anderson was a great detective, and usually ensured his professionalism was put before his personal proclivities.

'I'm fine, mate.' Anderson lied through gritted teeth, pushing himself straight and then offering his friend a pained smile.

'You look like shit.'

'I feel it.'

'Good night, eh?'

A shudder rushed down Anderson's spine. He wished it was a hangover and a regrettable one-night stand that hindered his body, but it was far darker. After being placed in a cab by his mysterious, yet generous friend, Anderson had found himself unconscious. When he was dragged out of the back of the Uber, he recalled seeing the lights of the car round the corner of the run-down industrial estate. The alcohol slowed his train of thought, and before he could connect the dots that he'd been abducted, Mendoza had driven the wind from his body with several thunderous body blows. Unable to defend himself or fight back,

Anderson had been dragged into a nondescript abandoned warehouse, where Mendoza had already set up shop. When Anderson had tried pathetically, to fight back, Mendoza aimed every blow to his ribs, ensuring not to leave any visible marks.

Ribs were broken, and after a brief, one-sided struggle, Anderson was strapped to a chair, with his bottom half stripped naked. Mendoza had rolled up the sleeves of his shirt, revealing a plethora of gang tattoos, and he told Anderson then and there that he had essentially been an off-the-books hitman for both Fidel and Raul Castro during their reigns over Cuba.

Then, as he showed Anderson the selection of tools he had for their meeting, he conceded that he was a dangerous man.

Anderson had begged to be let go, immediately crumbling under the threat of torture, and he guaranteed Mendoza that he would give him whatever he wanted. But that wasn't enough in Mendoza's eyes.

He needed to show Anderson what danger he was in.

And, more importantly, just what would happen to his friends and family if he tried to double-cross him.

The remit was simple enough. As the Derbyshire Police representative on the Sam Pope Task Force, Anderson had access to all the relevant information needed to locate the man. While the police were bound by law and procedure, Mendoza would be able to forge his own path to the wanted man and claim the large amount of money that came with it. With Pope situated in Anderson's back garden, the detective had more information to share than any other law enforcer in the country.

That made Anderson more powerful than he knew.

And Mendoza needed him to understand that any hint of betrayal, or any sniff to the other detectives that

Mendoza knew existed, would result in the slow and painful death of someone he cared about.

Despite his cries of understanding, Anderson was then subjected to an all-night session of pain, with Mendoza showing strict control on only ever taking the man to his limit, but never past it. To begin with, Mendoza had taken a metal meat tenderiser to Anderson's thighs. Ten vicious swings, which pulverised the man's quadriceps along with ripping the skin until it was mush. As Anderson had roared in agony, Mendoza had stuffed Anderson's own socks into his mouth.

With every swing, Mendoza had recommended he breathe through the pain, which Anderson did.

After that, Mendoza had removed several of Anderson's toenails by force, ripping them clean from the flesh of his toes.

An hour after that, he'd dripped vinegar onto the exposed flesh beneath them, causing Anderson to weep with agony. At some point during the barbaric torture, Anderson had a sudden rush of rage, and he spat the socks back at his tormentor and threatened him with the full force of the Derbyshire Police Force.

Mendoza had responded by taking a number of thumbtacks and sticking them into muscles around Anderson's knee cap, each one embedding into the skin and drawing blood.

By six a.m., after Mendoza had left the warehouse for an hour and returned with a coffee for them both, the sadistic hitman had promised Anderson one more reminder of discomfort before he left. Taking a basic nail file, Mendoza violently rubbed the implement against the bottom of Anderson's right foot, shearing away a couple of layers of skin until it was red raw. The pain had been unbearable, but when he then poured the vinegar over the exposed skin, Anderson had broken completely.

He promised Mendoza all the information he could find on Sam Pope, and only then would Mendoza step away from his promise of butchering his family.

Saddler's voice brought Anderson back from his torturous memory.

'Liam, you okay, buddy?'

'Yeah, just a rough night.'

'I figured.' Saddler held his friend by the shoulder. 'Do you need a doctor? I mean, I've seen you hungover, but you look awful.'

'I'm good. Think I took a fall and hurt my ankle. I'll be fine.' Anderson nodded to the group of uniformed officers rushing to a briefing room. 'What's going on? It's never this busy—'

'You don't know? We took in two Americans last night, both armed, one beaten to a pulp, the other with two bullet wounds, both in Spondon.'

'No shit?'

'Not much to go on with regards to witnesses, but CCTV on the ATM across the street showed a man fitting Sam Pope's description leaving the café, where we found the guy beaten to near death. It's fuzzy, but we're pretty certain it's him.'

'Did they get him?' Anderson asked, trying to hide the fear in his voice. Mendoza had made it clear there was money on Sam's head, and he shook at the thought of telling the man someone had beaten him to the punch.

'Nope. The two Americans aren't talking either. The woman who runs the café said she hid in the stockroom, so didn't see anything. You should see the state of the place.'

'So, nothing on Pope?' Anderson asked, before stumbling back into the room after foolishly putting pressure on his right foot.

'Christ, mate. Go home.'

'I will. But where are we with Sam?'

'Potential license plate on a vehicle. It's on the board in the main room. But look, all free hands are on this. I'll call by later and check up on ya.' Saddler looked tentatively at his watch. 'I gotta go, but I'll get some food in later and make sure you're all right.'

With another friendly pat on the arm, Saddler took off in a brief jog back up the corridor, leaving his pained friend to slowly amble to the main room. As promised, there was a license plate number, and grainy CCTV of a Range Rover with the same plate. Anderson sheepishly nodded to a few officers, who responded in kind and after taking a photo of the plate, he turned and headed back to the exit, stopping only once to vomit in the gents.

A combination of the pain and the threat of what was to come. As he splashed water on his face, he caught a glimpse of himself in the mirror. He was a ghostly pale, and if he hadn't have gotten so drunk and run his mouth, none of this would have happened.

Anderson knew he needed to make a change.

Be more like Saddler.

Taking a deep breath, he shuffled towards the door, ready to rendezvous with Mendoza and pass on the information, knowing there would be more anarchy to come.

———

The rich aroma of coffee gently guided Dana Kovalenko from her sleep, and she took a deep, satisfied breath before she rolled over onto her back. After successfully sending a group of elite contract killers after her brothers' murderer, she'd spent the rest of the day treating herself to a pampering session. It not only took her mind off what was to come, but it also allowed her to scrub away the dirt of the situation.

This was the type of thing Andrei used to do.

Nobody crossed her brother. Ever.

While she mourned the death of her other brother, Oleg, it was Andrei who her heart had belonged to and knowing that she'd set in motion the demise of the man who'd killed him filled her with excitement. Over the next couple of days, one of those men would deliver Sam Pope to her, hopefully alive. If they did, then she'd already cooked up a number of wonderful and brutal ways she would test the man's pain threshold, before bringing him to the point where he begged for death.

She would grant it, eventually.

But there was fun to be had beforehand.

Vengeance to enact.

Uri sat on the edge of the bed, a smile across his rugged face and the gormless stare of a puppy dog. Dana offered him a polite grin, knowing the previous night's sexual encounter was clearly still playing on Uri's mind. The power of sentencing another man to death had stirred something within Dana, and when she and Uri laid on the bed, she'd taken extreme control and was certain she'd treated her right-hand man to the most enjoyable night of his life.

The fresh coffee was just the first of what she expected to be many gifts to express his gratitude. She shuffled up the bed until her back was against the headrest, her naked chest sliding out from beneath the sheets to expose her breasts. Uri tried to avert his eyes, and his lack of subtlety caused Dana to roll hers.

She'd expected her brother's penthouse to have been seized by the police after his death and the dissolution of his empire, but to her surprise, it hadn't been in his name. It had been in hers, another sign of his love for her, and she'd expected the swanky apartment block to be the hive of activity it had once been. But the rumours of Kovalenko's misgivings had clearly spread through the residence, leaving the expensive building completely dormant and undoubtedly haemorrhaging money for whoever owned it. Dana didn't care.

The privacy of being the only resident in a four-storey building suited her perfectly. As she sipped her coffee, she looked around the room and imagined her brother still being there.

Being the one who had brought her coffee.

'I trust you slept well?'

Uri tried to start the conversation, sipping his own coffee with muscular arms that stretched the sleeves of his polo shirt. Dana knew she didn't love him but was certainly grateful for how dedicated he was to the family. The fact he was a former soldier certainly helped.

'I did.' Dana sipped her coffee. 'Any news?'

'I have kept the phone off. I thought you could do with the rest.'

'Well, go and get it will you?'

Obediently, Uri scuttled out of the room, leaving Dana to slither from the sheets and stride to the floor-to-ceiling window that offered a reasonably enjoyable view of London. The staggered buildings offered a glum, grey palette that mirrored the clouds above. Taking a few seconds to offer the world a glimpse of her naked body, Dana lifted a silk dressing gown from the chair nearby and slid it over her skin, tying it loosely at the front. She pushed the window open slightly, and then placed a cigarette between her lips and lit it. As the soothing smoke entered her body, she felt another twinge of excitement.

Sam Pope could already be captured.

Could already be dead.

As Dana contemplated the closing of this chapter of her life, Uri stepped back in, phone in hand and a look of bemusement on his face.

'What is it?' Dana demanded, asserting her authority.

'The news sites are talking about a violent episode in Derbyshire. Talk of armed Americans captured by the police.'

'The ones who took the contract?'

'It doesn't say. But I do not believe in coincidence.'

'Any news on Pope?' Dana puffed her cigarette with irritation.

'Not yet,' Uri said as he handed her the phone. 'But you have missed calls.'

Dana quickly snatched the phone and looked at the screen. There were seven missed calls, all from the same number. She didn't recognise it, but logic dictated it was one of the hitmen calling to collect the bounty.

Her hand shook as she returned the call.

A lightning bolt of excitement cascaded down her spine as the call connected.

'This is Dana Kovalenko,' she said before the person on the other end of the phone answered. 'Do you have him?'

The next ten words eradicated all that excitement and replaced it with a cocktail of rage and terror.

'Hello, Dana. This is Sam Pope. We need to talk.'

CHAPTER TWELVE

Six Months Earlier...

The warm spring morning had been overwhelmed by a sudden downpour, and the drizzle was pattering gently against the window to the bathroom of the Bethnal Green Youth Centre. Despite the weather, the place was its usual hub of activity, with a few dozen local teenagers finding their way to the building in hope of finding entertainment. Sam loved the energy of the place, watching as his late friend Theo Walker's legacy was living and breathing before him.

Once a highly respected medic, Theo had stepped away from the military life when he became disillusioned with Project Hailstorm, leaving with a handshake and a medal.

Sam had been airlifted out with two holes in his chest and a less than five per cent chance of survival.

But he did.

He was born to survive.

But since Theo's untimely and heroic death at the beginning of his crusade against crime, Sam had seen another friend, Adrian Pearce continue the good work Theo had started, building a community for the children who wanted a better life than the streets offered them.

Pearce was stricter than Theo had ever been, with his near three decades working for the Metropolitan Police, ingraining a sense of authority with every word he spoke. But Pearce was a good guy, one of the few people Sam trusted, and was the one who had offered him this second chance.

The world thought he was dead, killed in a drug war in South Carolina.

To everyone at the youth centre, he was Jonathan Cooper, an old police friend of Pearce's, and a quiet man who did the odd jobs. They smiled and said hello, but for the most part, they left him alone, and after fighting for so long, Sam had found a place where he could find a little peace.

A little redemption.

As the commotion grew louder from the main hall, Sam chuckled and then returned to his back, lying underneath the sink with a wrench in his hand.

'That outta do it,' he said with one final, powerful twist that caused the impressive muscles in his arm to strain.

'Yo, JC. You're looking wedge, man,' Curtis said with a chuckle, flexing his own arms.

'Thanks?' Sam raised his eyebrows. 'I guess that's a compliment.'

'Yeah. You need to take me to the gym, bruv.'

'I don't think you could keep up.' Sam chuckled as he sat up and held out his hand. Curtis took it and helped Sam to his feet. He was a good kid, one of the older ones that frequented the centre and a great role model for the others. As with most of the other kids who stopped by, Curtis was from a broken home but had made a decision to better his life rather than let that define him. He'd shown a keen interest in some of the jobs Sam had done and often shadowed him.

He wanted to be an electrician, and Sam and Pearce were both aligned in trying their best to make that happen for him.

'I don't know, JC. I reckon I could outrun you, still.' Curtis smirked. 'But I guess you don't need to run from anything, huh?'

'Oh, I'd still run,' Sam said, stroking the thick beard that hung from his jaw. Since returning under his fake name, Sam had grown out his beard along with his hair, which now flowed down to his neck in thick waves. The beard, tinged with grey hairs, itched like crazy, but he'd got used to it. 'Never stand your ground unless you absolutely have to, Curtis. You hear me? If you have the option to walk away from a bad situation, then you prove yourself right, and you run.'

Curtis nodded, understanding that Sam wasn't joking around anymore and was trying to impart some sage advice. At that moment, knuckles rapped on the door of the bathroom and the two turned to see the beaming smile of Pearce. For a man in his early fifties, Pearce was in great shape and as always, immaculately presented. His trimmed, grey beard was sharply lined to his jaw, and his black skin was the perfect contrast. He wore a buttoned-up Oxford shirt and chinos, and looked a million times better than the shabby handyman Sam had become.

'All sorted?' Pearce asked, nodding to the sink.

'Yup.' Sam smiled and patted Curtis on the shoulder. 'I think my apprentice here would make a hell of a plumber.'

'No thanks.' Curtis looked offended. 'I'll stick with the electrics, if that's okay.'

'A lot of money in plumbing, son.' Pearce offered.

'Yeah, and shit filled pipes.' Curtis immediately looked mortified. 'Sorry, Adrian.'

As a former soldier, Sam appreciated the level of excellence that Pearce expected from the regulars, and swearing was something he disproved of. Pearce shrugged.

'Don't worry about it.' He turned and looked over his shoulder. 'I think Becky is about to leave if you wanted to walk her?'

Curtis blushed, looked at the ground and then sheepishly to Sam.

'Hey, don't look at me. It isn't me she's interested in.' Sam joked and Curtis nodded, said his thanks and goodbyes and then scurried back through the youth centre in the pursuit of young love. Sam smiled to himself and began to gather up his tools.

'You're better at this than you think,' Pearce eventually said.

'What, plumbing? Meh, it's not too difficult, really.'

'No, I meant with the kids.' Pearce folded his arms and leant against the doorframe. 'They gravitate to you, Sam. They could learn a lot—'

'Trust me, they're a lot better off listening to you than me. If I can help Curtis get a decent start in life, then that's great—'

'Did you mean what you just said?' Pearce interrupted, stepping forward slightly. 'About walking away if you had the chance?'

'You heard that, huh?'

'I did.' Pearce reached out and patted Sam's rounded shoulder. 'It takes a lot for a man to know when to act and when to walk away. You, of all people, know that.'

'I'm done with that life.' Sam smiled and shrugged. 'I'm just a handyman now and for the first time in a long time, I'm at least content.'

'Good.' Pearce turned and stepped to the door. 'The only time a man should ever fight is for those he loves or for himself. What Wallace did to you, what he lied to you about, that doesn't define you. You know that, right?'

Sam gritted his teeth, struggling to accept it.

'Like I said, I'm done with that life.'

'You're a good man, Sam. I know you will only fight when you know you have to. But let's just hope that never happens.'

'Let's hope so.'

Sam did a small salute with his index finger to Pearce as he left the room, and once again on his own, Sam began to pack the last of his tools into his toolbox, contemplating just how many people there were left in the world that he would go to war for. There weren't many, but for those who made the list, any act or threat towards them would be the only reason he would fight back.

But with every fibre of his being, he hoped that would never be the case.

———

Sam held the phone to his ear, looking around at the abandoned crime scene which he'd just splattered with fresh evidence. Brandt's body was motionless, a pool of blood widening around it with fragments of skull scattered around. There was blood trickling from the dead man's right hand, and as Sam awaited a response from his clearly furious caller, he looked down at the severed finger in his other hand. He gently tossed it in his palm and caught it, briefly recalling removing a finger from a prisoner when trapped in the Grid over two years ago.

That was to keep his cover as he infiltrated the gang of the one of the UK's most notorious criminals.

This time, it was to speak to the person who had ordered his death.

He looked at the finger again and scoffed to himself.

Needs must.

It had been over thirty seconds since he'd announced himself on the call, and apart from the heavy breathing, he'd received nothing back. Then, the thick Ukrainian accent echoed through the device, the words laced with hatred.

'You are a dead man.'

'So they keep telling me.' Sam shrugged it off. 'Dana, isn't it?'

'You do not need to know who this is.'

'Dana Kovalenko?' Sam knew he was kicking the hornet's nest. 'I killed your brothers a few years back. Your uncle, too, right? Just so we are clear.'

Sam heard her move away from the phone and mumble something in her own language. He assumed it wasn't complimentary.

'You will pay for you have done to my family.'

'Well, according to your friend, who let me borrow his phone, it sounds like you're the one paying for it. A lot. So how many more of them are coming for me?'

'Fuck you, Sam Pope. You think this will make me call off what *you* started?'

'I would implore you to do so. Save a lot more people getting hurt.'

'Like my brother, Andrei?' Dana's voice shook, completely lost in her grief. 'You put a bullet in him and left him for dead.'

'Your brother was a bad man…'

'You hanged my other brother from the ceiling like he was nothing but meat. You travelled to my country, to my home, and killed the man who took us in when my father was killed. Many people have already been hurt. And now, it is your turn.'

Sam had always known there were ripple effects to what he did. Despite his targets always walking on the wrong side of the law, they still had people who cared for them.

Who loved them.

It was only a matter of time before Sam killed someone who would have someone who would care. Someone who wouldn't accept that karma came in the shape of a bullet and would seek the same retribution Sam had. Despite how cruel and calculating the Kovalenko family had been, they had been a family.

Sam had caused this woman to bury the three people closest to her.

Even in light of the man's crimes, she worshipped Andrei and for his death, Sam would be hunted.

There was only one way this could end, and Sam sighed, knowing that he would never be able to keep his promise to his son now, despite how hard he tried.

'I'm going to offer you one chance, Dana. Call off the hit, take your money and walk away. I know you hate me, and you want me dead for killing the person closest to you. Believe me, I know what vengeance feels like. I've lived it. But trying to kill me won't bring your brothers back, and it won't bring you peace. I killed your brothers because they abducted young girls and sold them into a life worse than death. You might be okay with that, but as far as I'm concerned, I did what was necessary.' Sam could hear her breathing escalating. 'I did what was right. And if I had to, I'd put a bullet in him again.'

'Then I would suggest you pray that they kill you before they bring you to me.' Dana's voice grumbled with evil intent. 'I will put your body through more pain than you ever imagined. You will beg me for death. But I will keep you alive. Just enough, so you can watch me bring in anyone you ever cared about and watch as I kill them, too.'

'Hate to break it to you, Dana, but I'm hardly Mr Popular.'

'You might have no friends, but you have people you care about. That old black detective. That woman police officer who my brother should have killed. Your ex-wife. You have people.'

'Don't give me a reason, Dana.'

'So did I. You took them from me. And now I have put your end in motion.'

'I'm afraid all you've done is make this inevitable.'

'Excuse me? I don't understand you.'

Sam's jaw clenched. His muscles tightened.

Blood red fury coursed through him.

'I've been trying, for some time now, either to leave this path and walk a different one. I've been trying not to kill people unless they mean harm to me, or the people I care about. I even made a promise to my son that I'd try to be a better man.' Sam took a breath, not wanting the emotion of his guilt to take control. 'But I am a good man. I know that, and for that reason, I'm going to make Jamie a new promise. A promise that I will do what I couldn't for him. I will protect those who mean something to me with every fibre of my being. So, if that means I have to kill more of your money-hungry soldiers, then so be it.'

'You do not want to start a war with me, Sam Pope.'

Sam's fist clenched as he delivered his final retort.

'I already have.'

With that, Sam hung up the call and tossed the phone onto the dusty metal table, along with Brandt's removed finger. Talking her down was always going to be a long shot, but it was worth a try. There was no point trying to be a better man and then not seek peace.

But there were no other options.

With the amount of money she'd put on him, more people would soon take the bait. Brandt and his operation were top of the line, and he'd intimated they weren't the only outfit in the running.

There would be more of them.

Dana Kovalenko was desperate for revenge, and she'd already told him the hand she would play if necessary. People he cared about would die for his sins, and he couldn't live through that again.

Theo.

Mac.

Marsden.

Sam had lost enough people since he'd begun this war, and now, that war had bit back. There was only one way to keep them safe, and one way for him to stop looking over his shoulder.

Dana Kovalenko needed to die.

And to do so, Sam was going to need to return home, load up his arsenal, and head off back to London, ready to take on some of the best hitmen money could buy.

CHAPTER THIRTEEN

'I already have.'

Sam's ominous threat was immediately followed by the line going dead. Dallow sat in his chair anxiously, wondering when the two men who had stormed his room were going to kill him. The young man, Defoe, whistled anxiously as he took off his headphone and sat back in his chair. The older one, Nash, sat still, unmoved by the conversation they had listened in on.

After what felt like forever, Dallow was delighted when Defoe broke the silence.

'He sounds pissed.'

'He sounds calm,' Nash responded, sliding off his own headset and handing it back to Dallow. After the young man had come-to following Defoe's needless blow to the jaw, Nash had explained the situation to the man in no uncertain terms.

He worked for them now. Any refusal to cooperate meant he wouldn't be going home.

Dallow was hardly one to put up a fight, and when they insisted he pack up his gear, he did so in a heartbeat. Thirty minutes later, he was carrying it out to their car, where they transported him across Derby to their own, more luxurious hotel. In the grand suite they'd taken up, Dallow was afforded more space for his set up, as well as the offer of dinner by Nash.

Despite being the kinder of two, Dallow feared the large, tattooed assassin the most.

There was something about his calm demeanour that unsettled him. Accompanied by the file he'd seen on the man, Dallow knew he was sharing a room and a conversation with potentially the most dangerous man he would ever meet. Defoe, on the other hand, had the same character as Cook, only his resume was more substantial.

The man was a prick, but he was dangerous.

All Dallow could do was play along, and when they tracked the signal of Brandt's phone once it had been reactivated, Dallow immediately hacked into the phone line. They heard every single word of the conversation between Pope and Dana, and Dallow had noticed the anger simmering behind Nash's eyes.

'So, what's our angle?' Defoe cut through the silence as he sat back in his chair, rocking on the back legs.

'We need to draw him out,' Nash stated coldly as he stood. 'Somewhere out of sight.'

'The fuck?' Defoe slammed the legs back down. 'He's going straight to her. Why don't we just follow the phone signal and jump him when he walks to the fucking door?'

'It won't be that easy…' Dallow offered but was shut down by Defoe's infuriated gaze.

'You stay the fuck out of this.' Defoe stood a little too aggressively for Nash's liking. 'He's worth more alive, remember?'

Nash stepped forward, towering over his colleague and immediately redrawing the balance of power between the two. Defoe tried to save face in front of their hostage by raising his chin, but Nash saw the little twitch in his left eye.

Fear.

Defoe knew who Jacob Nash was.

'The kid's right. You think a guy like this doesn't plan for every outcome? And even if he didn't, that he couldn't quickly figure one out?' Nash turned to Dallow. 'Your guys he took out. They were good, right?'

'Good?'

'Trained.'

'Oh yeah, very much so.' Dallow shrugged. 'I mean, they killed a lot of people and made a lot of money.'

'And he took them out like that.' Nash snapped his fingers.

'But they weren't the Foundation,' Defoe insisted. 'We've been doing what we do on a level they could never comprehend for years. This Sam Pope fuck, he might be a soldier, but we are the best of the best. The last thing I ever expected was for you, the mighty Jacob Nash of all people, to be scared.'

Nash chuckled and shook his head.

'Believe me, I'm not scared. Worried? Sure.' Nash turned away from Defoe. 'But if we are going to take this guy, doing it when he's ready for a gunfight with a woman he's promised to go to war with probably isn't the smartest idea, is it?'

'We outnumber him…' Defoe offered, realising he was losing the battle with common sense.

'So did those guys. And where are they now? Dead most likely.' Nash turned to Dallow. 'Can you contact him?'

'Who? Pope?'

'He has your boss's phone, right?' Nash leant forward, one hand on the desk, his mighty frame engulfing Dallow.

'Arrange something. An ammo supply. Intel. Anything. Be creative.'

'Lure him out?'

Nash smiled at Defoe, who scowled.

'Bingo.' Nash patted Dallow on the shoulder. 'Find somewhere remote, no CCTV. At least one floor up. If we remove as many advantages as possible, then the man will talk.'

'Talk?' Defoe asked, his eyebrow cocked with intrigue.

'Surrender. You know what I mean.'

Defoe sat back down in his chair and glared at Nash. The man never mixed his words and usually, the thought of ending a contract as swiftly and as clinically as possible was the man's only thought process. The whole trip had been strange, with Defoe noticing what he believed to be a hesitation in Nash that he'd never seen before.

He didn't like it.

It wasn't what the Foundation stood for.

'I'll start searching now, sir.' Dallow turned to his laptop, which was framed by the other monitors. 'I'll run a list of abandoned facilities in the area and then set it up.'

Nash patted him on the shoulder once more and then turned towards the door, stretching out his colossal back as he walked. Defoe was staring daggers at him as he walked, and without looking back, Nash stopped in the doorway to his bedroom.

'You have something to say, Eli?'

Defoe stammered, caught unawares.

'No. Just I think this plan is bullshit, but that isn't my call.

'You're right. It's not,' Nash stated firmly, pulling rank. 'Now, get some rest. It's been a long day, a longer night, and if we want any chance of bringing this guy in alive, I have a feeling we're gonna need our beauty sleep.'

As Nash stepped out of the room, Defoe chuckled to himself and called out after him.

'You need a lot longer than a few hours.' Nash ignored it, and Defoe turned to Dallow, expecting a courtesy smile. It wasn't forthcoming, so Defoe leant forward and clipped him round the back of the head. 'Get back to work, bitch.'

Dallow cowered, cursed under his breath and fought against the rising tide of exhaustion, knowing that he was simply prolonging his stay as a loose end.

When all was said and done, they'd want to make sure all of those were tied up.

———

The grey clouds hung over the high-rise flats in Wembley, only adding to the depressing decay of the area. While it was synonymous with the impressive stadium for the national football team, the surrounding area had been neglected. The strip from stadium to train station had been gentrified, bringing with it multiple outlet stores, an Amazon store and numerous bars and restaurants. Those travelling for the football could marvel at the expense of it all, but walking a few streets beyond, and the poverty of the town was as clear as day.

Dana had turned her nose up at the state of the area. Considering her late brother's penthouse was situated in Kensington, one of the more affluent parts of the capital, driving through Wembley was like being back in some of the worst parts of Kyiv.

Uri said nothing as he guided the car through the traffic, eventually pulling into an estate that was dominated by graffiti and small clusters of black youths, many of them with their hoods up. The government had long since abandoned those who lived here, and those that remained looked after themselves.

Their eyes lit up as the expensive-looking Mercedes pulled into a parking space, flanked either side by a BT repair van and an abandoned car covered in parking tickets.

'Stay here,' Uri said firmly, stepping out of the car and fixing a furious glare at the approaching gang. Immediately, they all looked hesitant, but clung tightly to the idea of strength in numbers.

'Oi, bruv. Nice car.'

'Man looks like Vladimir Putin.'

'Defo a fuckin' foreigner.'

Uri slammed his door shut and stepped around the front of the car, his powerful frame stretching his bomber jacket and almost beckoned them forward with his eyes. Again, they hesitated. As the standoff began, Dana rolled her eyes at the pathetic display of machismo and threw her door open and stepped out. Instantly, the threats turned to catcalls, as the rowdy young gang gawped at the striking woman who wore a tight black jumpsuit and a leather jacket.

'Do you boys live here?' Dana pointed to the decrepit block of flats behind them.

'Damn straight, girl,' the apparent leader said, rubbing his hands together. 'Wanna see my room?'

The gang all began to chuckle, and Dana sighed.

'You wouldn't be able to handle it,' Dana replied, rolling her eyes.. 'Do you know Leon Barnett?'

'Yo, what you after Leon for?' One of them piped up and was immediately shut down by an elbow to the ribs. Dana pointed at the young man and Uri stepped forward, barging past the "leader" and a few others and grabbing the young man by the scruff of his jacket. The kid was no older than eighteen, and he struggled pointlessly as Uri marched him back towards Dana. The rest of the gang began to turn, and the spokesman reached into his pocket and pulled out a knife.

'Take your fucking hands off him or I'll fucking do you, bruv.'

Uri rolled his eyes, and then flashed the Glock strapped under his bulging arm, drawing a hushed panic from the gang.

'We are not here for trouble.' Dana assured them all. She turned to the terrified kid who had been brought before her. 'You know this Leon Barnett?'

'H-h-he's my cousin.'

'And he lives here?' Dana pointed once again. The boy nodded. 'Take me to him. Now.'

The cousin shot a glance to Uri, who returned one with such promised brutality that the boy quivered in fear. He nodded and then began to amble through his friends towards the door to the apartment block. Dana turned to Uri and the gang.

'You all stay here. Play nice.'

Uri folded his arms across his chest and then leant against the bonnet of the car, his eyes fixed on the hostile gang before him. They hurled a few words of abuse at Dana, but she marched on, following her reluctant guide into the stairwell of the flats and immediately gagged at the warm stench of urine.

'Lift's broken,' the kid said as he ascended the staircase. 'Has been for years.'

Dana ignored him and followed him up four flights until he stopped at a door. The paintwork had chipped, and the knocker was coated in rust. The entire building depressed Dana, who had lived in luxury for so long and every step through the neglected building was one step further into the terrifying past with her father.

The father who had tried to rape her.

The father her brother had killed to protect her.

The brother who Sam Pope had murdered.

The rage sent a burning sensation travelling through her veins and the mere sound of his voice on the phone call that morning had threatened to tip her over the edge. She'd dreamt of her revenge for years, but now, with one of her hired guns down, Sam had made it clear he was coming for closure.

To him, her brother was a target that needed taking down. She'd stepped into his place, and after she'd made threats to those Sam cared about, she knew she needed more than just Uri. Despite the man's loyalty, he was just one man, and Sam Pope, as detestable as he was, had proven he was a one-man army.

They needed help.

She needed more men willing to die for her.

And as the door opened, she offered a smile.

'Who the fuck are you?'

'Leon?' The man nodded. 'My name is Dana Kovalenko.'

The door slammed shut at the mention of her surname, and Leon's cousin shrugged. Dana huffed.

She had no time for the fragility of the male ego. She pounded on the door with a closed fist. It swung open, and Dana was taken aback by what she saw.

Leon Barnett had worked for her brother many years before, sending out his gang members to infiltrate parties and nightclubs to locate and target young women and teenage girls. They would then be taken and delivered to the Kovalenkos, who would then sell them into the sex trafficking trade in Eastern Europe. Barnett was responsible for over thirty abductions, which meant he'd sent over thirty families spiralling into disarray and over thirty girls to a fate worse than death. For that, Dana felt little sympathy for his obvious wounds.

The man's right arm was missing from just above the elbow, the stub a horrific tapestry of burns.

'I remember you,' Leon said coldly as Dana stepped into his small, unkept flat. It stank of marijuana. 'You were with your brothers when we set up the deal all those years back.'

'I remember,' Dana said coldly, looking around the apartment in disgust. 'I see you have fallen from where you were.'

'Well, some shit went down. In fact, I believe the motherfucker who marched my black ass outta here butt naked and then took my fucking arm off with a vat of acid was looking for your brothers.'

'Sam Pope.'

Dana saw the flicker of fury in the man's eyes at the mention of the name. He shook his head and stomped into what passed as a living room, reached down into his ashtray and pulled up his spliff. He took a long, pungent pull on it and then offered it to Dana, who waved it off.

'I heard he killed your brothers. Boom.' Leon made a gun with his fingers.

'He did.' Dana crossed her arms. 'Which is why I am here to offer you a job.'

Leon started laughing and took another pull on his joint before placing it back on the overflowing ashtray.

'The fuck makes you think I want to work for you?' He shook his head. 'Look, we lost a lot of shit because of your family. Credibility. Business. Fuck, me and my crew barely get by slinging drugs on these estates. I lost a fucking arm for your family, and I got nothing. So, you can shove your job up that fine arse of yours and get the fuck out of here.'

'I can offer you something no one else can.' Dana smiled. 'I can pay you and your crew handsomely. You need guns. I can get them for you. But I can offer *you*, Leon. I can offer *you* the one thing you want.'

Leon looked down at the grotesque stump that hung from his shoulder and remembered the horrifying moment Sam Pope stood over him and poured a vat of homemade acid over his arm until it melted beyond repair. How the man had taken everything from him.

He felt his lone fist clench.

'Yeah. And what's that?'

Dana flashed her perfect smile.

'The same thing I want. Revenge.'

CHAPTER FOURTEEN

Sam placed both hands against the tiles of the adequate shower cubicle and bowed his head, allowing the heavily advertised power shower to rain down on him. The Airbnb he was staying in offered the bare minimum of amenities, but the shower was certainly a welcome one. As the water crashed against his short, brown hair, and pushed it down against his forehead, he closed his eyes and took a few moments. A few months ago, he'd been close to happy for the first time in years.

The world thought he was dead, and he was spending time with good people, helping them to mould a better future for good kids. There were no pressures. No threats.

No deaths.

But the world had an awful way of turning, and Sam knew, as the water ran down his spine, that he was doing the right thing again. The months since he'd left London had proved it. The country was full of terrible people, willing to do abhorrent things to make money and seize power. With the government unwilling to change the state of the nation, more and more good people were falling on desperate times and made themselves more susceptible to those who played by their own rules.

Men like Daniel Bowker, who, for the right price, happily assaulted and killed in the name of a pharmaceutical company and their deplorable CEO.

Men like Slaven Kovac, who had shipped hundreds of weapons into the country and armed the criminals that walked the streets, selling the drugs that he imported.

These were dangerous people, operating outside the police radar and way beyond the line of decency. There was no limit for them, nothing they wouldn't have done to maintain their power, which was why Sam had to intervene. Innocent people, like Lynsey Beckett and Jack Townsend had been caught up in their violent operations, and had Sam not intervened, they would have just been more names to add to the list of good people who had been killed.

Names like Theo Walker and Helal Miah, caught up in the war on crime and brutally killed because of it.

Sam had stepped away from the path he'd trodden ever since that explosion at the London Marathon over three years ago, but the call of duty had pulled him back.

He had to break his promise to his son.

He had to kill these people.

Someone had to fight back.

The shower shut off and Sam stepped out, wrapping a towel around his waist and then he leant forward, grasping the sides of the sink and he took a deep breath. It wasn't just the guilt that was weighing him down.

His body was feeling the effects of war.

Adrenaline had carried him through the prior evening, but since executing Brandt and threatening Dana Kovalenko, it had begun to wear off, and after a restless few hours sleep, he'd been woken by her furious voice over a threatening phone call. Since then, he'd tried to rest again, but the aftermath of his fight with Cook had drained him.

His nose was likely broken, and there was bruising appearing under his right eye. His lip was split from being struck with the table leg, and whenever he moved his left arm, he felt a stabbing pain from his ribs. They had been broken a month previous when he'd been sent off a balcony within Slaven Kovac's burning mansion, and having Cook drive his solid boots into them had likely undone any of the healing since then.

The rest of his body was a tapestry of pain.

Despite being in peak physical condition, Sam's chiselled body was covered in scars. The right side of his torse was still smattered with decade old burns. His shoulder bore the scar of a stab wound he'd received from one of the Mitchell Brothers when he stormed the High Rise.

He had five bullet scars.

One in his leg from the shootout in the Port of Tilbury.

One in the shoulder and one through his stomach from his vengeful protégé, Mac.

Then there were the two that dominated his impressive chest. Like two white eyes staring at him in the mirror, they were a constant reminder of how treacherous the world was. Under the pretence of fighting for freedom, Sam had come too close to uncovering the truth of Project Hailstorm and General Ervin Wallace, the man who had given him his orders, and he was shot and left to die in the dark. He nearly didn't make it home, back to Lucy, back to the family he would have and the one that would be cruelly taken from him.

The cuts and bruises from the fights he'd survived had healed over time, but mentally, he remembered them all.

Edinson.

Bowker.

Oleg Kovalenko.

The Hangman of Baghdad.

Slaven Kovac.

There had been others, but Sam had survived. Barely, but he had survived.

He was built for it.

But now, as he looked at the damage he'd done to himself in the mirror before him, he wondered how much longer he'd be able to keep fighting. To keep putting himself through so much to put the world right. But right now, he didn't have a choice.

He had to fight back.

Dana Kovalenko had made it clear that the longer he stayed alive, the more desperate she would get. Her threats of hurting those close to him may have been widely optimistic, but they were swimming in dark waters. She'd already invested an eye-watering sum of money to see him killed, which meant he knew she wouldn't relent. If she needed to identify people he cared about, he was certain she would stop at nothing to do so.

Too many good people had been hurt because of him.

Too many had died.

Sam knew that one day his time would come, and when it did, he would die with a clean conscience for the things he'd done. Fighting back was the right thing to do, but not at the expense of others.

Good people.

Innocent people.

People he cared about.

With a resigned sigh, he splashed a little more water on his face, brushed his teeth, and then headed back to the quaint bedroom of the apartment. His clothes were laid out on the bed he wouldn't sleep in again, and he began to dress, easing his body into the clothing with as minimal discomfort as possible.

His body was screaming for a rest. For the fight to be over.

But until he'd taken out Dana Kovalenko and cancelled the bounty on his head, the fight was as dangerous as it had ever been. The price of his life had drawn the best of the best to the UK, each of them ready to hunt him down and take him in. Considering Dana was offering more for him alive meant she had something worse than death lined up for him.

But Sam would fight.

He was born to survive.

As he slid the black T-shirt over his body, he grimaced with pain. He needed to get some painkillers on his way to London, and he marched across the room to the sports bag on the table, which was stuffed with the remaining weaponry he had.

Two SA80 Assault Rifles.

Two Glock 17s.

Three grenades.

Sam had promised Dana Kovalenko a war, so he was going to bring her one. Until the final bullet flew from his gun or the last breath left his body, Sam Pope would fight back.

Then Brandt's phone pinged with an incoming message, and Sam suddenly had a chance to end the war before it had even begun.

———

'It's done.'

Dallow blew out his cheeks and placed his phone down on the table. He'd been held captive by Nash and Defoe, but not uncomfortably. Sure, his jaw still stung with soreness from the vicious strike from the younger man, but beyond the odd snarky comment, there had been nothing else forthcoming. Nash, while unbelievably imposing with every movement, spoke softly and politely, and had made it clear that as long as Dallow was useful, he'd be fine.

Dallow was desperate to prove himself just that, as he was certain that once the mission was over, the two Americans wouldn't want to leave any breadcrumbs.

Unfortunately, one of them was always in the room with him, making it impossible for him to either reach out for help or investigate them any further. He'd thought about calling the police secretly, but then he would have to explain his role in everything.

He'd end up in prison.

And his chances of survival there were slimmer than sitting in the reasonably comfortable chair he was in.

Defoe had his hands behind his head, leant back in the chair on the opposite side of the table, and he regarded Dallow with disdain.

'It ain't done. You sent a fucking text message.' He sat forward and lifted the handgun from the table. 'We're the ones who have to get it done.'

'I didn't mean anything by it…'

'Enough.' Nash entered the room, his arms stretching the white T-shirt to its limit and exposing the tattoos that ran the length of his arms. 'Good work.'

Dallow smiled and quickly withdrew it as Defoe stood, making a show of the weapon in his hand.

'So he's useless now, right?'

'Whoa, wait…'

Defoe started laughing. A needless display of power and one which drew the ire of Nash, who stomped forward and swiftly disarmed his colleague.

It was a show of skill.

Of superiority.

'What the fuck is your problem?' Defoe snarled.

'He still has his uses, and you don't need to dick measure with him.'

'Jeez, Jake, I'm just fucking around.' Defoe patted Nash on his shoulder. 'You should try to lighten up. Well, seen as how we got a few hours to kill, I am going to see what the spa's like downstairs and how much it will cost for the nice lady to jerk me off. You should come, big guy. Might ease some of that tension.'

'Get your hand off me, or you'll need to get her to pull your dick out next time you need to take a piss.'

Defoe scoffed but obliged and then stepped past his hulking superior and headed to the door. As he did, he looked at Dallow and then imitated shooting him with his finger. That swiftly turned into an upward middle finger and the door slammed behind him. Nash sighed and then placed the gun in the back of his trousers.

'Is he always like that?' Dallow asked meekly.

'Unfortunately.' Nash turned back to his hostage. 'But he does raise a good point. How useful are you?'

'Excuse me?' Panic began to set in, and Dallow began searching frantically for a possible exit. Nash held up his hand.

'Easy. I have no intention of killing you.' He then pointed at the row of monitors. 'I need you to do some digging for me.'

'Digging?'

'I want to know more about this Kovalenko woman. Eli, he's a pain in the ass, but he's married to the cause. The Foundation don't ask questions. Us assets, we get given a contract, we fulfil it and then we walk away. No trace. No footprint. No questions.'

'But you have some?'

Nash drew his lips together in a thin line and took the seat next to Dallow and then rubbed a hand over his bald head.

'Something just doesn't feel right. You heard that conversation. She's put money on this Pope because he killed her brother, but he saved kids from being sold to God knows what corner of Earth.'

'Brandt asked for the same information when we took the contract. All I could find were some news articles about it, but any police records about the incident have either been removed or archived way outside of my reach.' Dallow shrugged. 'The press claimed there were links with a mayoral candidate, and I guess, for the good of the country and the political landscape, they wanted to sweep it under the rug.'

'Politicians.' Nash spat with disgust.

'Can I ask you something?' Dallow gulped with nerves. Nash looked at him. 'Are you gonna kill me?'

Nash looked down at the carpet below his feet. For over two decades, he'd served as the blueprint for what a Foundation asset should be. There had been a lot of people who'd wanted to ask that question, but he'd never given them a chance. So many people who'd been in the wrong place at the wrong time, who had either seen or heard something that could be considered a breadcrumb.

Nash executed them without hesitation.

But years of serving the same master came with its own flaws, especially when the agenda changed without his input. Without a seat at the table, he was reliant on Callaghan to do the right thing. As a mentor and a friend, Callaghan was one of only three people who Nash trusted in the world, but even he knew that Callaghan's influence only stretched so far.

The notion of the Foundation being a covert force for good had long since evaporated, and this confirmed it.

They had accepted a contract from the vengeful family of a known sex trafficker.

There was no balance they were restoring. No moral gain for anyone.

The hit on Sam Pope was about vengeance, and the Foundation had accepted it for nothing more than cold, hard cash.

Blood money.

Money made off the back of lord knows how many young women and the sickening fate they'd been sold into.

Nash clenched his deadly fist and grimaced.

'You still want to be useful?' he eventually asked. Dallow nodded enthusiastically. 'Get reception to get you some sleeping pills, and then do exactly as I say. Then maybe I'll rethink this whole killing you thing.'

Nash offered Dallow a smile, which somehow reassured the young man, yet chilled him to the bone at the same time.

CHAPTER FIFTEEN

The license plate had been a dead end.

Despite the man putting his career in jeopardy, DS Anderson hadn't delivered an easy route to Sam Pope, despite claiming to be the man in the know. After a few hours of brutal torture, the man had claimed to Mendoza, through a barrage of tears and snot, that he could give him Pope on a plate. It turned out; he had a license plate for a hired Range Rover that had been rented out by a female American.

For that reason, Mendoza had made a pledge to kill Anderson once he'd collected his reward for Sam Pope's delivery.

After visiting the car rental shop and intimidating the middle-aged man behind the counter, Mendoza had decided to search the local news websites until he found the stories relating the attack at the café and the potential Sam Pope sighting. It was all broadly speculation, with the Derbyshire Police, quite rightly, playing down the incident as nothing more than a confrontation.

While the two Americans had been injured and taken into custody, there was no mention of Sam Pope, the missing SUV, or of any large German man. But Mendoza knew it was a smokescreen, and a quick search of the village on Twitter returned numerous, worried posts about potential gunshots in the area.

He had no other leads and a rapidly emptying hour-glass, so Mendoza decided to drive out to Spondon that afternoon, half expecting the place to be overrun by the police. To his surprise, the streets were empty, save for the elderly inhabitants of the village, who were walking their dogs and enjoying the rare day of sunshine as the weather began its descent into autumnal gloom. It was a rather quaint village, a world away from the poverty-stricken slums of Old Havana where he'd grown up. Having lived on the streets of the shanty towns, Mendoza was moulded into the unfeeling, dangerous man he had become, and watching as these middle-class folk strolled peacefully down cobbled streets, lined by flower gardens, sickened him.

They had no idea how lucky they were.

How oblivious they were, not just to the danger of the man in the car, but to the state of the world beyond their gate.

Mendoza pulled the car into the local car park, reversing it neatly between two parked cars, one of which had an elderly man struggling to lift his dog into the boot. Mendoza slid his window down.

'Need a hand?' Mendoza asked, masking his thick Cuban accent with a pretty impressive English one. The man nodded, and Mendoza stepped out of his Mercedes, adjusted his blazer, and then duly helped the man lift the dog into the back. The man slammed the door shut and then turned to his mysterious helper.

'Thanks, son.' He regarded Mendoza with a keen eye. 'You're not from round here, are ya?'

Mendoza held up his hands and grinned.

'You got me. No, I'm from north London. I'm just visiting the area for a wedding.'

'I see. Nice day for it.'

'It's not until tomorrow, but thought I'd take in some of the sights. This place is really nice.'

'It is.' The man seemed suspicious. Mendoza had ensured his blazer covered the tattoos down to his wrist, and the white T-shirt covered those that adorned his sculpted chest. 'Well, when the police aren't putting us all in a panic.'

'I heard about that.' Mendoza played along. 'Something about a fight in a café?'

'Mama's Café.' The man pointed up the road. 'I've been going there for thirty years and not seen as much as an argument. These damn tourists. No offence.'

'Hey, none taken.' Mendoza pointed at his face. 'Cuban dad. Means I get a hell of a tan, right?'

The man chuckled and wished him well, and Mendoza set off towards the café. As soon as the man dropped into his car, Mendoza dropped the fake grin and walked with purpose to the parade of shops. Once again, the expected police presence was absent, with a sign tagged to a lamppost asking for any witnesses to call them with information. To his surprise, the café was open, and he pushed open the door and stepped inside.

Whatever carnage had taken place the day before, there were no signs of it, and the only sign of life was a sweet old lady who was sweeping the floor. She didn't look up as she spoke.

'Afraid we ain't doing food today, my dear.'

'Any chance of a coffee?' Mendoza asked, his accent returning. She turned to look at him.

'Well, aren't you a handsome fellow?' She grinned. Mendoza's tanned skin suited his sharp face, with his neat beard compensating for his bald head. A flicker of a tattoo snuck up from the collar of his T-shirt, but he knew that in his smart, casual attire, he scrubbed up rather nicely.

It caught people unawares.

Put them off guard.

'Well, thank you.' Mendoza flashed his grin and motioned to a table. 'Can I sit here…?'

'Maggie,' she replied with a smile. 'But most folk round here call me Mama.'

'Mama it is.' Mendoza took his seat. 'The name's Charlie.'

'Charlie? You don't look like a Charlie.'

'I know. Sadly, I have Cuban heritage, but that's it. Everything else is English through and through.'

'That's not a bad thing.' Maggie gave a thumbs up and ambled behind the counter. The coffee machine hummed to life, and she pottered in front of it, the gentle clicking of porcelain as she got his mug ready. After the initial warm greeting, a silence had begun to filter into the room and Mendoza didn't want things to take a turn.

He was a cold-hearted killer by trade, but a harmless old lady wasn't high on his list of targets. If he could get what he wanted without going down the same route as with Anderson, he'd prefer it.

But if needs must…

'To be honest, I'm surprised you're open.'

'Open seven days a week, my dear.'

'I meant after the incident yesterday.' Mendoza caught her eye. 'From what I heard that is…'

Maggie sighed and shuffled out with the coffee. She placed it down on the table before him and then put her hands firmly on her hips.

'If you're a journalist, you can finish up your coffee and get out. I've already said to the rest of you all, nothing happened. Nothing of note.'

'Mama…' Mendoza reached out and gently held her

wrist. 'I was stationed with Sam Pope out in Afghanistan ten years ago. I served with him. He's my brother.'

'I don't know what you're talking about…' Maggie squirmed, her eyes darting around the room.

Mendoza knew he had her.

He stood, making no effort not to intimidate her with his strong build. He knew he looked like a soldier, and he'd rather lie to the woman than hurt her.

'He saved my life when we were out there, and now, I know I have the chance to save his.' Mendoza gave a fake concerned look to the door. 'I know the police are after him, but I know they won't find him. He's good. But I know I would never forgive myself if I didn't reach out and try to help him.'

'I know…' Maggie's eyes watered, and she looked down at the ground. Mendoza reached out and placed a caring hand on her shoulder.

'Please, Mama. If you know anything, it could help save his life. Especially if there are people out there trying to hurt him.'

The old lady sighed and then looked out of the window towards the road that curved away from the high street. It was where the local cemetery was, and where her late husband was buried. He was a good man.

Sam Pope was a good man.

And this young Charlie, well, if he knew Sam Pope, then he must be a good man, too.

'He's staying a few streets down. Not sure which one, but there are only a few guest houses available around here. Said he booked it online, but that's too confusing for me. He told me his name was Jonathan something, but I knew it was him. He just has that look about him, doesn't he?'

'Look?' Mendoza shrugged.

'Of a hero.'

Mendoza chuckled and then cracked his neck. He reached down and lifted his coffee, downing the whole drink in one go before handing the cup to Maggie. Bemused, she took it, as he pulled out his wallet, shifted out some notes, and tucked them into her pocket. He turned and headed to the door, as she fumbled with the mug and then pulled out over fifty pounds from where he'd stuffed it.

'Oh, Charlie. This is way too much…'

She was horrified by the thick, Cuban accent that responded, along with the evil sneer.

'Consider it a payment for your information. I will tell him where I got it, when he begs me for death.'

With that, Mendoza slammed the door open and stepped out into the cool breeze of the afternoon, already shifting through his phone to find accommodation in the village and headed in the general direction she had pointed him to.

It wouldn't take him long to find the right one.

And then he would collect his bounty.

Dead or alive.

As he turned the corner onto the street, he saw him. It was just a glimpse, but it was just enough for Mendoza to step backwards into a driveway and take cover behind a large hedgerow. His movement had been so fluid, there was no way Pope could have seen him.

But it was unmistakably him. About fifty yards down the street, hoisting a sports bag into the boot of a nondescript car. Short brown hair and stubble, with the physique of an elite athlete, the man was undoubtedly in his physical prime.

Peeping through the leaves, Mendoza noted the way he moved. The way he walked.

Like a soldier.

A man of purpose.

His face was littered with bruising and a severe gash across his lip.

Wherever he was planning to go, he seemed in complete control. There was no rushing, no panicked movements.

Mendoza waited for Pope to return to his abode before he took off and ran as quickly as he could back towards the car park. As he slid into the seat and revved the engine, he saw the black car turn out from the end of the road.

Moments later, Mendoza pulled out of the parking space and followed.

———

The message had changed Sam's plan of action.

While he'd intended to lay siege to London and rattle the right cages to find his way to Dana Kovalenko the hard way, a slice of good fortune had fallen into his lap. Brandt had clearly been working as part of an operation, and one could reasonably expect there to be someone off-grid running things from a logistics perspective.

It's how every high-end operation functioned, with someone being the eyes and ears from a remote location, feeding the assets the information in real time. Undoubtedly, that person would have been worried by the lack of response, especially with the arrest of both of Brandt's accompanying operatives. That would have hit the news and been swept up by any analyst worth their salt.

But in less than two hours, it would have been twenty-four since they'd engaged their target and whoever was behind that computer would have been none the wiser.

They wouldn't know that Brandt was dead.

Sam measured a guess that it would be another three days or so until anyone revisited the crime scene for the

Murphy case, and there, the police would be greeted by a dead body and another mountain of paperwork.

But the analyst had played their final hand. The message that Sam had received on Brandt's phone was laced with desperation.

Rendezvous: Powell House, Hudson Way. Exit Strategy 2 Initiated. Will bring ammo. 21:00. KD.

Whoever *KD* was, they had put in motion whatever Brandt had pre-planned. Although Sam had swiftly incapacitated the man, there was no denying Brandt's stature within Blackridge. Although he had never been part of Project Hailstorm, there was a reason why Wallace would have chosen the man to bring Sam in a couple of years ago.

Wallace only relied on the best.

Unfortunately for Brandt, his best wasn't good enough.

But KD would have access to information Sam needed. Potentially, more weaponry as well, as Sam was heading towards a fight he knew nothing about. Considering the artillery he'd faced when he took down her brother nearly three years ago, there were many people who were willing to die for the Kovalenko name.

Sam had proven it.

KD would likely have a direct feed to Kovalenko herself, and would likely be able to trace her location to within a reasonable accuracy, meaning Sam would be able to put all of this to an end as quickly as possible.

But as the sun began to set, he headed out of the door of his Airbnb and marched across the empty road towards the Renault Clio he'd traded his old car in at a local dealership. As he dropped the sports bag containing his weaponry into the boot, he shot a glance up the road.

Did he see someone?

There wasn't time to check, but Sam had a sneaking suspicion someone was watching. His training had kicked in, and as he walked back to the house, he saw out of his periphery the movement of a bald man rushing from behind the hedge and round the corner.

Whoever it was would have to be quick, because a minute later, Sam was behind the wheel, gliding up the street before he turned onto the main road and shot a regrettable look towards Mama's Café. Sam had just under two hours to make a less than twenty-minute journey, and that gave him plenty of time to lose any potential tails. Hudson Way was a side street, which looped around the back of Derby Train Station. The recently renovated station was on the edge of the city centre, offering a quick and easy walk to the large parade of shops, as well as the immaculate shopping centre. The one-way system around the city made it pretty simple to navigate, and a multitude of industrial estates snaked off of the ring road, offering large businesses an excellent location for their warehouses or head offices.

Hudson Way was one such road, which sat quietly behind the bulk of the station, and was lined by the train depot which was stacked with decommissioned trains. Sam had done some basic research on the place, enough to know that Powell House was an empty building that had run out of funding during its initial build and had therefore failed to attract any tenants.

Empty.

Secluded.

The perfect place for a drop off.

After finally accepting he wasn't being followed, Sam stopped at a drive-thru Starbucks and treated himself to a coffee and a toasted sandwich. It wasn't particularly nutritious, but he needed the energy. The caffeine was a plus, too.

Then, at five minutes to nine, he rolled the Clio to a stop on Hudson Way and killed the engine. Powell House was a hundred feet down the road, which was cloaked in darkness beyond the odd, working lamppost. There wasn't a soul in sight, and Sam eventually stepped out from his car, checked the Glock 17 securely pressed against the base of his spine, and then headed towards the building. Keeping as close to the shadows as possible, he entered the premises and approached the door.

It was unlocked.

Sam drew his weapon, carefully pulled the door open, and entered, knowing his training would eliminate any sudden surprises. He cleared the first floor swiftly and then headed towards the stairs of the two-storey building.

––––––

'He's in.'

Dallow's voice crackled through the earpiece and Nash nodded to himself. He stood, his arms behind his back and his hands clasped, looking out over the city of Derby. He was certain he would never return to this place willingly, and if his gut was right, then he probably wouldn't professionally.

Still, the view from the first floor of Powell House was quite enjoyable, and he knew he could only enjoy it for a few moments later.

Any minute now, the door would open, and he would have what he came for.

Sam Pope.

CHAPTER SIXTEEN

Jacob Nash knew there would be repercussions.

After Defoe had returned from his illicit liaison at what masqueraded as a massage parlour, Nash had greeted him with the same disdain as usual. There was no point playing it friendly, as that would have instantly aroused suspicion.

Defoe knew Nash didn't like him.

Nash didn't like many people.

He trusted fewer.

It was something that had been drilled into him from his time in the Marines; he trusted his brothers who fought alongside him, and he honoured and cherished every minute he spent wearing the uniform.

Serving his country.

Fighting for freedom.

It was why he had been intrigued by the offer of joining the Foundation when they approached him. It was Callaghan himself who had reached out to Nash, unable to look away from man's exemplary record of service. Nash was as near to perfect as a soldier could be, and he displayed the skills and aptitude that highlighted him as the perfect candidate to join the program. With little to no information, beyond the fact he would essentially become a ghost and go beyond what a soldier could in the name of liberty, Nash knew in his bones it was what he was destined to do.

Both his parents had long since passed.

A shotgun wedding in his early twenties had ended in an amicable divorce.

There were no kids.

No friends beyond his brothers still fighting for the flag.

Joining the Foundation had been his calling, and he quickly became their most valuable asset, combining his ruthless skills along with unwavering loyalty. For over two decades, he had been responsible for numerous, high-profile kills.

No questions asked.

The powers that be, who liaised with Callaghan, would denote the target and the names would be handed to the asset. A near limitless bank account meant Nash had access to the weapons and resources he needed and found himself visiting multiple countries and eliminating multiple targets.

But somewhere along the way, that impeachable loyalty had started to fray, and when he began asking questions, Callaghan regrettably had to shut him down. The man had been the nearest thing to a father figure Nash had experienced since his pre-teens and the man was clearly fond of him.

Questioning the Foundation wasn't encouraged, and Callaghan would try to appease Nash's newfound scepticism with promises of change.

Of trying to make him reconnect with the vision of an organisation who didn't keep the world in check because they wanted to, but because they were the only ones who could.

Defoe believed it. Beyond that, he lived and breathed

their creed, and seemed to enjoy killing people in cold blood. The man had a history of violence that should have blocked any path to such power, but while Defoe was a complete jackass, he was the most talented killer Nash has seen come through the system.

He was the heir to Nash's throne as the jewel in the Foundation's crown, and while Nash wasn't the egotistical type, he knew at times he needed to bring Defoe down a peg or two.

That's why, when the man returned from his rub down with a lurid grin on his face, Nash met him with the same contempt as always. As they prepped the location and potential takedown of Sam Pope, Dallow suggested getting in a beer or two. Defoe, ever the frat boy, enjoyed a cold beer before a simple mission and agreed.

Dallow did the rest.

He laced Defoe's beer with the sleeping pills, erring on the side of caution so as not to do any serious damage. Hopefully, it would just render the man unconscious for the evening. Putting the man's life at risk would certainly end his own, as Dallow was certain that although Nash clearly didn't like his younger colleague, killing him would cause untold problems.

Defoe guzzled the beer, chastised Nash for not partaking, and then not long after, retired to his room to get ready.

He collapsed on the bed and that was that.

Nash knew that Defoe would raise questions, especially as the man was a physical specimen that ruled out genuine fatigue. But this wasn't something he wanted Defoe's involvement in.

This was off the books.

Ever since the contract had been accepted and passed their way, Nash had questioned it with Callaghan. There seemed little to no political or military impact in bringing

Sam Pope to justice, whether alive or dead. The entire mission smacked of revenge, with Nash's investigation shut down by an irritated Callaghan who essentially assigned Defoe to join Nash as a quasi-punishment.

Defoe was also clearly keeping tabs on Nash's behaviour, probably under the reluctant order of Callaghan who was no doubt worried about Nash's seemingly crumbling dedication to the cause.

They were not ready to lose him yet.

They were certainly not prepared to let him walk away.

But Nash had to know and having pieced together the backstory through the minimal information Dallow could find, as well as the conversation they'd eavesdropped on, Nash knew he couldn't just blindly go along with it. From what he'd read, Sam Pope was a hell of a soldier and clearly a capable fighter, but Nash had little worry in subduing the man.

There hadn't been a soul he had come across whom he couldn't put down.

Taking Sam Pope wouldn't be the issue.

It was the reason why that he needed to know.

The Foundation would never tell him.

Dana Kovalenko had three to five million reasons why she felt she didn't need to.

So that left Pope himself. If Nash was going to kill this man, or at least lead him to his death, for reasons that didn't resonate with him, then he needed to know.

Which was why, as Dallow crackled in his ear to inform him of Sam's arrival at Powell House, Nash nodded and then disconnected his earpiece. Dallow wasn't part of his team, despite his assistance, and any conversation to be had was between him and Pope.

Man to man.

Soldier to soldier.

If it didn't go well, then Nash would do what he had

to do. But even if he did, there would be repercussions. Defoe would see to that, and in the back of his mind, as he heard the careful footsteps ascend to the first floor, Nash couldn't help but think that whatever the outcome, his time with Foundation could soon be coming to an end.

Nash stepped silently back behind the door to the gutted office, and moments later, it opened gently, and a Glock 17 slid into view as Pope scanned the room. Nash whipped his hand out, disengaged Pope's grip expertly, and then hauled the man into the room. Pope spun free of his clutches, took a step back and raised his fists and Nash couldn't help but smile.

The man was a fighter.

And now, in the dimly lit, abandoned office block, Jacob Nash had finally come face to face with the infamous Sam Pope.

———

As Sam pushed open the door of the stairwell to the first floor, he kept his Glock up, his arm tucked slightly to his chest and his eye down the sight. As part of Project Hailstorm, he had been on countless sweeps behind enemy lines, clearing out dark, seemingly abandoned hideouts. It was closer combat than what he'd made his name in, with his expertise lying hundreds of yards away behind the scope of a sniper rifle.

But Sam had excelled at pretty much every form of combat during his days in the military, from close quarters firearms to hand-to-hand combat. It was why he had been recruited by General Wallace all those years ago. His mentor, Sergeant Carl Marsden, had once described Sam as the ultimate killing machine.

Not only because he had skills beyond most.

But because he had the humanity to know when to use them.

A sudden twinge of guilt echoed through Sam, rocking his heart at the memory of holding Marsden in the dark, underground bunker in Italy as he bled to death in arms.

Another good man lost to the fight.

Sam carefully walked stepped through the door and cleared both corners of the corridor. This was a simple drop off, but his training had ingrained in him to assess every situation for danger. The one time he dropped his guard, he'd ended up on life support with two holes in his chest.

He was lucky to get a second chance.

There wouldn't be a third.

He stepped carefully towards the ajar door to the open-plan office floor. The lights, although dim, were a clear signal of occupation, and he took a deep breath.

He was about to catch the last of Brandt's team unaware, and if there was more than one of them, there was a strong chance of hostility. They were expecting a hulking, bearded German to bound through the door and dish out the next set of orders.

What they would be getting was their target, armed and ready to fight.

With the barrel of his gun, he pushed the door open as gently as he could, pushing it open enough to guide the gun into the room. Like a coiled snake, a hand shot out, wrapped around his wrist and twisted with the strength of an industrial strength vice. Sam felt the tendons of his wrist strain and eventually, they subsided, relinquishing hold of the weapon, before he was hauled forward into the room, his shoulder crashing into the door on the way through. He struggled, freed himself from the grip and spun to face his opponent, fists up.

Whoever the man was, he didn't look impressed.

He also didn't look ready to fight.

That wasn't to say the man didn't look capable. Sam had seen some soldiers in his time who looked like they were ripped straight from a comic book, but the man before him was intimidating on a whole new level. The bald head gave some indication to his age, along with the wrinkles that danced around his dark, beady eyes. The man's skin was tanned, although judging from the tattoos that peeped above his shirt and the sleeves of his blazer, most of it was covered in ink.

He towered over Sam, and was as broad as he was tall, with the sleeves of his blazer struggling to survive. The man looked down at the gun in his hand, holding it with the respect it deserved, and cast an expert eye over the weapon. Sam quickly realised he had been set up, but a strange feeling sat in his stomach.

He didn't feel under threat.

Not yet, at least.

The man's soothing, calm voice only added to the unease.

'I take it you were expecting someone else?'

Nash tucked Sam's gun into the back of his own trousers, almost daring Sam to try to reclaim it. Sam felt his fists clench, but he relented.

'You're American?'

'Unfortunately.' Nash grinned. 'Does it matter?'

'I had a bad experience with one yesterday.' Sam shrugged. 'Recency bias and all.'

'That's understandable. From the police reports, it looks like you did a real number on them. And the German? I assume you killed him.'

'I gave him the chance to walk away.' Sam solidified his footing. He needed to stand his ground and try to show he wasn't afraid of the change in circumstances.

'Five million dollars is a lot to walk away from.' Nash

ran a powerful hand across his stubbled jaw. 'That's for you alive.'

'Three million dead, right?'

'So the German talked?' Nash shrugged. 'See, if I wanted to claim the bounty, then I could put a bullet in your skull right now, drive you down to London and had you over to Kovalenko myself.'

'Then why don't you?' Sam tilted his head. 'I'm not big on small talk.'

'Me neither.' Nash sighed. 'But I wanted to hear from you what I haven't heard from anyone yet.'

Nash stepped past Sam and took a few steps into the unfinished workspace. There were lighting rigs affixed to the ceiling, with large halogen bulbs locked in place. Due to the incomplete work, only a few of them were wired into the circuit, offering a dim glow across the office. The halogen bulbs were fading like the rest of the building.

'And what's that?' Sam called after the mysterious American.

'The truth.'

Sam took a step forward, keeping enough of a distance between them so he could react if the mood changed. He had also made sure he was in line with the door, which had rebounded from his collision to be almost closed. There was enough of a gap for his hand, which meant he could throw it open if he needed an exit. There was no fire escape on the side of the building, meaning the only way down from the first floor was the staircase he'd ascended. Sam had done a quick scan of the building before he entered, noting that the chain-link fence that separated the Powell premises to the train depot was only a few feet from the building itself. There was nothing beyond the narrow alleyway, with a train stationed so close to the fence, it acted as another wall.

There was only one way out and Sam made damn sure he had at least a shot of making it.

Nash walked towards the window, gazing out over the stationary trains. A gentle drizzle had intruded into the evening, gently tapping against the glass, and he shook his head.

'I've been doing this a long time. A real long time. For years, the organisation I work for has put names in front of me, pointed me in the right direction and that would be that. People would die. The world would change for the better and life would go on.' Nash chuckled to himself. 'It's funny, when I read some of the files on you, I didn't believe it.'

'Believe what?' Sam asked, tentatively stepping further into the room.

'I didn't believe that someone had just had enough and decided to do something about it.' Nash turned and looked Sam dead in the eyes. 'You were a highly decorated soldier. One of the best, apparently. If you wanted to put away your gun, you could have taken a post anywhere in the world. Trained the next batch of soldiers. But instead, you went after the establishment. You went after the people no others would dare. Why?'

Sam took another step, his eyebrow arched in confusion. For someone who looked so composed and direct, Nash seemed to be wrestling more with his own conscience than whether he was worth five or three million. Eventually, Sam offered the only reason he knew.

'It's the right thing to do.'

Nash tried to hide his grimace with a grin and nodded to himself.

'That's the thing, isn't it? Knowing the difference between right and wrong.' He sliced the air in front of him with his hand. 'Seeing things clearly. Knowing, in your heart, that what you're doing is for the greater good. When it isn't clear, that fog covers everything.'

'As nice as it is to talk ethics with you, what the hell does this have to do with me?'

Nash frowned, his curious disposition morphing instantly into one of intense power.

'Is what you said to Dana Kovalenko true?' Nash took a purposeful step forward. 'That the only reason for this contract is because you killed her brother?'

'I'd say with a hundred per cent certainty that's a yes.'

'And that you killed him because he trafficked young girls into Europe?'

'Well, I was searching for one girl. But yeah, that's pretty much the gist of it.' Sam felt a sense of pride fill his chest. 'And I'd do it again in a heartbeat.'

'Fuck,' Nash uttered to himself and stepped past Sam, running a hand over his bald head. Whatever was troubling him, Sam quickly realised that the hulking man was now between him and the door.

His exit was blocked.

'Look, I don't know why that matters, but if you're going to hand me over to her, at least know I won't go down without a fight.'

'We used to stand for something,' Nash said, not to anyone in particular. 'The Foundation used to be about freedom. But this…this is blood money.'

'If it's any consolation, I worked for an organisation that prided itself on being a force for good. Turns out, we were just killing targets to make the rich a little bit richer. You think you're doing good, but in reality, you're just another spoke in the wheel. Another weapon at the disposal of those who are untouchable.' Sam shrugged. 'I fight to show those people that they *can* be stopped. That *no one* is untouchable. That someone *has to* fight back.'

The American took a deep breath and then nodded to

himself, clarifying his thoughts. He turned back to Sam with a smile on his face and extended his hand.

'The name's Nash. Jacob Nash.'

Sam extended his own, but before he could clasp it, and potentially solidify an easier way to ending his escalating war with Dana Kovalenko, a muffled gunshot emanated from the doorway, and seconds later, a burst of blood and a bullet exploded from Nash's left shoulder, sending him spinning to the ground in agony.

Sam lifted his hands, staring at a furious-looking man and down the barrel of a proven loaded gun.

CHAPTER SEVENTEEN

Elias Defoe was many things, but he wasn't an idiot.

Having proven himself as a valuable asset to the Foundation in the years he had been in their employ. Over thirty kills, all of them without incident, and he knew Callaghan and the higher ups saw him as he saw himself.

Indispensable.

That's why Jacob Nash was envious of him. Until Defoe began to make his name, Nash was the crown jewel of the organisation. A sure thing, whenever a name was passed his way, Nash had built a legacy that nobody ever expected to be challenged. But Defoe relished the chance, and now, with Nash showing signs of fatigue, he was ready to tread on Nash's throat and choke him from his throne.

Callaghan knew it.

Nash knew it.

Over the past year, signs of doubt had begun to creep into Nash's work. Nothing obvious, but Defoe could read people like an open book and there were subtle signs that Nash had begun to question what the Foundation stood for. Nearly two decades older than Defoe, the old man still held on to the ridiculous notion that they were making a difference. That what they did was vital to ensure the world span on a peaceful axis. It was naïve, and Defoe was more than willing to accept what they were and the lucrative life it gave them.

They were mercenaries.

Hired guns.

Killers for the highest bidder.

After discussions with Callaghan, Defoe knew it would take more than words to show the old man that Nash was on the brink. He had to prove it, and so he had insisted that Callaghan send them both for the Kovalenko contract. It was everything Nash despised about their work, and Defoe was certain he could chip away at Nash's wavering commitment on the job.

It was working.

The legendary hitman had been hesitant to rush in and take Sam Pope out. They both knew they were more than capable of doing so, but Nash needed to know more.

You didn't question the Foundation.

But he was. At every turn.

Defoe had been passing the messages back to Callaghan, updating him on Nash's apparent disillusion with the cause and with a heavy sigh, Callaghan had given Defoe the go ahead to remove him from the process.

Nash wasn't to know it came from above. But if Defoe made it quick and untraceable, then Callaghan could make the right moves to ensure Defoe's safety within the organisation.

Foundation members didn't turn on each other. That was written in the blood of their founders.

But they had no room for those who'd lost their way and an asset as valuable and knowledgeable as Nash couldn't be allowed to just walk away.

Defoe had spent two hours discussing it with Callaghan, under the guise of going for a seedy massage and he laughed at the fact that Nash and that nerd, Dallow, would ever believe a man of his stature would need to pay for a woman's touch. Defoe may have been an arrogant bastard, but he was handsome enough to not care. When he returned to the hotel that early evening, Defoe knew Nash would have been plotting a way to get to Sam without him, knowing Defoe was watching his every move.

When Nash suggested Dallow get them a beer, Defoe had to hold back from laughing at how obvious a ploy it was. He pretended to swig from the bottle as he made his way to the kitchen of the suite, before tipping the contents of it into one of the large plants that sat elegantly in the corner.

Then he groggily stumbled to his bedroom and collapsed on his bed, giving himself a pat on the back for his stellar acting. Twenty minutes later, when Dallow ducked his head in and ushered 'he's out' to Nash, Defoe knew he had them.

Nash had betrayed the Foundation.

He had decided that their way wasn't the right one, which was all the signal Callaghan had said was needed.

Lying completely still, Defoe listened intently as Nash and Dallow spoke, catching the odd phrase through the slight gap in the door.

'I need to know…'

'It can't just be for money.'

'I'm tired of killing good people.'

For over two hours, Defoe didn't move a muscle, but as soon as Dallow and Nash left for their rendezvous with Pope, Defoe pushed himself off the bed, changed into a new shirt, and then checked his handgun to ensure it was loaded.

He wouldn't need much else.

A Glock 17 and the element of surprise.

Lethal.

He'd taken a cab to Derby Train Station and then walked the back streets to Powell House, using the map on his phone to help navigate the alleyways. The back of the station gave way to a vast train depot, with many of the decommissioned vehicles pressed right up against the fence and a few feet from the building itself.

It didn't take him long to spot Dallow. The useless novice was sitting in a car, half a street down from the building. The light of his laptop screen gave his position away and Defoe went to make his move until he saw a car pull to a stop not too far from Dallow's vehicle. At least the young man slammed his laptop shut, cutting off the light and trying his best to stay hidden.

As Defoe slowly twisted a silencer to the end of his pistol, he watched as a broad, powerful looking man stepped out of the car and Defoe immediately recognised Sam Pope from the articles he'd read on the internet. The man walked with a purpose, showing no fear despite the fact he knew he was being hunted by some of the deadliest people on the planet. Defoe admired the swagger, and somewhere deep within, he despised it as well.

Defoe insisted on being feared, and it took every shred of his willpower not to eliminate Sam Pope there and then.

But it would give the game away, and he now needed to not only incapacitate Pope for the healthy payout, but he needed to handle some housekeeping.

He needed to take out Jacob Nash.

As soon as Pope disappeared into Powell House, the light of the laptop screen re-emerged, and Defoe stepped out from the shadows, marched across the road and threw the driver's door open.

Dallow screamed in terror, the colour draining from his face, as he threw his hands up in a ridiculous notion of self-defence. Defoe didn't even offer the young man the option of any last words, and he squeezed the trigger twice, painting the inside of the car a deep shade of red.

Then he turned on his heel and headed quickly across the silent road towards the building, where both of his targets were waiting. With the young man's death not even registering on his conscience, Defoe made his way into the building, knowing he was headed for the first floor. As he approached the top of the staircase, he softened his footsteps, keeping his gun up and his eyes open. Through the gap in the door, he could see the dim lighting of the office space and, more importantly, he could hear the soft, purposeful voice of Jacob Nash.

'The name's Nash. Jacob Nash.'

Defoe felt his blood boil.

Nash didn't introduce himself to people he was willing to kill. As far as legends go, Nash's name was already etched in stone, but if Defoe needed any more confirmation, beyond the intended poisoning he'd sidestepped, this was it.

Nash was on first-name terms with the man they'd been hired to kill.

There was no coming back now.

The Foundation stood for many things, but betrayal was not one of them.

Carefully, Defoe prodded the door further open, revealing his hulking partner and Sam Pope, stood across the room, looking out over the sea of forgotten trains. Defoe didn't know if it was instinct or rage, but he drew his weapon and fired.

He hadn't aimed to kill.

Not yet anyway.

In proximity and an enclosed space, the silencer made little difference, and he saw Sam Pope's head turn in shock as the bullet zipped through the dilapidated office and plough through Nash's shoulder, sending the man spinning to the ground. Defoe stomped forward, gun trained on Pope, who lifted his hands. Nash grunted through the pain and rolled onto his front, pushing himself to his knees with one powerful arm.

'You missed.' Nash scoffed; his teeth gritted.

'You know that's not true,' Defoe retorted, not taking his eyes or gun off Pope. 'Sorry to interrupt this mother's meeting, but I felt a little offended I wasn't invited.'

'You're a mother?' Sam asked, raising his eyebrow. The lack of fear in the man clearly riled Defoe.

'Shut your fuckin' mouth, dipshit.' Defoe took a few steps closer. He was roughly the same height as Sam, but probably gave away ten to fifteen pounds in weight. Considering there wasn't a shred of fat on either man, it meant Sam would hold the power advantage. But Defoe was confident in his ability, having never fought a man he couldn't wipe the floor with. 'You're a popular man, Sam Pope.'

'I know.' Sam edged towards Nash slightly. 'It's annoying.'

'I can imagine.'

'You're making a mistake, Elias…' Nash began to speak, but Defoe drilled a boot into the man's bullet ridden shoulder.

'Shut the fuck up.'

Sam moved towards Nash, feigning concern, but in reality, he knew his only gun was firmly tucked into the back of the man's trousers. Without the weapon, his chances of surviving were non-existent. Defoe quickly retrained the gun on Sam and motioned for him to step back.

'Why don't we all just start from scratch so no one else gets hurt?' Sam said, taking a few more steps back. He glanced over his shoulder.

It was a long drop from the window.

'People get hurt, Pope,' Defoe said arrogantly. 'This is the world we live in. We see names on screens, we put bodies in bags. Bullet by bullet. We are the Foundation of our great nation, and the organisation that tips the scales of justice in the free world. Unfortunately for the people who make our list, people have to die. And worse still, for those who turn their back on the cause…Well they have to die knowing they turned their back on the people who gave them everything.'

'I get it. But if you want to make this world a better place, you put a bullet in the head of Dana Kovalenko.'

Defoe screwed up his face.

'Not when she's paying me three million dollars.'

'I thought it was five million.'

Sam's eyes widened with realisation as Defoe adjusted his grip on his gun.

'That was if you were still breathing…'

He pulled the trigger.

Sam closed his eyes, and visions of Jamie laughing and running through the park filled his mind. They were giggling together, with his son kicking a ball at him. A few flashes of his career as a soldier rushed by, followed by watching Lucy walk down the aisle towards him.

Jamie's dead body.

Amara Singh.

Jamie's smile.

It took Sam only a split second to realise the bullet never hit him, but even then, a myriad of images swept over his brain like a tidal wave, and he felt disorientated. A few seconds later, he watched as Nash, fighting through the pain barrier, struggled with Defoe. His powerful hand gripped the wrist holding the weapon and Sam quickly surmised that Nash had diverted the shot. Without a weapon, Sam was helpless, and Defoe, clearly overpowered, desperately swung a fist at the bullet hole that was pumping blood from Nash's shoulder. Nash roared with agony, loosened his grip, and Defoe struck him with a vicious hook to the body, followed by a few expert rising knee strikes.

Sam made a move.

Defoe pulled the trigger again, just as Nash drove his good shoulder into his gut, skewing the shot and sending the bullet through one of the windowpanes behind Sam. Defoe drilled his elbow down into Nash's spine, who kept running forward, driving himself and Defoe back towards the door. Eventually, he caught the back of Nash's skull, knocking him woozy, and as the man stumbled to his knee, Defoe gripped the back of his head and drove it forward, directly into the raised knee.

Nash hit the floor, spitting out blood, and to his own shock, seemingly out matched.

Maybe he had underestimated Defoe.

Maybe the man was as good as he constantly claimed to be.

Maybe, this was where Nash hit the end of the road.

No.

As Defoe stood to put a final nail in Nash's coffin, Nash kicked out, driving his foot into the side of Defoe's shin and knocking him off balance. There was little hope of getting to his feet, but Nash refused to just lie back and take a bullet to the skull.

If Defoe wanted him dead, then he'd have to earn it.

Sam watched on, and as Defoe stumbled from Nash's kick, he made an ill-advised dash to the door. Even off balance, Defoe pulled the trigger, and two more bullets hit the wall to the side of Sam, coming within an inch of his chest. Sam skidded to a stop, realising there was little hope of escaping. Despite the valiant attempt, Nash was struggling to his feet, and Defoe regained his composure and then stomped viciously onto his spine as he tried to get to his feet.

Sam was pinned in.

There was a good twenty feet from the wall to the door and Defoe had him cornered. By the devilish glint in his eye, the man was about to execute Nash and also agreed that three million was more than enough.

Defoe was in control.

The next few moments would be entirely predictable.

With a deep breath, Sam reached inside his jacket pocket and shook his head in disbelief at what he was about to do. Defoe noticed and swung the gun in Sam's direction.

'Hands where I can see them.'

Sam pulled the pin and finally breathed.

'You got it.' To the dismay of Defoe, Sam rolled the grenade into the room. 'Nash, run!'

The invitation wasn't needed, as Nash had already ignored the pain of his shoulder and scrambled to his feet. As he darted to the door, he heard an impressed Defoe behind him.

'You crazy son of a bitch.'

Defoe followed Nash a few steps behind him.

Sam ran as fast as he could away from the grenade, covering the ground between himself and the window as fast as he could. One step away from the window, he pressed down on his standing foot, wrapped his arms around his chest and leapt.

Behind him, the grenade exploded, the roar of the explosion rattling the room, and the force of it sent him hurtling through the window. As he soared through the glass, he tried his best to turn his body, watching as the blast of fire and smoke missed him by inches.

Then he felt the world beneath him rush forward to greet him.

CHAPTER EIGHTEEN

The blast of the grenade shook the entire Powell building to its foundations, and the propulsion sent Defoe slamming into the wall of the stairwell and tumbling down the last few steps. Any lighting that was still hooked up to the electricity grid was blown out, and some of the cheap panels that lined the ceiling collapsed to the ground. Smoke filled the building pretty quickly, with the thick, grey concoction already threatening to overwhelm his lungs.

Defoe spluttered and then covered his nose and mouth with his jacket, trying his best to ignore the ringing in his ears.

As he pushed himself to his feet, he tried to stretch out the pain in his spine and he stumbled forward, through the door which had been rocked off his hinges and into the smoky reception room of the office. The desk that had been fitted on the far right still stood, but a few of the other features were scattered across the floor. The wall fixtures hung loose, and debris from the falling tiles littered the walkway.

It was dark, and the smoke was already pumping into the room at an alarming rate.

Pope had rushed to the window. It was the last thing Defoe had seen, which meant the man was likely lying in a crumpled heap somewhere outside the building. Undoubtedly, the emergency services were on their way, which meant he had a matter of minutes to find his man and get the hell out of Dodge. A slick, wet sensation trickled from his eyebrow, and he cursed inwardly that Pope had drawn blood from him.

The man would pay.

Three million would be more than enough, as he had no intention of taking him alive.

The glass entrance doors had been blown completely out by the blast, meaning every step he took towards freedom was met with a loud crunch. It was almost impossible to see more than a few feet ahead of him, and Defoe lazily held the gun out.

There was still business to be done.

'Jacob,' he roared loudly, before coughing as the smoke slithered into his throat.

Allowing Sam Pope to survive made his task at hand harder. Not killing Jacob Nash would be potentially fatal. Despite his cocksure attitude and apparent lack of respect, Defoe knew exactly who he was dealing with, which was why the element of surprise was so important for taking Nash down. Having shown his true colours, Defoe had made an enemy of Jacob Nash, and he had seen first-hand what Nash was capable of.

His best chance of taking Nash had already passed.

A few feet from the door, Defoe could already feel the fresh air beckoning him to safety, and at that moment, he dropped his arm.

It was swiftly followed by a vicious boot to the stomach, and Defoe doubled over, the air driven from his lungs, and he coughed and spluttered as he dropped to his knees. Nash stepped through the smoke, his arm hanging loose from the bullet wound, and he followed it up with a crunching sidekick to Defoe's head.

Defoe crumpled to the glass, unconscious, the shard slicing his pretty face on impact.

Nash reached down and grabbed the back of Defoe's collar, and for the final few feet to freedom, he dragged his fallen foe to the outside, allowing the glass to mutilate his face as it peeled the skin from it.

The pain was enough to shock Defoe back to consciousness, and his howling screams echoed through the night sky and in tandem with the steadily approaching sirens. Once they were out of the building, Nash released Defoe and stepped back, admiring his handiwork as Defoe trembled on the ground. The treacherous assassin was obsessed with his looks, and now, as he struggled to all fours, blood gushed from the deep lacerations that weaved across his face like a tribal pattern.

'My face. My fucking face.' Defoe screamed in agony, his hand shaking with shock as he dabbed at it.

The end of the street began to illuminate with bright-blue lights, and Nash knew this wasn't the end of their issue. He needed to disappear. The Foundation's consider-able influence reached across the Atlantic, meaning Defoe's inevitable arrest would soon be quashed and the man would be set free.

As for himself, Nash knew there was no way that Defoe had gone rogue. The man was too much of an egotist to not want to be the Foundation's golden boy.

Which meant the order came from above.

It meant Jacob Nash needed to speak to Callaghan.

And it also meant he needed to be gone when the boys in blue showed up.

'This isn't over, Eli. Not by a long way.'

'Fuck you.' Defoe spat, before Nash drilled him in his mangled jaw with another expert kick, shutting his lights out and sending him sprawling across the concrete. Ignoring the cathartic pleasure landing that blow offered, Nash picked up the pace and raced back towards the vehicle he and Dallow had arrived in. As soon as he approached, he saw the splatters of blood, and he was surprised at how guilty he felt at the obvious murder of the young man.

Defoe had been clinical in his execution, and Nash felt his fist clench with fury at the needless death of the young man. Yes, he had intimated that Dallow would be killed if he didn't help them, but it had only been a subtle threat.

Nash didn't believe in killing innocent people.

He hadn't for a long time, and now, as the guilt intensified as he hauled the bullet ridden corpse from the car, he knew his change of heart was complete.

The sirens wailed down the street, and Nash brought the car to life, slid it into gear and then turned the wheel sharply. The car spun out and into the road, and Nash accelerated towards the incoming blue lights, racing past a fire engine and three police cars, knowing that the carnage left behind would be enough of a distraction to allow him to disappear.

They'd find Dallow.

The mangled, unconscious Defoe.

The building, ablaze from the first floor, which had been rocked by an explosion.

There was even a chance they'd find the broken remains of Sam Pope, but something told Nash that the man was a survivor.

The only thing Nash knew, as he looked in the rearview and saw a police car making a lame, and ultimately fruitless attempt at turning round to give chase, was this whole situation was far from over.

———

The wailing of the sirens eventually punctured Sam's consciousness, and he felt himself begin to stir. His entire body ached, especially his spine, and as he tried to push himself to a seated position, his wrist buckled under the pressure. His knuckles were bleeding, and as he succeeded on his second attempt, he took a few moments to try to bring his spinning vision to a complete stop. Everything was cast in a blur, and all he could ascertain was something was on fire and the emergency services were arriving imminently.

'Time to leave.' He chuckled, and then groaned at the thudding pain in his lower back. Battling the stiffness that ran the length of his spine, Sam arched his head upwards at the train before him, and then the burning building behind it.

He had caused that.

As if someone had clicked their fingers, Sam's memory of events returned to him, and he recalled being blasted through the window by the grenade he'd rolled into the room. As he sailed through the air, he landed on the top of the train, the sheet metal bowing slightly as it absorbed most of the impact of his fall.

It still hurt like hell but landing in the centre of the carriage had meant he had saved his life.

It was the subsequent roll and drop onto the hard concrete that had caused the damage.

Beaten.

Burnt.

A little broken.

But alive.

As he staggered to his feet, Sam stretched his back out, before a smile spread across his bloodied and soot covered face. He'd been accused before of enjoying the path he had taken, with a few people questioning whether it was as selfless as he made it out to be. Sam had always been clear in his mind that it was always for the greater good, fighting back for those who simply couldn't themselves.

A way for him to make peace with the loss of his son, and his failure as a father to protect him.

But maybe they had a point?

Maybe he just wanted to see how far he could push himself, how much turmoil and trauma he could subject his body to, and still continue on. Still keep fighting. Amy Devereux would have had a field day with his current mind state, as during their therapy sessions over three years ago, Sam would offer the odd grunt or cliched response and then stare at the clock. All she had wanted to do was help him to manage the trauma and deal with the very real pain he suffered. In the end, he had helped her, saving her from a murderous crime lord and a treacherous Metropolitan Police detective.

But now, with his mind wandering, she would have been eagerly infiltrating his mind, trying to discover the real reason as to why he would roll a grenade into a room where his only viable exit was through a first-floor window.

When a man had nothing to lose, he had nothing to fear.

Sam knew his fight against crime wasn't for him. It was his penance for failing his boy, and as long as he kept that at the front of his mind, he would continue to pick himself up.

Continue to fight.

Continue to survive.

But unlike all the others, this fight was for him. Before, he had Amy or Jasmine to fight for. People he cared about, like Sergeant Marsden, Alex Stone or Sean Wiseman.

People he had loved, like Mac or Amara Singh.

But this time, he was fighting for his life.

The smoke billowed from Powell House, and Sam shuffled through some of the broken glass to the edge of the train and peered around the side of it. Between the train and the building was a chain-link fence, and through it, he could see the emergency services hard at work. Firefighters were bravely beginning to tackle the fire, while the police had Defoe on the ground, his hands behind his back.

The unmistakable figure of Jacob Nash was nowhere to be seen, and Sam wondered just how powerfully the people he worked for would now be hunting him. As dangerous as Nash appeared, he had clearly seen enough to know that Sam wasn't the bad guy in this feud.

Dana Kovalenko was, and Sam knew that with every passing hour since he'd threatened her life, he'd given her more time to prepare for his arrival. The option was there for him to just walk away, but according to Brandt, there were more than a few people who had lined themselves up for a big payday.

Until Sam had cut off the source, then he would forever be running.

And he didn't run.

Wasn't trained to.

Somewhere along the way, he was certain Jacob Nash would be back. The Foundation had resources that would have made Paul Etheridge vomit, and Nash would likely use them to either cash in on Sam and disappear or try to change his own narrative. Either way, Sam had to make his way to London, and he needed to end this once and for all.

With the blazing fire, the arrest of Defoe and the discovery of a dead body on the street, the police were occupied enough for Sam to weave his way through the train depot and disappear himself.

It was time to get going, and as Sam began to navigate his way through the corridors of old, abandoned trains, he heard the unmistakable crunch of glass underfoot echo from behind him.

He stopped, his bloodied hand instinctively reaching

for the Glock that wasn't there, and he cursed Jacob Nash under his breath. The only lighting was that of the flickering flames beyond the fence, and the intermittent flash of blue from the emergency vehicles.

Another crunch of glass.

Sam stood, fists clenched, and every part of his body begging for mercy.

Then, as the glass crunched again, an immaculately dressed man stepped out from the shadows, a carriage length away from Sam. The open collar shirt revealed an impressive display of tattoos, and the man confidently stood, his hands clasped and resting in front of him.

Sam squinted, trying to get a look at the man, and he had a familiar feeling, as if he had seen the man somewhere before, even if for a split second.

It didn't matter. Something told Sam that the man wasn't there to help him home.

'Can I help you?' Sam eventually offered. The man responded by reaching into the pocket of his blazer and making a display of the sharpened knuckle duster that he slid over his tattooed fingers.

'That depends, *vato*.' The man's accent was thick and menacing. 'If you want to do this easy way or the hard way.'

Sam sighed, clenched his fists, and stepped towards the inevitable.

CHAPTER NINETEEN

After catching up with Pope as he'd left Spondon, Mendoza had carefully maintained enough of a distance between himself and his target as he followed him back through the city centre. It was a relatively easy task during the final remnants of rush hour, with the one-way system becoming a hindrance to those in a rush, but a godsend for those with patience. As he followed, Mendoza mused on what Pope was up to, and considering the heat he had brought upon the city of Derby over the past few days, he was surprised the man hadn't cut and run.

Throughout his years as a weapon for the Cuban Revolutionary Armed Forces, Mendoza had pursued many a target, all of whom had felt the full force of his fury. The regime in control of the country governed with an iron fist, and Mendoza found his method of extracting information or eliminating his targets a fitting tribute.

The sharpened, metal knuckle duster that hung heavy inside the pocket of his blazer was all he needed when it came to hand-to-hand combat. He carried a gun, of course, as some people were smart enough to try to run or foolish enough to open fire.

But it was when he was up close and personal, ripping flesh from faces with expert fists, that Mendoza extracted the most pleasure. He was certain that Pope would put up a fight, especially after the state he left the Americans in at the café, and that was a tantalising prospect.

Mendoza was already a rich man.

But fighting a warrior like Sam Pope to the death for three million dollars was an opportunity he couldn't turn down. He had done his own research and quickly saw enough to know it was worth the fight. There was a bigger bounty if he took Pope alive, but while the cash reward was bigger, the reputational reward wouldn't be.

The man who took down Sam Pope would become a legend.

Mendoza was ready to etch his name in history.

There were a few moments where he considered initiating Pope, but he held back. He watched tentatively from the darkness of the car park as the man ventured into a Starbucks for some food, and then followed him as he did some recon on a large building behind the train station. There was no concrete proof, but Mendoza logically guessed that Pope was meeting someone, and that meant there were outcomes he couldn't plan for.

Who was he meeting?

How many?

Were they armed?

The best tactic Mendoza had was to step into the shadows and observe, and once all the pieces were in play, he would step in and flip the board. Once Sam drew his car to a stop on the road leading towards his previously scouted building, Mendoza had cut his engine and watched from the corner shrouded in darkness. Sam made his way tentatively towards the building, and then, after scanning the perimeter, he revealed his weapon and stepped in.

He was armed.

There was a dim light on the first floor, and Mendoza kept his eyes trained on the windows, hoping for signs of movement. Eventually, he saw a hulking figure move past the window and his mind rushed back to the meeting the day before, with the two Americans.

The disrespectful one and the intimidating one.

They were here. Which meant the time to move was imminent. Just as Mendoza was about to push open the door to his car, he saw the arrogant American he'd wanted to murder in cold blood storm down the street.

A clear trap for Pope?

With nowhere for Pope to go, it appeared the two Americans were about to make their move, and Mendoza knew he would have moments to hijack it. Despite the man's arrogance, Mendoza was under no illusion that the American would be a tough target.

Then, to his complete shock, the man threw open the driver's door to a car halfway up the road and unloaded a few bullets into the poor soul sitting in wait.

What was going on?

As the American disappeared into the building, Mendoza pushed his door open and stepped out into the street and quickly scurried to the now blood-spattered car. A nondescript man lay in the driver's seat, a bullet hole in his stomach and another through the side of the head. The death would have been quick, but it was apparent the man wasn't from their world.

Mendoza turned his attention to Powell House, knowing that at least three of the most dangerous men on the planet were somewhere inside.

His gun was tucked neatly in the holster under his arm.

His knuckle duster available with a quick dip into his pocket.

It was time to make his move.

As he marched to battle, a light drizzle began to coat

the street in a moist haze, and the cooling water was a relief.

Twenty feet from the gateway to the building, a flash of light, followed by a roaring explosion ripped through the first floor of the building, shaking the street and echoing back towards town.

Then he saw it.

A man blown from the first-floor window, over the chain-link fence that cut off the train depot, only to land back first with a sickening thud on the top of a retired train carriage. The metal absorbed most of the impact, but the momentum sent the body rolling off the side and into the labyrinth of abandoned vehicles. A shower of glass rained down on the trains, clattering off the metal.

The emergency services would be there in minutes, their focus surely trained on the explosion and the potential findings of three bodies. Mendoza battled his way through the bushes that lined the walkway until he reached the fence and, with minimal fuss, he scaled it, dropping down into the depot, shrouded in darkness.

Nothing but large, empty train carriages were in view, all of them in varying stages of decay.

The drizzle drummed against each of them.

With careful, considered footsteps, he made his way towards the carriages near the now burning building, hoping that the man who had fallen from the sky had been Sam Pope.

And now, he had landed in what Mendoza planned to be his own personal hell.

———

As Sam took a step forward, his boot crunching on the rough gravel beneath, a gust of wind swept between the carriages, splashing both him and his adversary with a sterner wall of rain. The drizzle had thickened, and the narrow alleyway between the trains had created a wind tunnel. Mendoza showed no fear, stepping forward with the confidence of a man who had done this many times before and lived to tell the tale on every occasion.

Whoever this man was, Sam knew he was in very real danger. The fee that had been placed upon his head ensured only the elite would hunt him and judging by the man's expensive suit and custom-made weapon, he was pretty sure he'd collected on a number of contracts.

As they eliminated the space between them, Sam's mind harkened back to some of the brutal fist fights he had endured over the past few years. There was the brutal and bloodied fight with one of the Mitchell Brothers at the top of the high rise, which ended when Sam drilled a knife through the man's eye. His near death at the hands of Oleg Kovalenko, which was only avoided when he managed to plunge a rusty hook through the man's throat.

Buck, in an underground bunker in Italy.

Farukh, atop the dilapidated High Rise, as he clung for his life on a rickety scaffolding.

Edinson.

Bowker.

For a man who had built his entire legacy off his prolificity through the scope of a rifle, Sam was surprised at how many people he had beaten to death with his bare hands. And now, a few steps away from another murderous enemy, he knew that the only way he was walking away was if he added another to the list.

Mendoza wasted little time in unloading a few rapid jabs with his bare-knuckled fist, which Sam managed to avoid, before throwing his own. Mendoza was fast, quicker than Sam could ever wish to be, and the man's slighter frame meant that the agility was in his favour. As he weaved under Sam's thundering right hook, he swung out a swift sidekick that planted Sam clean on the thigh, causing a slight wobble. Sam adjusted his foot against the gravel, only to be rocked by a swift left hook.

Sam stumbled a few steps to the side, wiped his jaw with his hand and then raised his fists again. The two men circled each other slowly, and then Mendoza burst forward with another flurry of jabs. One of them caught Sam on the cheek, but the next one he evaded, before retaliating with a swift strike to the man's solid stomach.

Mendoza stepped back, smirking.

'You got some fight in you, *esse*.' Mendoza raised his eyebrows in approval. 'I like that.'

Sam lunged forward with a hard right cross, but Mendoza ducked, drilled a knee into Sam's hip and then finally rocked him with a clubbing blow with the metal knuckles. The sharpened point sliced across Sam's cheek, pulling open the skin and sending a small splatter of blood against one of the trains.

The rain washed it away instantly.

Mendoza wasted little time, racing forward and ducking the wild swing by Sam and burying his shoulder into Sam's mid-section and driving both of them into the train behind. Sam's already sore spine slammed against the metal, but he locked his arms around his Cuban attacker and began to swing his knees up as hard as he could. A few of them connected firmly with the man's body, but on the third one, Mendoza latched onto Sam's leg, and then swept the other from under him.

Sam hit the gravel hard and then roared with agony as Mendoza drilled a brutal, metal-clad fist into his thigh. Unrelenting, he fell on top of Sam, and began raining down brutal right hands, all of which Sam absorbed with his forearms, the sharp blades ripping his leather jacket to shreds. Eventually, one of the fists got through, and the fist struck Sam flush on the jaw, ripping the skin open and sending his head snapping back against the gravel.

Blood gushed from his jaw.

His brain rattled in his skull.

He was losing.

'This is too easy, *vato*.' Mendoza chuckled, and then drilled Sam with another one, this time imprinting a few more cuts on Sam's cheek. The pain was instant, and with every brutal strike, Sam felt the fight getting away from him. The man was too quick, and unlike Sam, hadn't just been blasted through a first-storey window.

Sam could fight back against most things.

But there was only so much his body could take.

A few more blows, and it would be over, and Sam could only hope that his attacker would rather kill him than drag his beaten body to London. Dana Kovalenko had made it clear that Sam would experience more pain than he ever thought possible, and that involved going after the people he cared about.

The people he trusted.

The people he was willing to fight for.

Mendoza slammed his fist down towards Sam once more, looking for that killing strike, but Sam's moment of clarity caused him to shimmy to the side, and Mendoza's balled fist hit the jagged stones. He howled in pain, and Sam locked his arm around the man's wrist and then, with all the power he could muster, he rolled his entire body weight over it, bending it back over itself and hearing the satisfying snap of bone. Mendoza roared with agony and fell backwards, the metal sliding from his limp fingers, and he scurried back to his feet and fell against the train, trying to manage the pain.

Sam pushed himself up, the rain crashing against his beaten body and bloodied face, and he locked his eyes on Mendoza.

Valiantly, Mendoza tried to throw up a hand to block the incoming blow, but Sam made it through, rocking the man with a thunderous right that disconnected his jaw bone, before he grabbed him by the collar of his blazer, drove his forehead into the man's nose, and then slammed him face first into the train.

The front of Mendoza's face was flattened, his nose obliterated as blood gushed over his slack jaw. He slid down the train, his legs sprawling out beneath him.

There was no begging for mercy.

Even if the man's jaw was working, Sam knew the words would never come.

They had made a silent promise that it was to the death, and as he raised his boot, Sam knew he was keeping his word.

He thrust forward as hard as he could, the bottom of his boot connecting with such velocity with the side of Mendoza's head that it compressed viciously against the unforgiving metal of the train. His skull cracked, but it was the unmistakable drooping of his head that told Sam that the neck was broken.

Mendoza flopped forward onto the gravel, blood pumping from his face, his eyes wide and lifeless.

The death had been quick, but brutal.

Sam felt nothing. There was none of the enjoyment he had been worried about. There was also no remorse. The corpse before him had been hell bent on killing him, a man he had never met, for cold, hard cash.

The dead man was a hired gun.

And in that line of work, there was always the possibility that your next target would be your last.

Sam lifted his face to the sky, the chilled rain soothing the searing pain that emanated from the lacerations across his skin. He felt like hell warmed up, and as he slowly trudged across the gravel and away from the man he'd just killed, he wondered how many more were coming for him.

And what Dana Kovalenko would do when she found out another one of her potential assets had been eliminated.

Beyond the cover of the train depot, Sam could still hear the emergency services battling the fire, while the streets were now alive with activity, with nosey residents being ushered further back by irritated police.

There was too much noise.

Too many people.

Too many phones.

Sam's car was somewhere on the street, his dwindling arsenal in the boot of the vehicle. There was no way he was getting to it, with the ever growing crowd meaning someone was sure to spot him, especially with the battle scars of his fight with Mendoza on display.

There was also no chance of sticking around and waiting it out. Eventually, they would sweep the area and he needed to be gone.

It meant he needed to head to London without a gun in his hand, or any plans on how to get one.

It was becoming a long few days, and as he limped through the narrow gaps between the trains, he didn't expect it to get any easier any time soon.

CHAPTER TWENTY

Dana Kovalenko slammed down her laptop in anger, shutting off the news broadcast she'd been watching. It was all over every news channel, with the Sam Pope narrative dominating the headlines as another confrontation had seemingly taken place, once again in Derbyshire, with another dead body and another seriously injured man, taken into hospital.

No matter the calibre of the hitman she'd sent after the man, the fact annoyingly remained the same.

Sam Pope simply wouldn't die.

When she had learnt of his return from the dead, Dana had fantasised about the revenge she would enact on behalf of her beloved brother. Pope had tried to justify Andrei's death by the empire he'd created, but Pope had no idea where Andrei had come from.

The life he had endured.

The things he had to suffer to keep her and Oleg safe.

Yes, the lives of many people were ruined by their trafficking business, but it had been a necessary step in providing the Kovalenko children with a life that they had deserved due to the awful hand they'd been dealt. They had never asked to be raised by an inadequate and abusive father, and had Andrei not intervened or loved her, then Dana would have been raped multiple times over by the person who was supposed to protect her.

Would Sam Pope have murdered people to protect her from such a fate?

It was what turned her stomach. The man preached about right and wrong, yet he ruined as many families as her brother had. He had certainly killed more people, yet he believed he was justified in his actions.

It was why she craved her revenge, and it was why, with her hitmen falling one by one, she could feel her anxiety heightening.

The multi-million bounty was supposed to draw the best of the best to her door, with Uri diligently vetting each one to verify that they were up to the task. When she had sat in that crummy warehouse two days before and given them the terms of the deal, she had regarded them all as killers.

Men capable of getting the job done.

She didn't care which one of them would end up knocking on her door, either with a corpse or a man on death's door, looking to get paid.

She had just expected it to happen.

But now, another piece had been taken off the chess-board. The news report had described the dead man as of Latin-American descent but had yet to be identified. She knew it was the man who had sat in the warehouse, with a revered history working for one of the most dangerous governments in the world.

Yet he'd found himself beaten to death in a train yard.

Because Sam Pope simply wouldn't die.

The identity of the man taken to hospital still eluded her, but with Brandt and his team eliminated, it meant that one of the Americans was still in play. She hoped it was the strong, silent one, as the arrogance of the younger hitman had turned her stomach.

But either way, they needed to change things.

They needed to bring Sam to them, as out on the streets, they were in his domain, and he was once again reminding them all that he was built for the war they were bringing to his doorstep.

'Uri,' Dana called from the plush dining room of the penthouse.

'Yes, dear.' Uri entered, offering a modicum of affection as he did. It wasn't reciprocated.

'Get Leon and his crew in here. Now.'

Uri scurried out of the room, leaving Dana to stand and fix her hair in the mirror. Despite the fury and the increasing panic, she was a Kovalenko, and she knew she needed to represent the power that had been bestowed upon that name. She straightened the front of her fitted black dress and then sat back down at the head of the table, sipping the coffee she had been enjoying while watching the news. Eventually, Uri re-emerged, followed by the one-armed thug and a few of his crew.

'Sit,' Dana commanded, and all the men obliged, with Uri making a point of sitting beside her. An empty display of authority.

'Whaddya need?' Leon asked, slouching in his chair.

'I need you all to be ready,' Dana began. She splayed her immaculately manicured fingers out on the table. 'As you know, Sam Pope is not going down without a fight. We are losing the people we sent after him, and once the final one goes, then there is a strong chance he will disappear for good.'

'Run like a lil' bitch?' Leon chuckled.

'That cannot happen. For nearly three years, I have mourned my brother. When they announced that the fucker who killed him was dead, I lost my way. But now, I have been given a chance to put right what he did. To make him suffer for the things he has done for my family.' She turned to Leon. 'The things he has done to people who work for me.'

Leon shuffled uncomfortably in his chair. The sleeve of his hooded jacket had been pinned at the elbow, emphasising the missing limb.

Uri sat forward, his eyes on Dana and his hands clasped in his lap.

'What do you want to do?'

'I want to bring him here.'

'Excuse me?' Uri sat back, startled.

'Out there, even with the element of surprise, it's his turf.' Dana spoke calmly. 'Several of the men we sent after him are dead. So, if we want to bring that bastard to his knees, then we need him here. Where we control things.'

'Makes sense.' Leon shrugged.

'And how do you expect we do that?' Uri asked, shaking his head in disbelief.

'None of the men know this location. They have not been here. We have not told them. But we know which phone Sam has access to. So, I want you, Uri, to send this location to the other numbers on the list and see which one comes to us. Then, with them here, I will reach out to Sam and invite him here myself.'

'That is insane.' Uri threw his hand up.

'You scared, bruv?' Leon raised an eyebrow. A member of his crew chuckled.

'Fuck you.' Uri spat back. 'I have seen and done things that make your missing hand look like a fucking scratch.'

'Yeah, but you ain't been through this have you?' Leon lifted the remainder of his arm in fury. He turned back to Dana. 'Boss, bring that motherfucker here and I'll put him down myself.'

'That's very sweet.' Dana rolled her eyes. 'But what I

need you and your boys to do is stay alert. When I make the call, I expect him to come here looking for a war.'

'And then what do you plan to do?' Uri asked, clearly displeased with the whole plan.

Dana smiled cruelly.

'Give him one.'

The men around the table all shared a quiet look, knowing full well the gravity of what Dana was planning. She had made a clear threat against Sam Pope and the people he cared about, and now she was inviting him to their front door. The chances were, he wouldn't knock politely.

Dana stood, gave them all one more authoritative glare, and then strode back across the room, goading them all to look at her as she left. Men were easy to rein in, and she knew that despite Uri's misgivings, he would obediently send the message to the remaining contract killer.

Once they had a positive response, then she would take the final step towards her revenge.

She would call Sam Pope and tell him exactly where to find her if he wanted her dead.

———

The beeping of hospital equipment echoed through the hallway, and Defoe felt his fists clench in frustration. With his entire body shaking with pain, every beep felt louder as it pounded against his eardrum. The paramedics had done their best to alleviate the pain, but it wasn't until he was taken to the hospital that the nurses finally pumped him with painkillers.

It had been enough to dull the agony, but the pain still clung to the edges.

He had only been able to look at his face once.

The brutality of Nash's actions hadn't been lost on

him, and he realised, upon the only inspection of his wounds, that it had come from somewhere beyond survival. Defoe had walked into the building with the very clear objective of eliminating both men, and Nash, as they had been trained to, had fought for his life. The man had killed countless people in the name of The Foundation, yet instead of putting a bullet through Defoe's skull, he did something worse.

He obliterated his identity.

Defoe knew he was egotistical. It was a small consequence of being such a talented assassin, coupled with his dashing looks. He took pride in his appearance, and it had never been difficult to sway a woman's gaze from a table and use his considerable charm to bed her.

But that had been taken away.

Nash had literally peeled back the skin of his face to reveal the monster beneath, and there were no painkillers in the world that could dull that damage.

Defoe had been rendered a monster.

Five, deep, brutal scars had been carved into his face, one of them ripping through a nostril, while the other had come close to blinding him. A cosmetic surgeon had been rushed in for emergency surgery upon Defoe's arrival at the hospital, and although they had successfully patched him to ensure his survival, it hadn't been the same man looking back when he finally faced his reflection.

His face looked like an old, discarded jigsaw. Numerous black stitches criss-crossed his face like a tatty old football.

If he wasn't handcuffed to the side of the hospital bed, he would have already been hunting Nash to the ends of the earth.

But that would have to wait.

A nurse entered to check some of the notes on the clipboard that hung at the end of his bed, and Defoe greeted her with a grunt as he sat up.

He needed to see himself again.

To make peace with what he had become.

Before he could ask her for a mirror, there was a gentle tap on the door to the room, and he turned his mutilated gaze to it. Two young men, both decked out in cheap looking suits and average haircuts entered, trying their best to exude authority.

Defoe was instantly irritated.

'Fuck off.' Defoe spat, swinging his legs over the bed and glaring at them through his scars.

'Rough night?' DC Anderson asked dryly, before he shifted uncomfortably on the spot. The effects of Mendoza's torture were still palpable and he was trying his best to contain them. Next to him, DC Saddler tried a different tack.

'Can we get you anything?'

'You can take these fucking cuffs off me.' Defoe raised his arm as far as he could.

'I'm afraid I can't do that.' Saddler shrugged. 'Not until we get to the bottom of what's going on.'

Defoe began to chuckle.

'You have no fucking idea what's going on.' He turned his attention to Anderson. 'And if you did, you'd hobble the fuck back to whatever hole you came out of.'

'Well, unless you start speaking buddy, I can find a nice, dark hole for you to sleep in tonight.' Anderson replied in anger.

'Forgive Detective Anderson, here. He's not feeling well.' Saddler elbowed his friend in the rib. 'I'm Detective Saddler and…'

'And I've already made my phone call. So any minute now, you boys will be told to let me go and then I suggest you get the fuck out of my way.'

'This ain't the wild west here.' Anderson spat again,

just as Saddler's phone buzzed. 'In England, we treat our law enforcement with a little respect and…'

'Understood sir.' Saddler said with a sigh and then pocketed his phone. He arched a worried eyebrow at the brutally scarred and obviously dangerous man who sat before them and then anxiously stepped forward and undid the lock on the cuff. 'You're free to go.'

'What the fuck?' Anderson exclaimed.

Defoe stood, stretched out the aches in his spine and then rubbed his wrist. With a maniacal grin, he barged between the two detectives, but not before threatening to headbutt Anderson, who stepped back and collided with the door.

'Bitch.' Defoe snarled and then stomped through the corridor, ignoring any attempt by one of the nurses who demanded he needed more care. He threw open the door to the stairwell and walked his way down to the ground floor, ignoring any glass panel on the doors as he passed. As he stepped out into the main reception, he knew every face had turned to him in shock and awe. It should have mattered, but it didn't.

The only thing that mattered now was revenge.

The automatic door to the hospital welcomed him to a sunny morning and a surprisingly chilly breeze and only then did he realise he had been unconscious for almost nine hours.

Nash would be in the wind right now.

So would Sam.

Before he could ruminate on the thought of hunting them down, a non-descript man approached with an anxious look on his face.

'Mr Defoe.' The man swallowed his nerves and he handed Defoe a car key. 'The vehicle is in car park B with your replenished arsenal in the back.'

With an angry swing, Defoe snatched the key from the

young man who quivered slightly, trying his best not to look at the brutal injuries.

'Fuck off.'

The man turned and slipped into the stream of people walking around the hospital, and Defoe stomped his way towards the instructed car park. The Foundation's ability to override his arrest and provide him with what he needed was as swift as it was impressive, and had he not been dragged face first through a metre of broken glass, he would have appreciated it.

But the sharp blades hadn't just stripped him of his looks.

Defoe felt nothing.

Nothing but rage and a thirst for revenge.

As his phone bleeped with an incoming text message, he threw open the car door, dropped inside it and got ready to go hunting.

CHAPTER TWENTY-ONE

The room of the hostel was cramped and cold, with the 'clean rooms' advertising a generous claim by the owners. But Jacob Nash didn't care.

As he slowly opened his eyes, he realised the sun had come up, which meant he had been asleep for at least five hours, and as he tried to rise from the bed, the dull, agonising pain from his shoulder kept him stuck to the mattress. The paracetamol had provided a little respite from the pain, and Nash grunted as he rolled off the side of the bed, and then lazily slapped his hand on the flimsy bedside table until he found the box. He pushed two tablets through the foil and then slammed them back, swigging the lukewarm water from the bottle he had bought the night before.

He felt like shit.

Probably looked it to.

He shuffled backwards until his back was leaning against the bed and then tried to gather his thoughts. The sleep, while welcome, had caused a slight disorientation, and he knew that was due to the blood loss. After speeding away from the burning building and the anarchy he, Pope and Defoe had caused the night before, it hadn't taken him long to shake the police tail and disappear. He had sped back to the luxurious hotel as quickly as he could, marching to the room and clearing out as much as he could.

He had left Defoe alive, which meant that as soon as he could make contact with the Foundation, they would shut them down. Remove any and all traces of their participation in the events, and then reload Defoe if he was ready to get back into the game.

As for himself, Nash knew that until he had spoken to Callaghan, he would be excommunicated.

His phone wasn't working, the access revoked meaning he could only receive messages. As quickly as he could, Nash packed his expensive clothes into his suit case, along with the backup Glock that he had stashed by his bed and the bullet proof vest in his wardrobe. As he looked at the paltry arsenal remaining, he cursed himself for underestimating Defoe.

The man had clearly cottoned on to his misgivings about the mission, and had played both he and Dallow into thinking he had drunk their spiked beer. They thought he had been unconscious, but the man had laid perfectly still, absorbing everything Nash had said to Dallow, and all of the questions he had about the Foundation's motives.

Defoe would have relayed that back.

Nash had gone rogue.

He would be surprised if even Callaghan could help him now, but he knew he needed to speak to him. They had worked together for two decades, and the man was the closest thing Nash had to a father figure. Maybe there was hope for him yet?

Nash also packed up the computer system that Dallow had left in the room, hoping that once he connected to another internet account he would be able to at least try to figure out his next move while remaining off the grid until they tracked him down. Defoe would undoubtedly provide them the information for Dallow's now fatal assistance, and the computer buffs that worked extensively in the background would likely track him down through some unique identifier.

Which meant he didn't have much time.

Nor many options.

Within five minutes of arriving, Nash was packing the car up once more, dumping the weapons, clothes and computers into the boot of the car, and then speeding back out towards the city. There, he found a cheap hostel, dumped the car in a nearby parking lot and then trundled back to the building, stopping in a small supermarket to buy painkillers, cotton wool pads, bandages, Vaseline and Iodine. Then, he stumbled into the hostel, paid the man and disappeared for the night.

Nash took another swig of water and then looked towards the private bathroom. The room was tiny, barely big enough for his hulking size, and the sink was littered in bloodied cotton wool pads.

Treating the bullet wound in his shoulder had been a treat.

Throughout his career, Nash has rarely been hurt, with many of his targets either not seeing him coming, or unable to lay a glove on him if they did. But any injuries incurred were treated by the Foundation, who's funding meant the best healthcare was provided for their assets.

Sitting in a crummy bathroom, biting down on a towel and slapping an antiseptic laced cotton wool pad against the open wound was a far cry from what he was used to, and every developed muscle in his body had tensed with anguish as he did.

But he had treated the wound. Stopped any chance of

infection, and had covered it with enough bandages to stem the bleeding.

He felt weak, but he would survive.

He had to.

As he finished off the bottle of water, he tried to roll his shoulder, gritting his teeth and grimacing as the damage rippled through his muscles. With one arm, he was still a dangerous proposition, but it meant he was at a disadvantage. Especially without any support.

The Foundation were most likely looking for him, and as he brought his phone to life, he was inundated with messages, each one causing the phone the rumble in his hand.

Callaghan.

'Extraction Protocol Enacted.'

'We need to talk.'

'Defoe has requested a resupply. You have been stepped down from the contract.'

'Jacob…I can help you but you need to come in.'

'Jesus Christ, Jacob. Don't make this worse.'

Nash felt a twinge of guilt in his gut. Callaghan, despite his history as a dangerous killer, was a good man. He believed in the Foundation, in the good that it did, and Nash was certain that the old man was fighting his corner back in the States. You don't turn against the Foundation, and very few people get to walk away when they have served their purpose. But Callaghan had considerable power, along with respect, and Nash was under no illusion that the man was trying to use both to keep him out of the Foundation's crosshairs.

But would it be enough?

It didn't matter. Callaghan had already told him that Defoe had requested a resupply, which meant he was alive and already back on the hunt for Sam Pope. Nash had no loyalty towards Pope, but if he had sided with either a vigilante or a child trafficker, Nash knew where his morality would take him.

He might have been wounded, but he was still walking, and that meant he could still try to do the right thing.

A final message buzzed through and Nash didn't recognise the number. But the first sentence was an announcement to any contractor still alive.

It was from Dana Kovalenko.

It was a change of plan.

A clear idea to lure Sam Pope to them, the text message provided an address for a building in London, and the very clear instruction to be there as soon as possible.

It was a standard message which would have been sent to every person who had agreed to the contract. Those who had been in that room, and Nash had no idea where the Cuban hit man was or when he would appear.

But Brandt was dead. Sam had made that clear.

Defoe was still very much alive, and having requested a resupply, it meant he was likely heading there with the full force of The Foundation behind him.

Whatever the outcome of this entire mission, they would know by the end of that day, and Nash knew, with one arm out of action, he might not even see another sunrise if he went.

But he had never walked away from a mission in his life. Never failed on a contract.

And even if the goal posts had been changed, Nash pushed himself to his feet with a renewed purpose, and knew that there was one play left to make.

——————

As the water from the shower pelted down on Sam, he closed his eyes, pressed his hands against the tiles of the wall and dropped his head. The water slithered down his spine, offering a crumb of comfort as the impact from his fall had begun to kick in. His spine felt like the vertebrae had been cemented together, and once the adrenaline of being confronted with a fight to the death had worn off, the pain took over.

Luckily for Sam, he had slept well.

After leaving the train depot, Sam had ambled into a low quality fast food shop down a dodgy looking side street. A few of the patrons turned to look and immediately gasped at the bloody, dishevelled man who had stumbled in. Those working behind the till spoke little English, but when Sam asked to use the bathroom, they had been more than accommodating, and one of them even brought him a bottle of water and some wet wipes. As he had wiped the blood from his face, he stared into the mirror at the broken man before him.

Broken. But not beaten.

One of the slices on his cheek, caused by a violent fist by his deceased attacker, refused to stop trickling blood, and after a while, Sam just held a wipe against it before he left. As he made his way back into the chicken shop, one of the workers slid him a bag with some questionable food in and Sam smiled thankfully.

A kindly and well timed reminder that there were good people in the world.

With his car now likely seized and his weapons gone, Sam kept his head low and walked towards the city centre, hoping that a bright, well lit sign for a hotel would soon come into view. He didn't have to wait long, as the unmistakable white letters of *Premier Inn* soon arrived. Despite the receptionists misgivings, Sam was able to provide his fake ID and enough money to cover the night's stay and he soon found himself collapsing on a bed that was surprisingly comfortable.

Either that, or his body was so drained that anything

would be welcome. Either way, as soon as he hit the pillow he was asleep, and the sunshine was a welcome sight when he opened them.

In the shower, Sam took a moment to inspect the bruising on his ribs. Like his spine, they felt like they had been fused together, and his forearms and elbows were littered with cuts and scrapes from the swan dive he had taken out of the window. One day, he wouldn't be so lucky, and although he had tested his body's threshold on countless occasions, the time would come when it would get too much.

But until then, he'd keep going.

Keep fighting.

After he dried himself off and put his clothes back on, he opened up his phone and thought about his next move. There was no way, with his face covered in cuts and bruises that anyone would let him rent a car. Even if he lied about them, the next logical possibility was that he had been in a car accident, which wouldn't help his application. He navigated to a website to purchase a one way ticket to King's Cross St Pancras, where a multitude of trains travelled to from Derby throughout the day. It would take a little over an hour and a half, and Sam chuckled at the idea of having some quiet time to read but not having a book.

The thought of tucking into a book always reminded him of Jamie, who had been an eager bookworm from the get go. It was a trait he had clearly gotten from his mother, as Sam had never been the biggest reader. Lucy, when they were together and happy, was often found curled up with the latest thriller, gasping as a plot twist caught her by surprise or crying when the author reached out and tugged her heart strings. It was something Sam had always found fascinating, how someone she didn't know could write something that connected with her on such an emotional level. Jamie often spoke excitedly about the books he was reading, and upon Sam's return from Project Hailstorm and his retirement from duty, he had promised to read more with his son.

When Jamie died, Sam had tried to stick to it, working his way through the most critically acclaimed books in the world and found them to be a little difficult to enjoy.

There had been countless promises he had made to his son that he had broken. But Sam decided that if he survived the next few days, and walked away from Dana Kovalenko with the chance to keep going, then this would be a promise he would keep.

With a grim smile, Sam spoke to himself.

'I promise you, Jamie. I'll read more.'

With a surprising croak in his voice, Sam blinked away a tear that the memory of his son had brought forward, and then booked his train ticket. He could get any train that day, so he was in no rush. All he knew was he was heading to London. That's where Dana Kovalenko was, and although it was a big place, Sam knew there were cages he could rattle that would eventually lead him to her. The only issue was, he had no gun.

When he first begun his war on crime, he had made a concerted effort to stash weapons around the capital in lock ups and storage facilities. It was part of his plan to relentlessly fight back against the criminal underworld, but once the Sam Pope Task Force, in it's first iteration, found his home address, they uncovered the locations for all of them and promptly seized them.

That's what happens when someone as diligent as Amara Singh is hunting you.

His heart ached at the thought of Amara, wondering where she was and how life had treated her over the past few years. While he had turned down the offer to join an elite, covert government operation, she had taken the opportunity and that was that. He still remembered their one evening of passion together, the taste of her lips on his and the soft, smooth feel of her naked body.

In another life, he had told her.

He still believed that.

But as he looked around the charmless hotel room to ensure he hadn't left anything behind, he wished he still had his rainy day fund. A stash of weapons that he had buried in his good friend Theo Walker's garden, which he had dug up when all of this began. Frank Jackson, the crime boss who ordered the hit that killed Theo, had been on the receiving end of Sam's vengeance, but it meant that it was also another dead end.

With his back stiffening and a groan of pain accompanying it, Sam headed to the door, intent on buying some new clothes, grabbing some food and then heading to Derby Train Station. He had one play left in the hopes of attaining a weapon, and if that didn't work out, then he knew he was heading back to London, to walk into a gun fight empty handed.

CHAPTER TWENTY-TWO

'You all right there, Liam?'

Detective Saddler watched on with concern as his friend, Detective Anderson, gingerly lowered himself into his seat. It had been over a day and half since he had been abducted by the mysterious Cuban man and then tortured for information, and apart from the searing pain in his legs, it was Anderson's pride and ego that had suffered most. Outwardly confident and boisterous, Anderson was seen as one of the 'alpha males' within the Derbyshire Police Service, and the last thing he wanted was for anyone to know that not only had he foolishly made himself a target with his drunk behaviour, but that he was also reduced to quivering, weeping mess.

'All good, baby.' Anderson smirked, trying to ignore the pain. Saddler arched his eyebrow.

'You sure?' Saddler shrugged. 'I thought a day's rest would have sorted you out. You want to take another day?'

'What, with all this Sam Pope stuff going on? No way.' Anderson turned back to his desk to try to busy himself. 'Besides, I've got a call with the Met liaison in an hour.'

'I'm surprised they haven't sent some guys up to help out.'

'Besides, however bad our day is going, at least we don't look like that yank at the hospital. Man, that was messed up.'

Saddler contemplated the confrontation that morning, and the horrific scarring that had wrecked the man's face.

'Yeah, it didn't look good.'

'It was fuck ugly.' Anderson chortled.

'You think it was Sam Pope?'

Before Anderson could respond, a young, female officer hurried towards their desks, drawing his attention.

'Hello Officer…'

'Miller.' She ignored the charming twang in Anderson's voice. 'There is someone here to see you.'

'Me?' Anderson's shook slightly. A vivid flashback to the Cuban slamming the meat tenderiser against his thigh causing his anxiety to peak. Despite the man's apparent death, Anderson was still on edge. 'Who is it?'

'I don't know. Some old lady who said she had information about the body that was found last night. She's in room one.'

'Want some company?' Saddler offered, as Miller turned and headed back to her front of house duties. Anderson struggled to his feet and then straightened his tie.

'Sure.' He shrugged. 'Let's go see what she has to say.'

Saddler hopped up and followed, watching with concern as his friend and colleague made an effort not to pressure on his right foot. He was clearly hurt, but Saddler knew best not to keep prodding. Anderson was a good friend, but any question of his toughness was usually met with needless aggression. Whatever was going on with him, whether it was the pressure of the Sam Pope Task Force or an illness, Saddler knew Anderson well enough to let him speak when the time was right. As they approached the door, Anderson turned back to Saddler.

'Let me do the talking.'

Saddler held up his hands in agreement, and the two men stepped in, greeting the elderly lady with their best grins.

'Hello, there. I'm DC Anderson, this is my colleague, DC Saddler. How are you?'

'I'm well thanks. I'm Maggie. Maggie Scowen.'

'You run the café, right?' Saddler said with a smile as he sat down. 'Mama's café.'

'Yes, that's right.'

'Banging bacon butty.' Saddler offered her a warm smile again. 'We met yesterday, didn't we? After the incident in your café.'

Instantly, Maggie stared at the table, and Saddler looked to Anderson who had a glint in his eye.

'So, Maggie. Do you have any further information for us?' Anderson asked, resting his clasped hands on the table. 'You said in your statement that you weren't in the café when the fight broke out, so I'm not sure what we can do for you?'

'I heard about the incident last night.' Maggie spoke, clearly nervous. 'That a man was found dead with no identity. However, the description was…'

'Latin American. Tattoos.' Saddler helpfully interjected, and noticed Anderson shuffle uncomfortably on his chair.

'That's right. Well…he came into the café yesterday and…'

'You saw him?' Anderson sat forward, his brow furrowed.

'He said he was…he was…'

'Look, Mrs Scowen, you won't be in any trouble…' Saddler offered.

'What did he say?' Anderson demanded.

'He said he was a friend of Sam Pope.' Maggie eventually said. 'There was a man who had come in a few times called Jonathan Cooper. He was on his own, clearly ex-military...'

'You believe he was Sam Pope?' Saddler asked, trying to ignore the clear irritation in his partner. Maggie nodded.

'But you don't have CCTV to corroborate that, nor do you know for a fact if it was?' Anderson sighed. 'And this man, this tattooed man, how do you know it's the one who died?'

'I don't.' Maggie said firmly. 'I just thought telling you was the right thing to do.'

Anderson pulled his lips into a thin line and forced a smile as he pushed himself to his feet, using the table to steady him.

'Thank you for coming in, Mrs Scowen. It's been helpful.'

The lack of sincerity in his voice hung heavy and Saddler shook his head as Anderson marched out of the room.

'Ignore him. He's had a rough few days.' Saddler stood and then helped Maggie to her feet. 'Thank you, I will write this up and do some digging and if I need anything else, I know where to find you.'

'They'll be a bacon butty waiting.' Maggie smiled, impressed by the affable detective. 'Always is for the boys in blue.'

Saddler thanked her, held the door and then walked her to the front of the station where he saw her off. The police got enough stick from the public as it was, and Saddler saw it as little effort to ensure that anyone who took the time to help had a positive exit from the station.

It went a long way.

Once he returned to his desk, Anderson was on a

phone call, and he looked at Saddler and motioned with his hand that the woman was blabbing. Saddler politely chuckled and then sat down at his desk, tapped his fingers on the wood and then pulled his keyboard towards him. While he wasn't sure that Maggie Scowen had seen the dead mystery man, she had at least piqued his interest.

With his fingers clicking over the keys, he decided to start doing a few searches for Jonathan Cooper, to see if her regular was in fact the most dangerous man in the country. Considering Anderson had already dismissed it straight away, Saddler thought it was the least he could do.

Sam Pope had to be somewhere, and maybe, just maybe, Saddler would be the one to find him. Within ten minutes, he found himself racing out of his chair, knowing it was just a short drive to Derby Train Station and was either a waste of time or the most important trip he might possibly ever make.

———

By the time the waitress brought over Sam's chips, he had already eaten the toasted sandwich he had ordered. He smiled, almost in shame, but the woman offered him a kind smile and asked if he wanted anything else. He politely declined and then devoured the chips as quickly as his body could let him. Since returning from America over two years ago, Sam had made positive changes in his life and one of those had been an increased focus on keeping himself healthy. The rejection of alcohol had helped massively with the eternal grief and guilt of his son's death, and that had gone hand in hand with healthier food. But as the thick, calorific lunch hit his system, his body thanked him for the treat. After the prolonged evening before, and the pain that echoed through his body like a lion's roar, the comfort food was just what he needed.

He was heading to London empty handed.

The least he could do was not go on an empty stomach.

The young waitress approached again, offering him another smile and trying not to look at the cuts that adorned his otherwise handsome face. Sam nodded his appreciation as she took his plate and then he finished his bottle of water, left a five pound note for the young girl under the empty bottle and then headed for the door. The traffic was slowly crawling through the one way system that strangled Derby city centre, and he looked to the left where the large shopping centre loomed large over the high street. Sam had no idea what day it was, as the last few days had removed all concept of time. It was early afternoon, and Sam turned right and began to walk down the street, passing a number of specialist shops and salons, all of them bustling with activity. At the end of the street was the train station, and Sam knew the trains were roughly every forty minutes, so he was in no rush. Once through the barriers, he would board the first one towards King's Cross, and from there, he'd make one quick stop before he began to track down Dana Kovalenko. He had no idea how long it would take, but there was only one way to end the chaos of the last few days, and one way to keep the people he cared about safe.

Kill Dana Kovalenko.

There were still pockets of criminals he knew about, those that sprung up in the few years he spent trying to lead a quiet life of peace. Like weeds, no matter how many you pulled up, more would always follow. He'd start there, scaring them out of whatever information they had and hope it took him to Dana's front door before the next hitman looking to make a few million tracked him down.

It could take a lot of time, which was unfortunately, a commodity that Sam didn't have.

Just as he the train station came into view, the inside pocket of his new bomber jacket rumbled, and Sam fished out Brandt's phone.

He recognised the number and answered the call.

'Dana.'

'*This needs to end.*' Her voice crackled with venom.

'I agree. I'm getting tired of killing the people you've sent after me. I'm starting to think maybe I should collect that money myself.'

'*Then it is time for you to come and collect.*' Sam could feel the apprehension in her voice. '*Marlow Heights. Mayfair.*'

The phoneline went dead.

Dana Kovalenko had just invited Sam to her front door, and as he slid the phone back into his jacket, Sam frowned. While he now had the location, there was clearly a plan in place. A certain trap was being set, and Sam knew that someone as conniving and vindictive as Dana Kovalenko wouldn't allow her rage to blind her from the task at hand.

They would be waiting and surely certain that they would capture him, otherwise they would never open their door to him.

She didn't want him dead. Not yet, at least.

Which meant Sam could be willingly walking into hell, but as he approached the automatic glass door to the modern looking train station, he knew he didn't have a choice. They would keep hunting him until they found him, and if him walking right to them meant Kovalenko stayed away from the people he cared about, then it was a walk he would have to make.

Sam stopped on the concourse of the station, looking beyond the crowd of people and assessing the queue for the Starbucks kiosk. He had half an hour until the next train to London arrived, and he fancied a coffee. With his mind racing at what was to come, Sam didn't even notice the footsteps behind him.

———

DC Saddler watched in disbelief as the man approached the station, crossing the road from the high street with a phone clasped against his ear.

It was Sam Pope.

Saddler couldn't have been more certain.

Working closely with Anderson had meant he had been privy to a myriad of photos of the man, but Saddler didn't need to recount them. He could tell it was Pope, simply by the aura of the man. The way he walked, his shoulder's wide and his back straight. His head held high.

The broad, muscular physique that stretched the bomber jacket to it's limit, and the powerful steps he took towards the station.

A man with purpose.

The strong jaw was littered with bruises, and a few prominent cuts across the cheek and eyebrow which drew a few concerned looks from other passing civilians. In his entire career within the Derbyshire Police Service, Saddler had been proud of what little fear he had for the job. Breaking down doors and raiding houses had it's own potential pitfalls, but he always had his team with him. The same with responding to an emergency call.

Or interrogating a dangerous and heavily scarred man, as had happened that morning.

This. This was different.

This was just a routine check-up on a lead from a sweet old lady who clearly felt guilty about having nothing to offer the police. For the life of him, Saddler never thought it would play out.

But when he found an Airbnb booking in the name of

Jonathan Cooper, his interest rose. Then, when he found an online booking for a train to London for that afternoon, he knew he would regret not at least checking it out.

He had expected to grab a coffee, stand around for a few hours and then, when nobody arrived, he could go back to work with a clear conscience.

But watching Sam Pope hang up the phone, take a deep breath and then stomp into the station, Saddler let his instinct take over and he followed. He probably should have called for back up, but having seen the carnage of the last few days, the last thing he wanted to do was provoke the dangerous vigilante into action.

As he fell in step behind Pope, his mind raced. What if he was wrong?

What if he was forcing an identity on this poor man?

He'd apologise and move on. The public predominantly hated the police anyway, so annoying an innocent man for a few minutes wasn't going to have any impact.

The man stopped in the queue for a Starbucks, and Saddler took a breath and then stepped forward, latching his hand around the man's elbow and guiding him to the side of the growing line of customers.

Pope spun, but then stopped when he saw the badge.

Saddler tried to keep his face stern and his hand from shaking.

He was looking into the eyes of the most wanted man in the country.

'Jonathan Cooper.' Saddler felt the adrenaline pumping through his veins. 'DC Saddler. Derbyshire Police. I'd like you to come with me.'

CHAPTER TWENTY-THREE

As he slowed his car to a crawl, Defoe gazed through the passenger window at the building. It was a pretty plush looking apartment block in one of the most expensive parts of the city. Considering Dana Kovalenko had put millions on Sam Pope's head, he wasn't surprised that her residence was so luxurious. What did surprise him, were the clearly armed thugs who were situated in the lobby.

They didn't hold any fear for him, but they stood out in such a place.

Defoe pulled the car to the curb, and then got out, adjusting his jacket and then the balaclava that he wore over his face. The autumnal wind had grown colder, and as it whipped by, he welcomed the warmth it provided. It also kept the world from seeing the brutal injuries that he was suffering with.

The hideous deformation of his face.

He slammed the door shut, then retrieved his bag from the boot of the car and then marched to the glass doors at the front of the building, watching as two of the men in the lobby readjusted, ready for action. They were likely hired as protection, and Defoe raised his hands in surrender at the door, hoping they didn't mistake him for Sam Pope. A taller, leaner man approached, a gun in his only hand, and the sleeve of his other arm pinned above the elbow. Defoe felt a strange kinship with the man, knowing he too had been scarred in battle.

Leon pulled the door open and pointed the gun at Defoe's face.

'You ain't Sam Pope.'

'You the brains of the operation?' Defoe cracked, and Leon smirked, showing his gold tooth.

'You the yank, I take it?'

'What gave it away? My accent?'

'Nah. Just the usual arrogance.'

'Touché.' Defoe lowered his hands and stepped in, as Leon lowered his weapon. 'Where is she?'

'Follow me.'

Defoe fell in line behind Leon, who swaggered back through the marble floored foyer of the building towards the lifts. Two of his crew stood to the sides, their eyes fixed on Defoe and their fingers itchy on the trigger. The elevator doors slid open and Leon motioned with his gun for Defoe to step in. Chuckling, Defoe obliged, and Leon followed, hit the button for the penthouse and then stood next to Defoe as the doors shut. As the lift began its ascent, Defoe looked to Leon and then his arm.

'What happened to your arm?'

'None of your fuckin' business, bruv.'

'Fair enough.'

The lift slowed as it came to the top floor.

'Why you got that balaclava on?'

'None of your fucking business.' Defoe turned and cracked a smile through the gap of the wool. 'Bruv.'

Leon smirked as the doors opened, and the two men stepped out into the main room of the penthouse. Defoe knew getting the apparent leader of the street gang onside could only be useful, and as he followed Leon into the pristine penthouse, he gazed at the extravagant apartment and whistled.

'Nice, isn't it?'

The sultry sound of Dana Kovalenko's voice drew both men's attention as she stepped into the room. Dressed in a slick, black blazer and well fitted trousers, she looked as stylish as ever. Her blonde hair was pulled back into a tight ponytail and her cruel lips were painted blood red. Defoe nodded in approval, drawing a glare from the hulking Uri who followed her into the room.

'Lose the mask.' Uri demanded, pointing a finger at Defoe.

'I'd rather not, buddy.'

'It wasn't a request.'

'And that wasn't a negotiation.' Defoe snapped back. 'You know, you remind me of someone. Someone I'd very much like to put in the ground, so how about you back the fuck off?'

'Excuse me?'

Uri stomped forward, his meaty chest pumped, and his fists clenched. Defoe licked his scarred lips in anticipation, readying himself for the opportunity to unload some of his anger until Dana's voice sliced through the tension.

'Enough,' she spat. 'You men and your constant need to dick measure. It's pathetic.'

Uri stepped back, a few feet behind her.

'Sorry, Dana.'

'Good dog.' Defoe goaded.

'Please take off the mask.' Dana said politely.

'I think it's best for everyone if I don't.'

'I don't do business with people I cannot see.' Dana crossed her arms. 'Take it off, or Leon here will put a bullet through it.'

Defoe turned to Leon, who shrugged and then he

sighed. Slowly, he pulled the wool balaclava off his head, keeping his head low. He could already feel the pain of his stitches as they ran messily across his face like the Underground train map. His immaculate hair line had been butchered, with the stitches wrapping up over his forehead and onto the dome of his skull.

He was hideous.

To the gasp of Dana, he lifted his head and glared at her.

'Fuckin' hell.' Leon uttered involuntary. Defoe turned to him.

'I know. Put's your arm into perspective, doesn't it?'

Dana stepped forward, approaching Defoe who turned away from her. Throughout his life, he had welcomed the approach of beautiful woman with a charming smile and smart quip.

But that had been eroded away, like the skin from his skull. To the chagrin of Uri, she reached up and gently placed her hand on his torn up cheek.

'Who did this to you? Sam Pope?'

'He wishes.' Defoe joked, then winced at the smirk. 'My partner.'

'Nash?' Uri interjected.

'Don't say his fucking name.' Defoe felt his blood boil at the mention of it.

'He turned on you.' Dana observed. 'Betrayal is a horrible curse that can cut deep. Very deep.'

'He isn't my concern right now.' Defoe let his sports bag slope from his shoulder and hit the ground. 'Let's not fuck about here, why did you call us in?'

'Because you kept dying,' Uri said, rolling his eyes.

'I'm still alive, you fuck. Look at my fucking face. Do you think they can kill me?'

Dana ignored the needless display of machismo between the two men.

'I have given Sam Pope this location. I have threatened the people he cares about. He will come.'

Defoe leant down, opened his sports bag and pulled out an impressive AR-15 assault rifle. Leon's eyes lit up, and Defoe made a show of it to Uri, before resting it against his shoulder like a marching soldier. He turned to Dana and through his slashed face, his expression told her that she was dealing with a man with a lot of anger within.

His words tried to convey an element of control.

'And I'll be ready for him.'

———

Sam looked around the train station. The concourse was full of civilians, different people all going about their lives without realising what was happening. A couple of middle aged men in suits were staring up at the departure screen with mild irritation. A group of young lads were loitering near another kiosk. Families were happily making their way through the station.

Innocent people.

Children.

There were too many people around for any move he made to be inconspicuous, and so he fought the temptation to incapacitate the young detective, who was just doing his job. But the situation wasn't the only reason for Sam's anxiety. He was furious at himself for finding himself in the situation to begin with.

The last few days had put him on high alert, as he had been ambushed on a few occasions by highly skilled mercenaries, all looking to cash their cheque and end his life. For some reason, Dana's invite had lowered his guard. It seemed like a last throw of the dice from her, which had made him feel safe in his surroundings. But eventually, when you leave a trail of destruction like he had over the past forty eight hours, someone was always going to follow the breadcrumbs, and he scolded himself for allowing this situation to manifest.

DC Saddler watched carefully, clearly seeing the cogs turning Sam's mind, and tightened his grip.

'Let's not make a scene, okay.'

'You need to let me go.' Sam's words were cold. Saddler stuffed his badge into the back pocket of his trousers, and then fished his phone out from his blazer jacket.

'One call and I'll have this place surrounded with armed response in minutes.' Saddler did his best to keep the nerves from his voice. 'Now I'm going to let go of your arm, and I want you to do nothing.'

Saddler made a show of his thumb hovering over the call button on his phone and then let go of Sam's elbow. Obediently, Sam stood still.

Saddler let out a deep breath, a clear sign of his relief, but he held the phone tightly, ready to make the call at any moment. Realising the tension was rising, Saddler offered Sam a respectful nod.

'You're a hard man to find.'

'Obviously not hard enough.' Sam shrugged. 'Seems to be the case recently.'

'So, "Jonathan",' Saddler accompanied the name with a finger quotation. 'What the hell is going on?'

'Well, I was about to get on a train and leave this city for good…'

'Very funny. Do you know how much chaos you have caused over the last few days?'

Sam pointed at his face.

'I'm pretty aware of it.' He sighed. 'Look, you seem like a good man and a decent detective. Bringing me in will probably get you a few back slaps and maybe your name thrown in for some promotions. But if you don't let me go, things will just get worse.'

'We can protect you…'

'Not from this.' Sam shook his head. 'You want to know what's going on? Fine. Here's the deal. Three years ago, I tore London to pieces to find a teenage girl who had been taken by a sex trafficking ring, who was on the verge of sending her and three other girls into the abyss. I put the family responsible for it in the ground, and I'd do it again in a heartbeat. Girls that the police could never have saved.'

'Well, there are rules and regulations that…'

'That don't apply in my world. I know I'm a criminal. I know that what I do is against the law, but what I do and what I am is necessary. The family I killed, they were funded by people who had links to our government. The same government who pressured the Met to bring me in. There might be a clear line between right and wrong in your book, Saddler. But from my stand point, the whole justice system is a shade of grey.'

'I can't speak to what happened before. But I know, right now, there are people who want you locked up and it's my job…'

'There are people who want me dead.' Sam cut him off, drawing a shocked look from the detective. 'Don't be surprised. I'm hardly in the business of making friends. But the family want revenge, and they have stuck a big fat bounty on my head. That's what's been going on. There are some very dangerous people, capable of inexplicable things, who have come after me, knowing they will get paid millions if they put me down.'

'Jesus.'

'So I have been fighting, detective. Fighting for my life, and if that's caused you and your boys back at the station a few extra hours of paperwork, then I apologise. But this won't stop until I end it. If you lock me in your station, they will just send people who will burn it to the ground. Right now, I have put a few of their guys down, but there will be more. There is always someone who wants to get paid, and until I cut off the money at the source, things will just get worse. More people will die. Innocent people will die.'

Saddler took a step back and blew out his cheeks. He had consumed every report that had been sent to Anderson from the Sam Pope Task Force, and half of it, he couldn't believe. The man before him had gone to war with some of the most dangerous criminals in the country, as well as government officials, and there wasn't a hint of regret in his voice.

No fear in his posture.

Saddler found the conviction of the man, despite the number of offences he had made and the people he had killed, to be admirable. There was a report, one written by DI Amara Singh, who had been in charge of the original task force, where she surmised that while Sam Pope was indeed a criminal, he wasn't a bad man.

Saddler could see the truth in those words.

Eventually, after registering everything that Sam had said, Saddler sighed and looked at him, more in hope than anything else.

'There has to be another way.'

'There is.' Sam said sadly. 'But it puts a lot of lives in danger. So let me get my coffee, walk through those gates and head back to London. You'll never see or hear from me again, and I promise you, these last two days will be the only trace of it. This isn't your fight. It's mine. So let me go and fight it.'

Saddler ran a hand across his cleanly shaven chin, clearly battling the situation before him. He took a lot of pride in being a good detective, and everything he did, was by the letter of the law.

But he was also a good man.

There was right and wrong, and then there was the thin layer between. The place where Sam Pope existed.

The place where, and Saddler hated to admit it, Sam Pope was needed.

Sam glanced up at the departure board, and then back to Saddler and waited patiently for the answer. After a few more moments of contemplation, Saddler stepped to the side.

'I'll file the report, saying the Jonathan Cooper lead was a dead end. Should give you a bit of peace and quiet on that front.'

Sam, slightly startled, extended his hand.

'Thank you, detective. You're a good man.'

Saddler nodded unconvincingly, and then took it and shook firmly. Sam stepped passed him and ordered his coffee. As he waited, he watched as Saddler stood, hands on his hips, obviously battling with the decision he had just made. It would hang heavy on the man for a while, but Sam knew, deep down, the detective was one of the good ones.

The barista handed the coffee to Sam, who turned and headed towards the barrier. As he fished out his phone to scan the ticket, Saddler stepped forward.

'Good luck.'

'Cheers.' Sam tilted his coffee cup in Saddlers direction. He had five minutes until the train arrived, and he was anxious to get out of the city.

'What are you going to do?' Saddler asked, and Sam pulled the ticket up on his screen, held it to the sensor and the gates popped open. He turned back to Saddler, with his eyes focused and his head held high.

'What I do best.'

Sam stepped through the barrier and headed down the platform, leaving the detective and the city of Derby behind him.

He was heading back to London.

To Dana Kovalenko.

To finish things once and for all.

CHAPTER TWENTY-FOUR

As the autumnal evenings drew darker quicker and descended into a frosty chill, Adrian Pearce noticed that fewer people were attending the youth centre. It wasn't a surprise, it happened every year, but he wondered if he was experiencing a strange form of 'empty nest syndrome' when the halls of the Bethnal Green Youth Centre were eerily quiet. The place had become a haven for the community over the past few years, an idea born from the generous mind of Theo Walker. As a black man, Pearce had always wanted to set an example to the younger generation, and his near thirty year career within the Metropolitan Police certainly helped.

But Theo Walker was something else.

As a role model, the man was ideal, with his dedication to helping people seeing him enjoy a well-respected career within the military as a medic, before he left to champion progression within the black community. As a man of considerable means and experience, along with effortless charm and a million-dollar smile, Theo was able to get the community centre off the ground, having it renovated and taking it on as a full time passion project.

Theo reached out to the streets of London, and he persuaded swathes of youths to spend their time with him, bettering themselves and sculpting the young minds to search for more.

To break down the obstacles that would be put before them in their lives and seek to achieve beyond expectation.

The message had certainly gotten through, and Pearce had only known Theo briefly before his untimely death, but he understood why the man meant so much to him.

It was why his name was displayed proudly on a plaque above the entrance to the building, and the constant flow of kids that attended all of the sessions that Pearce worked tirelessly to book or run himself, was a testament to Theo's legacy.

He had made a difference.

Pearce was just keeping it going.

It had been nearly two and a half years since he had retired from the Met, his reputation as a Detective Inspector within the Directorate of Professional Standards had made him as feared as he was hated. Nobody wanted someone snooping around their work, and Pearce always tried to use his smarts and his smile to break those barriers down.

But ultimately, his compulsion to do the right thing meant he didn't care about or need the approval of the other officers, and the staggering number of colleagues he had proven to have broken the rules was all the vindication that he needed.

He was a vital component of the Met for many years, and his diligence and refusal to give up was why he was so great for the kids who now attended the centre.

Pearce would never give up on them.

He couldn't.

Sat at his desk in the office at the back of the centre, Pearce drew his attention away from his computer screen and to his phone. He had three messages from Sally, a woman he had met through a dating app that the older teens had forced him to join. Usually a confident man, Pearce found his stomach flipping at her name appearing on his screen and he realised it had been a long time since he had been happy in the company of another woman.

It had been years since his divorce from Denise, who stated he had been unfaithful with her, as he was already married to his job.

Now, retired and working a calmer but equally fulfilling job, the gaping hole that Denise had left in his life had become more prominent and every evening he had spent with Sally had made him wish he could see her again sooner.

His thumbs began to tap out his response, when he heard the door to the youth centre open, and then slam shut.

'Hello?'

Pearce called out, stepping from his desk and marching briskly down the corridor to the main hall. As he stepped into the dimly hit wall, he stopped dead.

'Jesus.' Pearce smiled. 'You look like crap.'

A smile grew across Sam's face and he sheepishly lifted his hand as a greeting.

'I've felt better.'

'I see you're still keeping out of trouble.' Pearce chuckled and took a few more steps forward, before throwing his arms around Sam and hugging him tightly. 'It's good to see you, Sam.'

Sam held on. It was only for a few extra seconds but having been hunted by violently killers for the past few days, it felt nice to be in the company of someone who didn't want him dead. He then stood back, rested his hand on Pearce's shoulder and looked at him in sorrow.

'I'm sorry for what happened before.'

'Ah, forget it.' Pearce shrugged. 'You and I both know you did the right thing.'

Sam smiled uneasily. A few months earlier, in that very hall, Sam had engaged in a knife fight with a violent man who had threatened one of the kids. It ended how most of them did, with Sam adding another kill to his conscience. The man was involved in the brutal beating of a friend of Sam and Pearce, and when he had come looking for more trouble, had threatened one of the kids at the centre.

Sam had stepped in and shut him down.

Eventually, Sam confronted the elephant in the room.

'How's Sean?'

Pearce sighed.

'He's on the mend, but it's slow. They did a real number on him.' He shook his head. 'Lynsey is still with him, which is nice and between us, one of us visits him every day. They think he'll make a pretty decent recovery, but there's likely to be some lasting damage.'

'I'm sorry.'

Pearce shrugged.

'We're both realists, Sam. We've seen the worst of this world many times over, which is why we cling to the little nuggets of good that shine through. You had peace, here, with me for a while, but this world is a messed up place. It pulled you back into the muck.'

'I walked back into it…'

'But for the right reasons.' Pearce interjected. 'I've sat across a beer too many times with you to know where this is going. So before you fall into some depressing mono-logue about how life has kicked the shit out of you, why don't you tell me who *actually* kicked the shit out of you and then what it is you're doing here? Because I'm doubting it's to see how an old fart like me's doing.'

Sam couldn't help but smile. Through his entire journey from the quiet man in the archive office to the most wanted vigilante in the country's history, Sam had made few friends along the way. But in Adrian Pearce, he found not only a fellow man who was bound to the idea of right and wrong as tightly as he was, but a genuine friend.

A man who understood pain and loss, and a man who looked beyond what Sam was doing to see the reason why.

There were only a few people in the world that Sam trusted explicitly, and Pearce was one of them.

'Stick the kettle on, then.' Sam joked, and Pearce obliged. When he returned a few minutes later with a hot cup of tea for them both and a half eaten packet of biscuits, the two men found a plastic seat each in the hall and Sam began. He recounted his venture to Suffolk and how following an illegal firearm had led him into a brutal and violent war with Slaven Kovac, and how an under-cover police officer had saved his life. Pearce approved, any praise that Sam gave the police was as rare as it was genuine.

But then Sam walked Pearce through the last few days, and how he had been ambushed a few times by highly skilled and deadly hit men. Pearce sat in astonish-ment as Sam walked him through the brawl with Cook inside the café, and then the subsequent confirmation that a five-million-pound bounty had been put on his head.

'Christ. I should take you in myself.' Pearce had joked.

But as Sam continued, the gravity of the situation grew on Pearce, and while Sam hardly swam in the safest circles, the man's life was very much hanging in the balance. As Sam wrapped up his story, he looked at Pearce, who was trying his best to wrap his head round it all.

Sam had omitted one key detail.

One that would have a personal connection to Pearce, and the one that would make him understand why there was no other option.

'The person who put the hit out on me is Dana Kovalenko.'

The name rocked Pearce in his seat like an uppercut to the jaw, and he fell back in his seat. It had been three years since he had heard that name, and instantly, he fully understood the gravity of the situation. He had helped Sam to track down Jasmine Hill, which had put Sam on the war path with the Kovalenko family.

They were the most dangerous family he had ever come across in his career, and the terror that walked along-side that name was well earnt.

Sam had killed Andrei and Oleg Kovalenko at the Port of Tilbury, and then ventured to Kyiv to finish the rest of the job. Dana Kovalenko had evaded police capture, and with no evidence to link her to her brothers' crimes, they stopped chasing her. But now, with the value she had placed on her vengeance, Pearce realised that there was no chance of a peaceful resolution.

Dana Kovalenko would hunt Sam until either one or both were dead.

After a few moments, Pearce lifted his mug to his lips and polished off his tea, his eyes wide and staring ahead. Deep in thought, he finally turned back to Sam who offered him nothing more than a shrug.

'You asked.'

Pearce nodded and raised his eyebrows, still processing the severity of the situation that was potentially about to arrive at his door.

'It can't be here.' He finally said, the authority returning to his voice. 'I can't have the police back here or any more dead bodies…'

'Adrian, I have no intention of bringing anything to your door.' Sam looked around the hall. 'You know, this place is one of the very few places I can remember being happy. In a long time. The work you are doing, and the work Theo did before, it's bigger than whatever it is I do. I'm out there trying to fix things that are already broken. In here, you're making sure they don't break in the first place.'

'Thank you.' The words hit Pearce hard. 'So what do you need?'

'A gun.'

Pearce almost dropped his mug.

'Give me a break, Sam. I'm not an arms dealer, for Christ's sake.' Pearce stood, his hands on his hips. 'Besides, you took the one I confiscated off the last guy you killed.'

'I know. I wouldn't ask you if I didn't have any other option. I could go and knock on some doors of some hot spots, beat the crap out of some gang members and see what they have in their pockets, but that's going to take time. And I don't have time.'

'I don't even know where I would begin…'

'There must be someone. This side of the line or the other. Someone you know who can get you a gun.'

Pearce scowled at Sam. He knew the man was desperate, and everything he did was for the greater good, but Sam had put him in a terrible position. It wasn't that it was impossible, it was that it was immoral. Pearce preached to the kids who relied on him to turn away from crime, and here he was, about to track down a firearm so a vigilante could kill a violent criminal.

It was hypocrisy at it's finest, and it made his skin crawl.

He lived and died by his principals, and the idea of betraying them made him tremble with anger.

'I'll see what I can do.' He eventually said through gritted teeth. 'When and where?'

'I'll be at the bench.' Sam said, a tinge of sadness. 'I'll give it until ten and then I'll be heading to Kovalenko, with or without the weapon.'

Sam stood, slightly towering over Pearce who still, even in his early fifties, was in great shape. Anxiously, Sam extended his hand to his furious friend.

'Thank you, Adrian. For everything.'

'I'm only doing this because you saved my life.' Pearce said, angrily snatching the hand and giving it one firm shake. 'But this is the last time, Sam. I can't have you coming back here again.'

'I understand.' Sam said regrettably, before reaching up and patting Pearce on the shoulder and stepping past him. 'For what it's worth, I'm sorry.'

As Sam trudged towards the door, knowing his request had damaged their friendship, Pearce sighed. He turned to Sam, and called after him.

'Just stay alive, okay Sam?' Pearce watched as Sam turned, smiled and nodded, before walking through the hallway and out the door. A gust of wind blew through, sending a shiver down Pearce's spine. Then, under his breath as he turned to collect the mugs, he muttered to himself. 'You always do.'

CHAPTER TWENTY-FIVE

SIX YEARS EARLIER…

'*Dad!*'

Jamie's voice echoed from his room into the dark hallway, and Sam, yawning, stumbled towards it. The relentless rainfall had evolved into a full blown storm, and as the water clattered against the windows of their family home, a flash of lightning lit up the sky.

Then the powerful roar of thunder.

Beyond the door, Sam heard Jamie scream once more, and he nudged the door open and peered in. Jamie's bed was empty, with both the child and the blanket missing. All that remained was his Buzz Lightyear plush toy, and the pillow. Sam sighed at what he saw on the floor.

Using the chest of drawers, Jamie had fashioned a precarious looking tent out of his duvet and another sheet, and through the gaps, the brightness of a torch shone through.

'*You okay, buddy?*' *Sam asked, arms folded and rested against the door.*

'*I don't like it.*' *The innocent voice was muffled by the blankets.*

'*What's going on?*' *Lucy entered the conversation, stifling a yawn* as she wrapped her dressing gown around her body. Sam nodded towards the sheet and Lucy pressed her hand to her heart.

'I'll handle it.' Sam said, leaning in and kissing his wife on the head. 'You go back to bed.'

Lucy yawned once more, nodded, and then gently stroked his shoulder before heading back to their bedroom. Another flash of lightning illuminated the room, and was quickly followed by another clap of thunder.

'When will it stop?'

Sam lowered himself down next to the make-shift tent, and rested his back against the wall.

'Don't you know? It's already moving on.'

'How do you know that?'

'Because I'm your dad and dad knows everything.'

'Ha ha.' Jamie mocked. For a five year old, Sam appreciated the sarcasm.

'After the lightening, you start counting. Then, when the thunder comes, that number tells you how many miles away the storm is.' Sam patted his knee. 'That's just science.'

'I didn't know that?' Jamie offered.

'I counted the last one, and it's already eight miles away from here which is super far.'

Jamie ruffled underneath the quilts. Sam wanted nothing more than to pull them back, scoop his son up into his arms and reassure him, but he knew it was a teachable moment and Jamie needed to get there on his own. Sam's father, William Pope, was a strong man, well respected within the military and was as stern as he was caring. He never neglected Sam, nor did he wrap him up in cotton wool.

'But I can't see the lightning so how will I know?'

'Well, you'll just have to come out and count with me won't you?' Sam suggested. He leant in and then peeled back part of the blanket until he saw his son. 'It's all good, I'm here with you.'

Tentatively, Jamie pushed away the rest of the blankets and began to scramble towards his dad. Just then, another flash of lightning struck and the boy panicked.

'Just start counting.' Sam said softly.

Jamie did, and once he got to eleven, a slightly quieter rumble of thunder echoed somewhere in the night sky.

'Eleven! It's moving away.'

The sheer joy on the boy's face filled Sam with a proud warmth and he wrapped his arm around his son's waist and hoisted him into the air as he stood up. Jamie giggled and Sam spun him round once before dumping him back on the mattress. As Jamie readjusted his pillow, Sam picked up the duvet and draped it over him. Jamie snuggled in and Sam stroked the hair on top of his head.

'See, kiddo. There's nothing to worry about. And I'll always be here to keep you safe.'

'What about the others?' Jamie said with a yawn. He was already drifting back to sleep.

'What others?'

'Everyone else?' Jamie was dropping. 'Who keeps them safe?'

Sam couldn't fight the smile. His son was one of the most caring people he had ever met, and he was only five years old. Pretty sure that his son was asleep, Sam stroked his head once more and whispered his answer.

'Hopefully, someone is willing to keep them safe too.'

———

The cold evening was turning into an even colder night, and Sam sat forward on the bench and bowed his head. The wind whipped down the back of his jacket collar and danced down his spine, as if someone had just danced across his grave.

It wasn't his death he was focusing on.

A few yards away from the spot where his son was hit by a drunk driver, Sam tried to channel the rage that was begin to course through his body. Not far from where he was seated was the Hendon Police College, where Sam had been in training to become an officer when the tragedy struck. With Jamie gone, Sam's desire to help the world had vanished. He soon lost his wife, who couldn't watch on as Sam shut himself away from the world outside.

Eventually he contemplated ending it all, only for his now deceased mentor, Carl Marsden to intervene when he needed him the most. He pulled Sam back up, and in a moment of blind rage, Sam tracked down the drunk driver with the intent to murder him. When he found Miles Hillock, he found an unstable, guilt-ridden man who Sam beat to a pulp, but couldn't murder in cold blood.

Sam was a trained killer, but a murderer he was not.

Hillock took his own life in the end, but that wasn't justice for Sam. What he had seen was a man beat a broken system that the country still stuck rigidly to. Only when he began peeling back the layers did he realise that those who played outside the constructs of law and order were the ones who were succeeding.

Drug dealers. Arms dealers. Sex traffickers.

All of them getting rich off the country's fear to confront them, and when they were confronted, they usually paid enough to have the law turn the other way.

Sam couldn't be bought.

He had found a measure of peace in fighting back. In helping those who couldn't help themselves. It had given him a renewed sense of purpose, and for every criminal he put in the ground, he didn't find himself any closer to his son, but he found the grief and guilt being slowly pushed away.

A light drizzle had begun to sprinkle the evening, only adding to the chill of the night sky, and Sam knew what he had to do. Pearce had come through for him, and a nefarious looking man had approached the bench an hour before and silently handed Sam a gun.

A Beretta M9.

It was in relatively good condition and Sam slid the

magazine from the stock and inspected the ammunition. It was full, but it meant he only had fifteen bullets to take down whatever Dana Kovalenko had waiting for him.

Sam inspected the gun once more, watching as the drizzle coated the top of it in a smooth, damp shine and then he tucked it behind his back until it was pressed against the base of his spine. Then, with his back still screaming for mercy, he stood gingerly and tried to stretch out the pain. He took one more look at the spot where his son's lifeless body had stared back at him from and he knew it was time to let go of the grief.

It was time to stop blaming himself for not being able to protect his son.

The hole in his life would always be there and it would always hurt, but he needed to keep going.

Keep fighting. Without looking back, Sam spoke.

'Someone needs to keep everyone safe.'

And with that, Sam marched away from the single most painful place on the face of the earth, making his way steadily to the train station to travel back into the centre of London, where Dana Kovalenko had beckoned him.

———

By the time he arrived on the street in Mayfair, it was nearly midnight. He had taken it slow, trying to give himself as much time as possible to formulate some kind of plan, but Sam still felt woefully under-prepared. He'd run headfirst into danger many times before, even as a soldier.

But back then, he always had his brothers to watch his back.

This time, he was walking up to the front door of a building he hadn't scouted and effectively knocking on it. There was no chance that Dana wasn't prepared, and he made the logical guess that there would be armed men waiting for him. How many? He couldn't even hazard a guess, but he knew that his element of surprise was minimal.

Dana Kovalenko knew he was coming.

It was just a matter of when.

The Marlow Heights building was a triumph of modern architecture, and even in the extremely wealthy area of Mayfair, it stood out in its extravagance. It didn't surprise Sam at all that the Kovalenkos had the millions at their disposal to live in luxury and put millions on his head. For years, they had successfully transported young teenage girls into Europe to be sold to a life of destitution and sexual abuse, for which many people were willing to pay a pretty penny. He wished he could hunt every single one of them down, bring them home and put their 'owners' in the ground, but he was just one man.

An operation like that would require too many people and too much co-operation between countries who no longer trusted each other.

He would do what was within his power to, and that was to eradicate the last vestige of the Kovalenko name from the world.

The front of the building was well lit, with the glass entranceway offering a view of the plush foyer, with its marble floors and expensive plants. Sam kept to the shadows and stayed low as he got as close as he could, and it didn't take him long to see an armed man sitting in one of the leather chairs, looking decidedly bored. The man didn't look like a usual member of Kovalenko's crew, which Sam had dismantled at the Port of Tilbury.

This man was black, with his hood up, and looked more like the group Sam had encountered when he lived in Hackney, gathering on the corners of the Blackstone Estate. Sam ducked away once again and made his way to the far end of the street, keeping himself hidden behind the extortionately priced cars that lined the streets. For such an expensive and sought after part of London, he was surprised and also thankful for how quiet it was. They were a good ten minutes from the bars and clubs that were frequented by the other half, all of them with demanding dress codes and expensive memberships.

The surrounding streets were quiet, and that played into Sam's favour.

He didn't expect to be quiet, but he wasn't planning on staying long. Whatever Dana Kovalenko had waiting for him, he now knew it involved men that weren't as loyal as the ones before.

Would they be willing to die for her?

He was about to find out.

At the top of the road, Sam looked over a few of the cars and then finally landed on a new model Range Rover. It was an impressive vehicle, with plush leather seats and a nice oak trim.

Whoever owned it must have been worth a pretty penny, and Sam deduced the owner was likely insured. Sam drew his elbow up, and with a firm swing, he drilled it into the corner of the window, shattering the glass. Swiftly, just as the alarm kicked into gear, Sam yanked open the door through the window, reached through and shut it down before it could grow any louder.

He waited.

Nobody emerged from the Marlow Heights building further down the street, and there was no curtain twitching in the surrounding buildings. He lifted the handbrake from the car, and then stepped outside of it, the driver door open. With the pain in his back throbbing, he thrust his entire body weight into the frame of the car, using his considerable bulk to slowly budge it forward. With the handbrake off, the Range Rover slowly began to roll forward, and Sam pulled the steering wheel to guide it out into the centre of the road before it collided with the car in front.

With the street empty, Sam straightened the vehicle out on the road and continued pushing, thankful for the slight decline on the road that helped the car pick up some momentum. Marlow Heights was on the left hand side of the street, which meant, as they approached, he was hidden on the right hand side of the vehicle. Eventually, as the car rolled in line with the front door of Dana's residence, Sam reached in and yanked the handbrake up, and then spun out from the driver's side of the car and dropped down. Keeping low, he scrambled around the open car door, and then pressed himself up against the front wheel arch.

It only took a matter of seconds for the sound of the glass door to Marlow Heights to open, and the unmistakable sound of footsteps.

'What the fuck is this?' A voice echoed, and then clearly turned. 'Yo, Chris, come and check this shit out.'

Sam kept his back to the car and shut his eyes. His instincts as a sniper were helping him to track the sounds, giving him a rough mental layout of the street, the building and where the voice was emanating from. The ability to aim and fire was never questioned, and it was something a lot of soldiers possessed. But Sam was able to map the trajectory of a shot with minimal information, and in such close proximity, he had already built a pretty clear map in his mind of where the man was standing.

The door opened again and another man stepped out.

'Whose car is that?'

'Dunno. It just rolled down the street. Think it's…'

Sam spun up from the ground, pivoting on his heel until he was facing the building. The two men startled, and then rapidly tried to reach for their weapons. But as he spun, Sam drew his M9 up expertly to his eyeline, and with one simple squeeze of the trigger, he sent a bullet zipping through the air and through the forehead of the first man. As the dead body dropped to the ground, Sam swung his arms to the left, just as the man known as Chris was finally gripping his weapon.

Sam squeezed the trigger once more.

The man's head snapped back, spraying a visceral red mist against the glass behind him as he dropped to the ground.

The gunshots were loud.

Meaning those inside the building were aware of his arrival, and those in the surrounding ones were likely calling the police. Sam rushed around the bonnet of the Range Rover and quickly scooped up the Glock 17 that the first man had failed to fire at him. He quickly slid out the magazine, noted it was full, and then slammed it back again.

Two guns were better than one.

As the drizzle began to morph into a downpour, Sam opened the door to Marlow Heights, ready to go to war.

CHAPTER TWENTY-SIX

Defoe stood in the bathroom of the penthouse, his head bowed, and his hands clutching either side of the curved sink. The entire room was decadent, with a standing, roll-top bath the key feature and the walls were decorated with expensive, herringbone tiling.

But none of it registered.

Above the sink was a circular mirror, affixed to the wall, with a wooden shelf running along the bottom of it.

Defoe couldn't lift his head.

He didn't want to see what was staring back at him.

Dana had been welcoming to him, but he felt her show of empathy was nothing more than pity. She wanted Sam Pope and she was willing to play whatever role she needed to in order to get Defoe onside, and he was aware of that. The woman was powerful, and she clearly knew how to bend people to her will.

But her lingering on his facial scars had become another trigger to him, and he could feel the anger boiling through his body. Uri, her right-hand man, had made it clear he was disgusted by the sight of him and had already made the mistake of saying Nash's name.

Just the mention of it caused Defoe to grind his immaculate teeth together and Uri had clearly taken objection to Dana leaning on other men for help. The way he followed her like a lost puppy was clear evidence that he loved her, yet she obviously didn't feel the same way.

When all of this was over, Defoe was very likely going to put the little puppy down.

With deep, concentrated breaths, Defoe slowly lifted his head.

As his eyes rose to the mirror, he grimaced at the jagged scar that obliterated his hair line, and the further he raised his head, the quicker his breathing became. He hadn't fully inspected the sheer destruction of his face this close, and what he saw repulsed him to his very core. The stitches that were holding his face together were thin, black strips, but they were sashaying across his face in different directions. One set was holding his eyebrow in place, as it trailed down under his eye and he was surprised he hadn't been blinded. Others were pulling his face back together, looping across his nose and several stitches were keeping his lips in place.

He had been mutilated.

Jacob Nash hadn't tried to kill him. That much was clear. If he had wanted to, Nash could have snapped Defoe's neck under his boot had he wanted to. But Defoe knew Nash, and despite being a ruthless killer, the man was also irritatingly noble. To him, Defoe's betrayal wasn't worthy of death.

Not yet at least.

As he thought about the pleasure Nash must have taken from disfiguring him in such a brutal manner, Defoe felt his knuckles whiten as he tightened his grip before letting out a ferocious roar of anger. It echoed through the bathroom and no doubt, alerted the others in the penthouse.

He didn't care.

He took a final look at the monstrous face in the mirror and then stomped to the door. He threw it open and marched back into the main room, where all eyes fell on him,

'Yo, you okay, bruv?' Leon asked, but Defoe ignored him and reached for one of the assault rifles. As he checked the chamber, his eyes were wide with frenzy, and Uri stepped forward.

'Do not fuck this up.'

Uri's threat sent Defoe's vision red, and the American dropped the rifle and struck the hulking Ukrainian with a vicious right hook. Uri's solid jaw absorbed the blow and he stumbled back once pace, before a smile spread across his face. As Defoe beckoned him forward, Uri's hand slipped to the inside of his blazer, but before he could retrieve his weapon, Dana clasped his hand.

'No,' she commanded. 'Stay focused.'

'Let him go.' Defoe goaded, his body shaking with adrenaline.

'No. Uri. Take a walk.'

'Excuse me?' Uri turned to her with surprise.

'Do not question me.' Dana snapped. 'I need you alive and I need him on Sam Pope. So do as I say, and take a walk.'

Uri's mouth curled into a furious snarl, and he shot a menacing look at Defoe before he turned and stomped to the door. He threw it open and stepped through without even looking back. Dana watched him go, knowing the man's pride had been hurt, but she knew of a few ways she could bring him back round again.

Men were so weak.

So easy to control.

Before another word was muttered, a gunshot echoed outside the building, followed swiftly by another. Leon rushed to the window and peered down to the street below.

There was an abandoned car in the centre of the road, and what he could just make out as the prone feet of one of his men. The building cut off the view, but he quickly surmised that the man was dead.

'He's here.' Leon said coldly.

'Right…' Defoe went to pick up his rifle, but Leon reached his hand out and stopped him.

'Let me welcome him.' Leon pointed to his missing arm. 'He's got a receipt coming.'

Defoe understood. What he wouldn't give for the same opportunity with Jacob Nash? Willingly, Defoe lowered the rifle and stepped to the side. As Leon marched to the door, flanked by a couple of his goons, Dana called out after him.

'I want him alive, remember?'

'He'll be alive.' Leon flashed a cruel, grin. 'Barely.'

———

As Sam stepped into the foyer of the Marlow Heights building, he was instantly drawn back to his first assault on organised crime. Hunting down Frank Jackson, Sam had swarmed the High Rise like a one man army, clearing it out floor by floor until he unloaded a full clip into Jackson's body. But that was over three years ago.

Then, he had grenades and an assault rifle. Now, he had two hand guns and no idea what was waiting for him within the building itself. He also hadn't been through such a crippling amount of punishment, and as he stepped carefully past the reception desk, his spine began to stiffen again.

His ribs ached.

His face throbbed.

He was as close to running on empty as he could be, and he knew he only had minutes before the armed response unit made it's way outside.

He had to be quick.

The doors to the lift opened on the other side of the foyer, and immediately, gunfire crackled into the room and Sam, instinctively, dived over the thick, oak reception desk and clattered onto the marble on the other side. Just before he had leapt, he had counted four men, all of them armed, and one of them was wielding what appeared to be an assault rifle. The bullets thudded into the thick wood separating him from death, and Sam drew a breath, calmed his senses and lifted the guns up. He counted down from three.

Two.

One.

Sam spun up from behind the desk, both arms stretched out, both triggers squeezed, and he unloaded a couple of rounds from each gun, sending two of his attackers spiralling to the ground. The other men scattered for cover, and Sam kept firing, scaring them into hiding before he spun back down to the ground and behind the sanctuary of the desk. The two remaining men unloaded another deluge of bullets in Sam's direction, each one sending wood chippings into the air. There was only so much the desk would be able to take, and Sam knew it wouldn't be long until he was completely exposed. As their shots died down, clearly to reload, Sam once again spun out, unloaded the remainder of both clips in their direction.

Then the guns clicked pathetically and he dropped down behind the desk again and tossed them onto the floor.

'I'm out.' Sam yelled.

'That's fucking disappointing.' Leon chuckled.

'She wants me alive, right?'

'Yup. She wants to fuck you up in ways you can't imagine.'

Sam rolled his eyes. Whoever this guy was, he spoke a tough game.

'I guess there's no chance you can let me go?'

'Stand the fuck up, or I'm gonna walk over there and put a bullet between your ribs.'

Sam lifted his hands first, proving he was unarmed, and then cautiously rose to his feet. He turned, immediately seeing the assault rifle trained on him by one man, before a man he recognised beckoned him out with his gun.

His other arm was missing.

'Hello, Leon.' Sam said casually as he approached them, still very aware of the damage an assault rifle did at point blank range.

Leon cracked Sam in the side of the head, the metal of the pistol splitting his eyebrow open and rocking him down onto one knee. Leon followed it up with a vicious knee to the face, and then drove his boot into the fallen Sam Pope as many times as he could. Eventually, he stopped and stepped back, admiring his handiwork as Sam rolled in agony, coughing and wheezing.

'That felt good.' Leon threw one more kick in for good measure. 'Now get to your fucking feet, bitch.'

Tentatively, Sam obliged, wobbling as he stood before the other guy prodded him with the gun, guiding him to the elevator. Leon followed, and a few moments later, Sam was standing, blood dribbling down his face and his head spinning. Behind him, Leon chuckled to himself, proud of the beating he had just given him, and his lackey stood silently, the gun trained on the back of Sam's skull. One false move, and Sam's brain and blood would be painting the doors.

The lift continued its ascent, passing the second and

third floor, and Leon was shaking with excitement as they approached the penthouse.

Sam was heading in with no weapons, guns trained on him and his body ready to collapse. What awaited him was probably a fate worse than death, and the best thing about all of it was, they were taking him exactly where he needed to be.

The lift stopped. The bell dinged.

Then the doors opened.

———

Uri had heard the gunfire bellowing through the building, but hadn't gone running.

Dana had made it clear that she had put her faith in men she barely knew, and the last thing Uri wanted to do was bail them out. He had questioned Dana's intention from the beginning, offering his own services in the bid to take Sam Pope out of the equation, but she had refused. Foolishly, he thought it was her affection for him that had made that decision, but moments ago, he had seen the truth.

She didn't believe in him.

She didn't think he was up to the job.

As he stomped through the hallway to the maintenance corridor of the building, he threw a mighty fist at the wall in frustration, cracking a knuckle or two, but ignoring the pain.

He had proven to her on several occasions that he was a real man, satisfying her between the sheets regularly. Her moans had been all the evidence he needed to know that, but her coldness to him afterwards had never registered as deliberate. He assumed she was still grieving for the slaying of her family and thus wanted the physical interaction but not the intimacy.

It had hurt him not to be able to provide it, but he had fallen so deeply in love with her that he would wait for it.

He would do anything for Dana Kovalenko.

Anything.

It was why he had obeyed her order to take a walk, and ignored the gunfight that was already tearing the building apart. She didn't want his involvement, so he wouldn't get involved. Hopefully, when the misplaced trust she had placed in the two cripples had been blown away by Sam Pope, she would call for him.

Beg for him to save her.

And he would duly oblige.

Until then, he walked down the dimly lit corridor, passing multiple storage rooms and a few massive water tanks. The thick, metal pipes that comprised the skeleton of the building were not hidden in this corridor, and he had to duck down to ensure he didn't bump his head on them. Eventually, he came to the CCTV operation room, and he booted the door open with a stiff kick and stepped in, hands on hips.

He wanted to get a view of what was happening without him, and on the main screen, he saw Leon brutally attack Sam Pope on the ground, laying in kick after kick until he ran out of energy. Sam was a broken mess on the floor, and Uri's heart sank.

They had him.

He'd called Dana's bluff and it had backfired.

What use would she have for him if the other men had done what she thought he couldn't?

With a furious grunt, he slammed his already broken fist onto the desk, clattering the keyboard and bringing up a different camera onto the screen. He went to leave, but then his attention was drawn to the screen.

It was the camera focusing on the metal door at the top of the fire exit at the end of the maintenance corridor.

The door was open.

Without thinking, Uri drew the Glock from the inside of his blazer, and stepped out into the corridor. A few steps ahead and he would round the corner and then be less than twenty feet from the open door.

With murderous intent channelling his every move, Uri headed down the corridor, his gun drawn and his patience completely gone.

CHAPTER TWENTY-SEVEN

EARLIER THAT EVENING…

It hadn't taken too long for Nash to make his way to London, and knowing that the Foundation was likely monitoring the CCTV at King's Cross St Pancras should he take the train, he had instead simply stolen a car. It wasn't hard to find one with insufficient security requirements, and after a quick twist of a few wires, he was headed to London. Luckily for him, the M1 wasn't far from Derby City Centre, and after a few miles down the strangely named Brian Clough Way, he had turned onto the M1 and from there, it was a near two hour long journey on the same road.

Before the sun had begun to set, he had dumped the car in Watford Junction train station, not far from where he had exited the motorway. Just on the outskirts of London, he was able to then take a direct train from the station directly into Euston, and from there, he took another train to Camden Town. The aim was to keep moving, and head to places that had never been on the Foundation's radar when accepting this mission. The Foundation had almost limitless resources, but they would still essentially be looking for a needle amongst a myriad of haystacks.

Before he stepped off and experienced the famous roads of Camden, impressed by the amount of diversity he saw among the passers-by, he adjusted the heavy sports bag on his shoulder. With his other shoulder out of action due to the bullet Defoe had sent through it, his one working one was beginning to sag under the pressure. Large stools were erected across the sides of the road leading down to the docks, which itself was decorated in some stunning graffiti. His large frame drew a few eyes, and as he shuffled through the crowds of people, some of the merchants tried to sell him their goods, which he politely declined.

He found his way into a local coffee shop, purely because it offered free WiFi. Once inside, he pulled Dallow's laptop from the sports bag and opened it on the table. As he struggled to connect to the internet, the polite young lady brought his espresso to him, which he thanked her for.

She gave him a wry smile, but he ignored any interest as the connection finally took and he pulled up the previous screens that Dallow had open before his untimely death. After flicking through them and immediately dismissing them, he finally landed on the screen he wanted.

It was the software they had used to listen in on the original phone call between Sam Pope and Dana Kovalenko, with the recording of the call displayed across the screen in a wavy, colourful pattern. He had little interest in listening to it back.

But it did have the number to Brandt's phone on display.

Nash knocked back his coffee and then beckoned the eager lady over, ordering another along with a hot sandwich. As she returned back to the till to place it, Nash tried to stretch out the pain in his shoulder.

He had managed to stop the bleeding, but at some point, the bullet wound would eventually render his arm useless. Going to a hospital was out of the question, as the Foundation was likely monitoring those, too.

He pulled out his phone, to be greeted by a few more messages from Callaghan, begging him to make contact.

He would.

He'd had to.

Nash skimmed through them and the message from Dana with the address of her hideout, and then opened a fresh message. He tapped in Brandt's number, wrote out his message and then sent it.

His sandwich and drink arrived, and Nash devoured them both quickly, and then he looked at the window and watched the world walk by. As he did, he reflected on all the times he had blindly followed orders, put some poor soul at the end of his gun and willingly pulled the trigger.

When had it changed?

When did he start thinking differently?

Before he could even begin to unpack that, he received a message back from Brandt's phone.

From Sam Pope.

It was a street in a place called Colindale and to be there at ten.

Nash had no idea how far away that was, but was relieved when a quick search on his phone told him he could get a direct train from Camden Town. He had a few hours to kill, so he took himself for dinner and then he made his way there as instructed. Once there, he wandered down the non-descript street until he saw a man, unmistakably Sam, sitting on a bench. As he approached, he raised his eyebrows at the state of his face.

'What happened to you?'

'Oh, you know. Fell out of a building. Was ambushed by a crazy guy with tattoos. Standard stuff.'

'Was he Cuban by any chance?' Nash asked, sliding the bag from his shoulder and gratefully taking a seat next to Sam.

'He was.'

'Nasty piece of work. Mendoza. They gave us a file on him. Where is he now?'

'The morgue.' Sam leant back on the seat. 'So what's the deal here?'

'No deal.' Nash nodded, confirming it to himself. 'Just somethings need to be put right. I see you have a weapon?'

Sam looked down at the gun in his hand. Pearce had come

through for him, most likely at the cost of their friendship going forward, and Sam hated what Pearce probably had to do to help him.

But he had needed a gun. In the long run, it could be what saves Pearce's life if Dana's threats were anything to go by.

'I do. But this is it.' Sam turned to Nash. 'You?'

Nash relayed to Sam everything he was able to save from the room before he had to disappear. They were out-gunned and out-manned, and both of them were severely wounded. At the top of their game, they were near untouchable. But in their current state, and with a vengeful Defoe still looking to factor in somewhere, they were up against it.

Nash told Sam his plan. Sam shrugged.

'It's the best shot we got.' Nash offered.

'Well, I've been through worse.'

'I can believe that.' Nash chuckled. Sam moved as if to leave and Nash spoke up. 'Why do you do it, Sam?'

'Do what?'

'What you do. No one's paying you. You're putting yourself through hell. What's it all for?'

Sam took a few moments, while Nash watched him intently. The hulking American wouldn't know that Sam was recounting a cherished memory of his son, the two of them talking thunderstorms. But Sam knew that they were cut from the same, violent cloth. Nash didn't need to know his backstory.

He just needed a reason.

Sam inspected his gun once more then stood, stretching his back out before taking one last glance at the road before them. Then, without looking back at Nash, he answered.

'Someone needs to keep everyone safe.'

With that, Sam disappeared off into the night, leaving Nash contemplating their plan, and understanding that to Sam, this was a compulsion.

He needed to fight.

That evening, after Sam had guided the car down the middle of the road towards the Marlow Heights building, Nash had scaled the *fire exit, waiting for the right moment to break through the glass and ambush from the top down. As soon as he heard the blast of gunfire, he smashed the glass with the butt of his Glock, slid his arm in and opened the emergency door.*

The corridor was dimly lit, and it was roughly twenty feet until a turn. There was no way to know what was up ahead, but Nash held his gun up, his finger rested expertly on the trigger, and he took considered steps into the building, ready to help Sam in whatever way he could.

———

The penthouse was just as expensive-looking as Sam had expected, and it was a world away from the Airbnb's and dingy flats he had frequented over the past three years. The lift doors opened up into the main hosting room itself, and as they pulled back to reveal him like a prize at a game show, his eyes locked onto Dana Kovalenko.

Her face contorted into a foul snarl as she made eye contact, and the seething rage caused her to step towards them immediately.

'Out.'

Leon barked, and then stamped into the back of Sam's knee, causing him to buckle forward and stumble down the two marble steps and onto the floor. Dana's heels clicked loudly against the marble as she approached, and behind her, a brutally scarred man loitered, pacing slightly as if to contain the pent-up violence within. Sam had been in some dangerous situations before.

Penned down by a sniper in the middle of the Amazon.

Hidden away in a small home in Afghanistan while the Taliban circled.

Strapped to a chair by a Mexican drug lord and interrogated.

This was another to add to his ever-growing list of situations he had willingly gotten himself into.

As Sam pushed himself to his knees, he sat back on his legs and looked up at Dana.

'Nice place. Shit hospitality.'

Dana put every ounce of her petit frame behind the slam, that connected with Sam's cheek with such venom that it drew blood. Sam rocked slightly to the side, then spat a little puddle of blood onto the pristine marble. Dana stared a hole through him, daring him to speak again. Behind her, the man approached, and only then did Sam realise it was Nash's partner.

Only it wasn't. This was Nash's partner if he had been dragged face first through the bowels of hell.

As he approached, Defoe twisted his horribly maimed face into a smirk.

'Not looking good right now, is it, Sam?'

'What? Your face?' Sam could see the trigger going off. 'What happened? Cut yourself shaving?'

Like Dana moments earlier, Defoe exploded forward, cracking Sam with an hellacious right hook that sent him sprawling onto his front, and more blood to spray across the floor. Dana put her hand on Defoe's chest to keep him in check, while Leon hollered his appreciation.

'You done fucked up now, Sam.' Leon bragged.

'You're right.' Sam agreed, and then turned to the man. 'Give me a hand, won't you?'

It was now Leon's turn to see red, and as he drew his gun up, Dana slammed her foot down so it echoed loudly.

'Enough.' She pointed at Leon. 'You stand down. I've had enough of this posturing. Look at you. The mighty Sam Pope, trying his best to show you he's not scared. But you should be, Sam. You should be very scared.'

Sam groaned as he pushed himself back up, wiping away the blood that was trickling from his lip.

'Why? Is lover boy here going to show me his face again?'

Defoe pushed past Dana, pulled the gun from the back of his trousers and pressed the barrel against Sam's forehead.

'Three million dead, right?'

Dana stepped forward and pushed his hand away.

'We have him now. He can say whatever he wants, but it won't matter.' Dana pulled one of the modern, expensive-looking seats from the dining table, letting the metal legs screech across the marble until she was a foot away from Sam. Defoe stepped behind Sam, then reached down and locked his arms behind him, leaving him defenceless to the vengeful woman. She confidently sat down, and then she lifted one leg and pressed the sharp heel of foot into Sam's thigh. Sam winced, which drew a gasp of delight from Dana, who pushed it once more and then slammed her foot down.

'I promised you pain, Sam. I promised you that you would pay for what you did to my family. To my darling Andrei. I am not going to kill you. Not for a long, long time. You see, I will take you back to Kyiv, where I have some very, very skilled doctors who will be paid very well to keep you alive.'

'That's very nice of them.'

Dana thrust her heel into his thigh again, drawing a grunt of pain.

'Silence!' Dana drew her foot back, and practically licked her lips with excitement. She leant in close, so her mouth was an inch from Sam's ear. 'They will keep you alive, but they will give you nothing for the pain. First, I will take off your fingers. Then your toes. Then your hands. And so on, and so on, until there is nothing left but a body and a head. Then, when there is nothing left to cut off, I will see how much electricity I can pass through what is left of you until you finally, finally beg me for your death. Then, when I am bored, maybe I kill you. How does that sound?'

Dana drew her face level with Sam's their noses almost touching, and her smile was one of sickening success.

She had won.

Sam smiled back.

'It sounds like a pretty shit first date, to be honest.'

Dana slapped him again, and Defoe shoved him violently to the floor. As Sam tried to push himself back up, Dana turned and angrily headed back across the room to the door to the hallway, and as she did, she dismissively threw a hand up in the air.

'Have your fun, boys. Just don't kill him.'

Sam got to his knees and looked at the three men, and Leon and his running buddy put down their guns, while Defoe cracked his knuckles and his neck at the same time. Sam's body ached, and his ears were still ringing.

Then a gunshot echoed from somewhere on the fourth floor, drawing a panicked look from all three men.

Sam smiled.

It had worked.

He had successfully stalled for time, and now, as he got to his feet, he looked at the three men, none of whom had a weapon, clenched his fists, and hoped he could last long enough for Nash to join him.

CHAPTER TWENTY-EIGHT

Taking slow, measured steps towards the turning in the maintenance corridor, Nash approached the corner when a hand shot out, pushed the gun from his grip, and then spun him round into the wall.

It was Uri.

Dana Kovalenko's right-hand man looked furious, but then a shocked realisation set across his face as he realised who he had just accosted. It had been a few days since they had met, squirrelled away in that remote meeting place. Back then, Uri had been certain that of all the men in the room, it was Nash who was the main threat to Sam Pope. The man had a resume that would make the devil himself quake with fear, but it was the man's demeanour that had given Uri the sense of danger.

Nash was calm and collected, and even now, having been disarmed and shoved into a wall, all he had done was stretch out his arm and adjust his jacket. Considering the state of his former partner's face, and the rants of the deformed American about betrayal, Uri wasn't an idiot.

Nash was sneaking in through the back door, confirming to him what Defoe had wildly spat.

He was in cahoots with Sam Pope.

Which meant he was here to try to help the man kill his beloved Dana.

Which meant he had to die.

The corridor was narrow, with the low ceiling making it feel even more enclosed. The dim lighting ran along the wall, offering a dull glow that added to the sombre atmosphere. Both men knew the situation, and as Uri clenched and drew up his fists, Nash sighed and did the same.

'There's still time to walk away from this.' Nash offered. 'We're not here for you.'

Uri didn't say a word, allowing his actions to speak for him as he swung a meaty right hook, which Nash absorbed in the arms he threw up to protect his head. The man hit like a sledgehammer, and it wasn't often that Nash was confronted by a man of similar size. Although he may have been an inch or two taller than the Ukrainian, they were similar in weight, which meant each clubbing blow that Nash blocked still hurt like hell. After raining down a few more violent punches, Uri launched forward with a knee, which Nash deflected before driving his elbow into Uri's jaw, sending him stumbling back down the corridor. The two men stopped, and Uri dabbed at his lip, saw the blood, and smiled cruelly.

Nash pushed himself off the wall, and now, with both men in the centre of the long corridor, there was more room to manoeuvre. Uri charged forward, swinging with a left that Nash ducked, but he caught him with a follow up right. The blow rocked Nash, who then absorbed a powerful haymaker to his solid abdomen. It didn't completely wind him, but it was enough for Uri to blast him with a sickening right hook that sent him spiralling to the wall.

Nash hit the brick, and then stepped back, and like Uri

before, he dabbed at his lip, and then nodded in admiration.

Uri smiled.

This wasn't going to be quick.

With a grimace, Nash tried to stretch out his shoulder, but the collision with the wall had re-ignited the agony of the bullet wound, and as he tried to lift his fists to go again, he could only lift one.

Uri noticed, and he tutted.

'Is a shame. I would like to have killed you at full health.'

Nash half shrugged.

'Shall we get this over with?'

Uri's eyes flashed with rage at Nash's nonchalance, and he charged forward again, but Nash expertly side-stepped and drove his knee into the man's thigh, knocking his leg back. A swift left hook rocked Uri to the side and then Nash charged, their two hulking frames colliding and Uri slammed into the exposed brick wall, his head slamming against the concrete. But the man was relentless, and he pushed himself back up, a gash now dominating the side of his head, and blood oozed down his face. Nash went to lift his fists again, the pain of his shoulder causing him to falter slightly, and that was enough for Uri.

He lunged forward, ignoring the errant fist that Nash threw into his thick body, and Uri latched his meaty hand around Nash's shoulder, digging his fingers in and brutally as he could and Nash roared with anger. Uri could feel the bandages and the hole underneath, and he dug in further, trying to bury his fingers into the wound through Nash's jacket, all the while, Nash was hammering him with his free hand. After a few violent swings from Nash, Uri relinquished his hold, but the damage to Nash was done, and the American was weak on his feet.

Uri charged forward and drove his elbow into Nash,

not caring where he landed it, but knowing that the collision would take the American hitman off his feet. It worked, and Nash hit the concrete floor hard, a little cloud of dust shooting upwards on impact. He groaned.

His shoulder was done, which meant he effectively had one hand tied behind his back and was now being picked apart by a man who had been forged by the Burket for years. With one hand, Nash began to push himself back up, but Uri drove his thunderous boot down onto his spine, and then followed that up by stomping down on Nash's compromised shoulder. Nash howled in pain once more, and Uri then rolled him onto his back with his foot.

'This was unsatisfying.'

The boot was raised again, and Nash watched as it rushed towards his face, the impact would surely snap his neck or shatter his skull. In the nick of time, he rolled to the side, propped up onto one knee like an Olympic sprinter, and then burst forward like he had just heard the starting pistol. With Uri's foot planted, Nash dived into the man's stocky body, and the impact sent both of them crashing to the floor below, the air driven from Uri has he hit the stone. The fight was getting scrappy, as both men had begun to feel the devastating effects of the blows that had landed, and as Uri tried to scramble to his feet, Nash latched onto him from behind, locked his one good arm around his neck, and then fell backwards, arcing Uri's body into a crescent and then, using his expert training, he locked his legs around his body.

Uri began to struggle, feeling the air supply to his body being cut off, and as Nash wrenched harder and harder, Uri became more desperate. His wild hand eventually found the bullet wound once more, and as he gasped for life, he furiously hammered the wound through Nash's jacket.

Nash tried to ignore the pain, but on the fourth blow, his own grip loosened, and Uri wriggled free, and then caught Nash flush in the jaw with a sickening elbow. Nash rolled back, his head spinning, as Uri scrambled forward.

His eyes lit up.

Nash's discarded pistol was beside him, and he scooped it up, stood, turned and then took his shot. But as he was getting to his feet, Nash shook the cobwebs of the blow and then let his survival instinct kick in, the adrenaline pushing him to his feet just behind the Ukrainian. As Uri turned and pulled the trigger, Nash fought through the crippling pain of his shoulder to push the man's arm upwards, causing the bullet to lodge in the ceiling above, sending a trickle of crumbling stone showering onto them. As Uri pulled the trigger, Nash drew back his good arm, and then drove the palm of his hand as hard as he could into Uri's nose.

The blow was sickening.

The sound of Uri's nose being driven backwards into his own brain was unlike anything Nash had ever heard, and he was thankful that the errant gunshot had dulled his hearing.

Uri fell backwards, his eyes still open, but his life very much over.

It had been a killing blow from Nash, one that had been taught to him by the Foundation during his initiation. He took a few moments to collect himself, to push past the pain that was emanating from his shoulder and the other blows his body had absorbed. He could feel the blood pumping down his arm and his chest and with a slight wobble in his step, he stepped across Uri's dead body, retrieved his handgun, and then began limping back down the corridor towards the door, hoping against hope that Sam Pope was still alive.

The gunshot had given Sam the briefest of openings, and he had used it to blindside Defoe, who had been standing nearest to him. As Defoe turned back to Sam, it was too late, and Sam threw his entire weight behind the right hand that he struck him with. It sent the disfigured hitman crashing to the ground, and then Sam stood before Leon and his henchman. The two men had tossed their weapons away under Dana's orders, and the fear of the situation was clear on both their faces. They quickly huddled together, with Leon taking a tentative step behind the other.

'Fuckin' kill this man.' Leon demanded, and Sam watched as the man stepped forward, reaching into his pocket and pulling out a small, sharp blade. The man held it up, trying to intimidate Sam, but the tremble in his hand gave it away.

He wasn't a trained killer.

Neither was Leon.

When they ran together as the Acid Gang, the entire crew had found strength in numbers. All together, they were an intimidating prospect, and if trouble ever came looking for them, they could band together to ensure they eradicated it. But now, separated and faced with a very different kind of threat, they were crumbling. Sam had already seen it in Leon before, when he had tortured him with home made acid which had resulted in the loss of the man's arm.

If you pull apart the gang and isolate them, they were just as scared as the people they preyed on.

'Fuckin' shank him, bruv.'

Leon, who was doing his best to not make his cowering obvious, was barking the orders, and the gang member stepped towards Sam, his eyes locked on him, but lacking any sort of conviction. Put a gun in the man's hand and he would have happily pulled the trigger.

But hand to hand was different.

It was more skilled. More personal.

It required a true killer's touch, something that this man clearly didn't have.

Sam stood patiently, taking a few deep breaths to help ignore the pain of the blows he had taken to his face, and he kept his eyes on the man, who shuffled inch by inch toward him. Somewhere on the ground behind him, Defoe was beginning to stir, which meant very soon, this would become a dangerous situation for Sam to be in.

This needed to be quick.

Sam forced the issue, stepping towards the henchman who, in his panic, lunged forward and tried to slash Sam with the blade. Instinctively, Sam dropped his shoulder, dodging the attempted murder, and he grabbed the man's arm by the elbow and wrist, and twisted it. The tendons in the man's joints crunched under the pressure and the man relinquished the knife with a feeble wail of pain, and Sam caught the blade before it hit the ground.

In the blink of an eye, he obliterated the man with three swift, deep stabs to the chest, before stepping past him. Leon watched in horror as the man fell to his knees, the quick blood loss making it impossible for him to comprehend what had happened, before he collapsed onto his front, the blood pumping from his body as he twitched through the last few seconds of his life.

'Fuck this.' Leon screamed and then tried to run towards the discarded weapons on the floor a few feet away.

As he did, Sam spun the knife so he was holding the blade between his thumb and index finger, drew his arm back and then threw it. The blade spun through the air before it embedded in the side of Leon's upper thigh, causing him to drop to the floor amongst screams of agony. Leaving a smear of blood, he began to pull himself across the marble, but his missing limb made it a futile task. Sam walked across the room, each footstep growing louder as he got closer and Leon began to weep with fear.

His hand was a few inches from the gun.

He could almost reach it.

Sam's boot came down on his only hand, crunching the bones as it did and pinning him to the floor. The pain of his broken hand and the knife embedded in his leg was overpowering, and Leon howled, begging for mercy as he did. Sam calmly reached down and retrieved the gun, let it get comfortable in his grip, and then, as he stood over the man, he aimed it squarely at Leon's skull.

Leon looked up at him, tears streaming down his face.

'Please. Don't kill me.'

Sam's face was emotionless.

Cold.

He pulled the trigger.

The point-blank shot eviscerated the top of Leon's skull, snapping his head back and sending the remnants of his shooting down his own back. The earlier gunshot and the subsequent fighting had drawn Dana's attention, and she stepped into the doorway across the room and she shrieked in horror.

Sam turned, gun in hand, and he lifted it, ready to put her down and end this once and for all. Just as the gun was about to be drawn to his eye level, he felt the full weight of Defoe slam into his side, and the American continued running, using his entire body weight to take Sam off his feet and the two of them shifted about eight feet across the room until they collided with the door that lead to the stairwell.

They exploded through it, crashing onto the expensive

carpet of the landing among a litter of wooden splinters and groans of pain.

Sam had dropped his gun as they hit the door.

Shaken, both men took a few breaths, before they slowly began to get to their feet, knowing the spacious, lavishly decorated landing was where one of them would die.

CHAPTER TWENTY-NINE

After pushing through the door of the maintenance corridor, Nash came upon a stairwell. He had no way of knowing whether Sam had made it to the penthouse or not, but he needed to stick to the plan. They had gone into this building blind, not knowing how many people she had invited to the dance, how skilled they were or even if they were armed.

But judging from the gunfire he had heard echoing from the building, there was more than enough fire power to blow both him and Sam off the face of the planet.

For all he knew, Sam might already be dead, but he doubted it.

Sam Pope was a survivor.

With that in mind, Nash took the stairwell, keeping his gun up as he took the stairs two at a time. The sound of a door being thrown open stopped him in his tracks, and two floors below, he heard the sound of footsteps clattering the stairwell, with a few voices nervously shooting back and fourth.

'He killed Chris!'

'Man's got it coming.'

'Dana wants us up there now.'

'I'll call the others.'

Nash processed the information and ascertained that Sam had done what he had set out to do. He'd reduced some of their numbers and had been taken alive. If these men were still needed up at the penthouse, then it meant Sam was being the nuisance Nash had him pegged as.

Sam would have thrived in the Foundation, yet Nash knew, there was no way their ideology would ever have meshed with the man Sam was. There was an inherent need to help people, driven by a trauma that Sam never discussed, but Nash had read in the reports.

Sam was fighting back because he had nothing to fight for. He had lost his son, and grief had opened his eyes to the cruelty of the world and the imbalance between those who played it straight and those who did as they pleased. Nash knew he fit the latter category, but his own morality had drawn him to Sam. Now, he was happy to fight along-side him.

If Sam was holding up his end of the bargain, Nash felt obliged to do the same.

He was there to even the odds.

Having already taken Dana's right-hand man out of play, Nash took a step back until he was pressed against the wall at the top of the stairs. Directly in front of him, at the bottom of the next flight, was the door to the third floor, and he held the gun up with his right hand. His left arm was practically useless now, and he could feel himself weakening from the blood loss. It wasn't as constant as before, but Nash knew he was bleeding out.

Agonisingly slowly, but if he didn't get medical atten-tion within the next few hours, he'd eventually run out of runway and hit the ground.

The footsteps grew louder, and as soon as Nash saw the first henchman round the corner to the flight of stairs he was watching over, he held his nerve. He fought the initial reaction to shoot and waited a few extra seconds.

The second henchman stepped into view, just as the first saw what was coming, but by then, it was too late.

Nash pulled the trigger and sent the second man spiralling back towards the door of the third floor, before pulling the gun to his right and blowing a hole through the first henchman's forehead. With a laboured grunt, Nash stood, and then calmly walked down the stairs, stepping over the dead body of the first henchman and approached the second. Leant up against the wall with his arms flailed, the young man was gasping for air, the first bullet ripping through his chest and piercing his lung. As it began to fill up with blood, he looked up at Nash for mercy, and Nash obliged.

He lifted the gun and put a bullet through the young man's head.

Before he could make his next move, three bullets exploded through the door of the third floor, the last one grazing Nash's upper thigh and dropping him to his knee. The door flew open, and another henchman launched out, shocked at the sight of two of his running buddies lying dead. He turned to Nash in a blind rage, but before he could turn his gun on the hulking murderer, Nash pushed up from his knee, yanked the man's arm up and let him unload the bullet into the stairs above. With his other arm redundant, Nash improvised, and drove his bald head into the man's face with such a force that it shattered his teeth. Woozy, the man dropped his gun, and Nash grabbed the back of his head, spun him round and slammed him face first onto the metal hand rail.

The man went limp, before rolling down the staircase and into a crumpled heap at the bottom.

Three down.

Nash fell back onto the staircase heading back to the

penthouse, and took a seat, taking a few breaths as he tried to mentally stifle the pain he was in. His body was beat up, and he leant forward and lifted his gun from the floor, before waiting a few more moments to see if anyone else had been drawn to the gunfire.

Nothing.

With a groan of pain, Nash lifted himself to his feet, turned, and began to walk back up the stairs to the penthouse, hoping Sam had held up his end of the bargain.

———

Sam had been in fist fights to the death before, but never had he seen such murderous rage. When he had survived against the likes of Edinson in South Carolina or Farukh atop the High Rise, it had been through his sheer will to live. To keep fighting. Those men had been skilled killers, lacking in any sense of any emotion. To them, it was business, and killing Sam would have been part of their job description.

But for Defoe, this was personal.

Although Sam hadn't been the one to drag his face through the blood-soaked shards, it was because of him it had happened in the first place. Sam was just one of a few names that would pay for the disfigurement, and it showed. Defoe unloaded on Sam with an avalanche of blows, and while Sam was able to block many of them, the skilled fighter soon broke through and he caught Sam with a two punch combo that knocked him to the ground. Defoe tried to follow up with a stiff kick to the ribs, but Sam spun, caught the foot, and twisted it, sending the man to the ground. Quickly, Sam rocked the contractor with a hard right, then mounted him, raining down with a few violent strikes of his own before he felt the man's knee drive into his already aching spine.

Sam fell forward, his backbone near to breaking point, and as he stumbled to his feet, he turned to see the man holding his face in terror.

Sam's fists had opened numerous stitches, and now the very fabric of the man's face was beginning to tear at the seams. Blood began to trickle through the openings and for all the violent deaths Sam had administered in his time, he had never seen anything quite so visceral. Clearly unstable, the man let out a blood-curdling scream and then charged at Sam. But Sam place one foot back, pressed his weight down and leant forward, absorbing the incoming collision and dropping down on top of Defoe, driving him to the ground. Lying face down, Defoe hunched up and placed his hands over his head as Sam drove elbows towards the man's skull.

Desperation was kicking in.

Soon, the police would be there and the likelihood of Dana getting away was strong. Sam would be sent to prison, and he was certain she had the money and the reach to get to him there.

Sam needed to finish this now.

Without a moments hesitation, Sam abandoned his elbow strikes and thrust his hands around the side of Defoe's face, his fingers clawing at whatever parts of the peeling face he could. As soon as he latched on, he pulled as hard as he could, and as he felt the skin start to come apart, Defoe rolled back and howled in agony.

Sam let go and stood, and Defoe rolled onto his back, desperately trying to hold his face together as the blood seeped through his fingers.

It was over.

Sam stepped forward to end the fight, when a gunshot echoed.

The bullet hit Sam in the chest and he stumbled back and hit the floor.

In the broken doorway, Dana Kovalenko stood, her hands clutching Sam's previously dropped gun. She lowered it slowly, her eyes wide with pleasure. Defoe was pushing himself to his knees, his hands reaching up to clasp anything and he hit the button for the elevator. The doors opened, but he just used the metal door frame of the lift to get to his feet.

'Motherfucker.' He spat in fury.

Before the two of them could finish Sam for good, another gunshot exploded from the stairwell beyond the lift, and the bullet hit the wall beside Dana. She shrieked in terror, and then looked to the stairs where Jacob Nash leant against the wall, his left arm hanging loosely by his side and his right arm getting ready to fire again.

Terrified for her life, Dana rushed back through the broken shards that framed the door to the apartment. Defoe, still leaning against the side of the lift, peered his head round the metal and his eyes locked with Nash.

Nash stopped in his tracks.

The sight of Defoe's face, with the tears now wide and the muscle beneath exposed caught him off guard and he tried to find somewhere within him that felt pity for the man. That had felt bad for what he had done.

But he couldn't find any.

All he found, was the want to point the gun and pull the trigger.

He did, but Defoe ducked back, and the bullet hit the side of the elevator. As Nash began to climb the other stairs, Defoe dived into the lift, hit the ground floor and begged the doors to close. For a man who had prided himself on his confidence and ability, he had been caught by surprise by the sheer terror that had enveloped him when he saw Nash. The trauma of what the man had done to him hadn't just scarred his face, but his mind as well, and just as the doors were closing, Nash stepped onto the landing, and they shared one last look before they shut and Defoe descended back down the building to his escape.

Nash lowered his weapon, and then turned to Sam, who was lying at his feet.

'You hurt?' Nash asked. Sam grunted and then pushed himself up to a seated position. He pulled down the hem of his blood stained T-shirt to reveal the bullet proof vest that Nash had given to him moments before they had begun their assault on the building. The bullet Dana had fired had lodged into the Kevlar, and Sam took the hand that Nash offered and got to his feet.

'I'll live.' Sam looked at Nash. 'You look like shit.'

'Thanks. You're hardly a basket of fruit yourself.'

'That's fair.' Sam grit his teeth and stretched his chest muscle. Although the vest had saved his life, the impact had hit like a freight train and his right pectoral felt like it was on fire. 'Where is she?'

Nash pointed to the door that Sam and Defoe had obliterated. Sam nodded, then to the lift.

'And scarface?'

'He'll be in the wind by now. He's my problem.' The sound of sirens began to fill the street, and Nash turned to Sam. 'You usually work alone, right?'

'Usually…'

'Then they'll only be expecting one man, right?' Nash tucked his gun into his belt, and then extended his hand. 'Good luck, Sam.'

Realising that Nash was giving Sam a way out, he took the man's hand. While he would never condone what Nash had stood for when he had arrived, it would be hypocritical to tar him as nothing more than a killer. Sam had done questionable things for even worse people in his past, and he knew, sometimes, people could change.

'Thanks. You too.' Sam smiled. 'I hope I never see you again.'

Nash smiled, turned and then bounded down the stairs two to three at a time. It took him no time at all to get to the ground floor, and as he rushed past the remains of Sam's gun fight, he passed through the glass doors as the police cars turned onto the road. Nash leapt over the two dead bodies by the door and rushed to the abandoned car in the middle of the street. Swiftly, he hot wired it, bringing the engine to life, before he turned and raised the gun at the fast approaching police cavalcade.

He fired.

The bullet expertly hit the body of the car, so as not to cause any harm, but it was enough to let them know he was armed.

In the bright lights of the street lamps and the now pouring rain, they wouldn't be able to idenfity him. He was roughly the same size as Sam, if maybe a few inches taller, but in that split second they wouldn't know. He dropped into the seat of the Range Rover, threw it into gear and then put his foot down.

The majority of the pursuing cars would chase him, he knew that, and hopefully, the dead bodies that littered the front of the building would give Sam enough time to sneak out of the back.

As he sped to the end of the road, he smiled as he was proven right, as the cars showed no sign of slowing, and they raced after him.

Nash turned the corner, raced through the gears and sped off towards the city, ready to lead them on a merry chase.

———

Sam bent down to pick up his pistol from the floor. Dana had dropped it in her panic when Nash ambushed them, and he then stepped through the broken door and back into the penthouse. There was no time to admire the carnage he had caused, and he walked past the motionless corpses of Leon and the unnamed man he had killed earlier. He followed the path Dana had taken earlier that evening, and was impressed by the sheer size of the apartment.

He could have fit the entire flat he had lived in Hackney just in the hallway, and he took silent steps as he ventured further in. At the end of the hall, one of the doors was open, and he heard a few noises of activity. He picked up the pace and then pushed open the door further, startling Dana Kovalenko, who was rapidly packing a suit-case. The leather case was open on the double bed, with clothes stuffed sloppily inside, and she took a step back, her face pale with fear.

The last time she had seen Sam, he had hit the floor thanks to the barrel of her gun. She had thought it was over. It might not have been the revenge she had courted with such dedication, but it had been revenge all the same.

But here he was.

Her worst nightmare, risen from the dead, and with a gun in his hand.

After a few moments to let the gravity of the situation sink in, Sam took one more step into the room. Realising the final grains of sand were tumbling through her hour glass, Dana took a step forward, lifted both of her hands in surrender and tried to do what she did best.

Control the situation.

'Look, Sam, I think…'

Sam lifted the gun, squeezed the trigger and sent a bullet expertly between her eyes.

Dana's head snapped back, an explosion of blood, brain and skull painting the wardrobe behind her like a firework. Sam lowered the gun, took a deep breath and then tucked the weapon into the back of his jeans. He adjusted his jacket and then turned, marching back through the apartment and then headed to the fire escape. Nash would have bought him enough time to at least get to the ground, and after that, then Sam would have to do what he always did.

Survive.

As he pushed his way through the metal emergency door and onto the rickety fire exit, the rain lashed down, bathing him in its cooling downpour. He tilted his head up for a brief moment, enjoying the feel of the rain on his skin. As the sirens pierced the night sky with their high-pitched squeal, Sam began his descent down the steps.

Dana Kovalenko was dead.

It was over.

CHAPTER THIRTY

Defoe had been running for ten minutes straight, the terror caused by seeing the man responsible for his condition was palpable and he felt his heart beat with every step that pounded the pavement. As he rushed through the backstreets of Mayfair, heading towards anywhere but Nash, Defoe ignored the gasps of shock and the few calls for his well being by passers by.

He just had to put as much space between himself and Nash as possible.

Eventually, he rounded a corner, dashing past a quiet, cosy pub and slowed down. His chest was heaving, clawing at the wet night for air, and Defoe drew in some deep, long breaths.

He was shaking.

Not from the cold of the rain, but through shock.

Nash had broken him, and he was now aware just how bad it was. All that existed inside him was a hatred for the man, and although he knew the trauma would take some time, if Nash had survived, then there would come a time when he could have his revenge. He needed to keep that notion in his mind's eye, because if he let go of it, there was a very good chance that he would completely unravel.

With his heart rate lowering and his breathing relaxing, Defoe took a seat on one of the wooden benches that was situated outside the pub, which had its own, tiny forecourt. The rain lashed against him, slapping against the torn skin of his face and he welcomed the coldness on his wounds. He'd never admit it, but he was in agony, but there was little he could do.

Defoe reached inside his pocket and slid out his phone. He found the number he wanted through the rain drops that splattered the screen and then held it to his ear. Once the call connected, he simply said one word.

'Extraction.'

The line went dead, and he awaited his further instruction. Just as he stood, the door to the pub opened, and two young men stumbled out. Clearly drunk and in the midst of their own, unintelligible conversation, they huddled under the cover that looped over the bench Defoe was standing by and huddled together to light their cigarettes.

One of them glanced up at Defoe.

'Fucking hell, mate. You been running with scissors?'

His friend howled with laughter, and Defoe, without breaking his stare, faked a smile.

He felt his fist clench.

As the joker chuckled with his friend, he turned to late to see Defoe approaching, and the subsequent right hand shattered the man's jaw on impact. The friend, shocked and tanked up on alcohol, foolishly tried to jump in, but Defoe hit him with a quick punch to the throat, hooked his arm and then slammed him face first onto the bench, breaking the man's nose and sending a few teeth rattling to the concrete.

Their pain felt good.

Before releasing the man's arm, Defoe wrenched it

away from it's socket, disconnecting it and leaving the man crying in pain as he turned to the man who had insulted him. The man was sitting lazily, trying to gather himself as his jaw hung slack. Defoe swung his foot, catching the man in the temple and sending him sprawling. Then, as the fury of what had happened to him and the fear of Nash looming large like a spectre, Defoe began to stamp down on the man's head.

He didn't stop.

Not until the feeling of flesh and bone was replaced with concrete.

With the horrendous act of violence gone, Defoe simply turned and marched up the road, just as a few other patrons rushed out to check on the commotion and their horrified screams echoed through the night.

Defoe's phone buzzed.

'Extraction Point 3 Available. Contract terminated.'

———

For nearly thirty minutes, Nash weaved his way through the streets of London, thrilled that the traffic was practically absent compared to the day. There had been a few close moments, and a few lights he had had to run, but ultimately, he had done well to draw the majority of the police away. Eventually, he had turned down a sidestreet, immediately recognised another sharp turn into a secluded, private car park and had expertly yanked up the handbrake, spun the wheel, and guided the car through before any of the his followers had rounded the corner.

As soon as he was inline with another car, he hit the brakes and killed the car, blending in with the rest of the expensive cars that could afford to be parked in central London overnight. In the rearview mirror, he watched with relief as the police cars sped by, and then he sat up.

Had he been arrested, he'd have been handed over to the Foundation.

Calling them for support, like Defoe had done after he had left him a shredded mess the night before, wouldn't have been an option. But the second he hit the police system, the Foundation's analyst would have picked it up, sent it on to the higher-ups, and they would have made the necessary calls to have him extradited back to the States.

What awaited him wasn't good.

The Foundation, while their morals were becoming more and more blurred, maintained a strict code of honour for their assets.

They were not allowed to turn their gun on their fellow asset.

And nobody walked away from the Foundation. Not without the consent of the powers that be, and Nash knew, his actions were evidence of both.

His only hope was Callaghan.

With no response from Nash, the man had relented in sending any more messages.

Hopefully, once Nash laid out all he knew, and the things that Dana Kovalenko and her family had done, they would understand why he refused to take down Sam Pope. Nash had never had a family, nobody within the Foundation did, but even he drew the line at young girls being sold for sex.

Callaghan was a good man. He would, too.

At least, he hoped.

With the last echo of siren disappearing into the night, Nash pushed open the stolen car door and stepped out. He would be able to justify his reluctance to take Sam to Kovalenko, but there would be serious questions about the assault of Defoe. Despite Defoe firing first, Nash knew the Foundation would condone Defoe taking out a rogue agent.

They would celebrate what he did, but when they see the mark Nash left on their golden boy, they would likely be out for blood.

Defoe, if he survived the night, would be out for revenge.

Nash leant against the stone pillar of the car park and looked back at his stolen vehicle.

There was little damage done to the car, and he was sure the owner would report it stolen within the next few hours. It would be returned to him, and the owner would have no knowledge of what had happened. That one of the deadliest men walking the planet had stolen it.

But that was the world Jacob Nash existed in.

A world where he was, essentially, a ghost.

But he had left scars behind, and those would not disappear. Defoe would be a walking monument to Nash's brutality, and the Foundation would most likely want him shut down.

Out of options, Nash tapped on his phone. A few moments later, Callaghan replied.

'Extract Point 5. It's a long way back from this, son.'

Nash pocketed his phone, marched across the car park to another car and drilled his elbow through the window. The alarm chirped to life, but Nash shut it down within seconds. Moments later, he was pulling out of the garage and heading towards the extraction point. As with all mission briefs, there were multiple extraction points and the assets were required to memorise the locations.

Nash was certain Callaghan would send him to one that wasn't being monitored so he could at least return home.

Then, he'd have to face the consequences of his actions.

Like Callaghan had said, it was a long way back.

DC Saddler had never seen the office so excited. As he had arrived for work, the rumour mill was swirling that Sam Pope had laid siege to another building in London, and that ten people were found dead inside. It had harkened back to the assault from over three years ago, when Sam Pope first came to prominence and the country began to hunt him.

Younger officers were tossing theories around the open-plan office like paper aeroplanes, and Saddler tried to pull the facts from the fiction.

Ten dead.

One of them a woman.

One of them a known gang leader who Pope had previously tortured.

Pope escaped and managed to evade the police after a lengthy chase.

Saddler took his usual seat at his desk in the CID section of the office. As he adjusted the seat, stifling his anger that someone had tampered with it, he shot a woeful glance to Anderson's desk.

After yesterday's visit from Maggie Scowen regarding the Cuban corpse that was found at the train yard, Anderson put his foot in own mouth when he stated factually that man wasn't as the old lady described. DI Anne Freely, one of the keenest minds in the entire Derbyshire Constabulary pulled at the thread and eventually, Anderson crumbled.

He hadn't been feeling poorly as he had let on, rather that he had been abducted by the man and then brutally tortured. The horrific state of his legs was soon discovered, and DI Freely demanded he go to hospital for treatment. Saddler could only imagine how scared his friend must have been, and how painful of an experience it was.

Stupidly, Saddler felt guilty for not being able to help, but Anderson's drunken behaviour had made him a target.

There would of course be disciplinary repercussions for him, especially as he never reported any of it, but the circumstances of why he gave up information to a contract killer would be taken into account.

Saddler hoped he'd see his friend soon, and then he turned to his screen. Once he booted up the computer, he returned to the document he had written the day before.

It was the write-up from Maggie Scowen's interview, which Anderson had dismissed. Saddler, ever the boy scout, had ensured he had written up a full report, especially after his investigation into her claims had led him to Sam Pope himself.

The report read as such.

He had promised Sam that he'd bury it, but when he sat down to write the report, his dedication to the job had controlled his fingers. The report stated that the name Jonathan Cooper was an alias for the most wanted man in the country, and that he even had a bank card number that could be traced to the man.

Saddler understood the gravity of the situation. He was about to submit a report into the police database that would help them pinpoint Sam Pope's location the next time he used the card. It would also help them trace his steps for the last few years and possibly help capture anyone who had colluded with the man.

His finger hovered over the enter button, knowing the moment he pressed it, his life would never be the same again. He'd receive infamy as the man who managed to track him down, and that would open doors to a career he probably never thought possible.

But he was hesitating.

He had wanted to take the night to think it over. Maybe even speak to Hannah about it.

But when he had walked through the door, he was treated to his favourite meal and a beer. When he questioned why, Hannah broke the news that she was twelve weeks pregnant with their first child, nearly two years after they had started trying.

The mental quandary he had been in disappeared, and Saddler and his fiancée spoke at length about their future venture into parenthood.

They were bringing a child into a world that Saddler knew, because he saw first hand, was a dark and evil place at times.

And as he stared at the screen, the only thing he could think of, was if Sam Pope hadn't been around, more girls would have been sent to the darkest corners of Europe for a fate worse than death.

Sam Pope was a necessity.

Saddler guided the mouse to the top of the screen, clicked the delete button, and figured he'd write a new report, one that didn't mention anything other than a sweet old lady who had made a mistake.

As far as he was concerned, the country needed Sam Pope.

Someone had to fight the good fight.

EPILOGUE

It had been an exhausting few days, and Maggie hadn't felt like opening the café that morning. But out of habit, she did, and it didn't take long for a few young tradesmen to step through the door, their spirits high and the banter flowing.

As always, she joined in, and within a few hours of the working day starting, she was happy her old habits refused to die.

The last thing she wanted was to spend the day thinking about the mayhem that had happened, potentially because she spoke to the wrong person.

People were dying.

There had been reports on the news website that morning of even more carnage in London, with Sam Pope, apparently killing ten more people.

Had it been her fault?

It was guilt that she was placing on herself, and she had tried to do the right thing by going to the police, but they hadn't taken her seriously. One of them had been more than polite, but she held little hope for any further information.

After the lunch rush, the usual afternoon lull kicked in, and Maggie found herself leaning over the counter, her head buried in a half completed sudoku, when the door opened.

She didn't look up but she offered her happiest voice.

'With you in a second, love.'

'Take your time.'

She lifted her head as soon as she recognised the voice. The man she knew as John Cooper was stood in the centre of the café, a smile across his face. She dropped her pen and stood, then marched around the counter to him. His face was a blanket of cuts and bruises.

He looked like he had been to hell, and walked back in open sandals.

'Look at you,' she said with concern. 'Are you okay?'

'I'm fine.'

'John, I am so sorry…'

'Please.' Sam shrugged. 'Just call me Sam.'

'Okay, Sam. I am so sorry. A gentleman came in saying that he was your old army buddy. I mean, I was suspicious, but you were so secretive about things and…'

'Mama, it's fine.' Sam took her hands and held them tight. 'I'm alive, aren't I?'

'He isn't is he?' She searched Sam's beaten face for any hint of empathy. There wasn't any. 'Well, it's a dangerous world out there, isn't it?'

'You're telling me.' Sam squeezed her hands and then let them go.

'What can I get ya?' Maggie asked, her chipper mood returning.

'Oh, I can't stay.' Sam shook his head. 'I've left too much of a footprint here. Besides, I promised a good detective that I'd take my fight away from here.'

'Well, let me fix you a sandwich for the road.' Maggie said, trying not to dwell on the sadness of him leaving. She was fond of Sam, but she understood. After two minutes, she returned with a white, paper bag. Inside were two ham sandwiches, a packet of crisps and a bottle of water.

'Thank you.' Sam smiled. 'For everything.'

'It's been a pleasure.' Maggie threw her arms around Sam, and pulled him down towards her. He winced, his back still feeling the effects of his second-storey swan dive, but he fought through it. Genuine affection was rare in his world, and he squeezed her back. As she hugged him tightly, Sam slid an envelope from his pocket and tossed it gently onto the counter. He finally pulled away from Maggie, who wiped away a tear of embarrassment.

'Take care, Mama.'

'You be careful, you hear me? The world needs people like you, Sam. Good people.'

Sam opened the door, offered her one final smile and then stepped out onto the street. Mama would find the envelope, read the note and then find the five thousand pounds. His note said it was to cover any damages that he had caused, but in truth, it was to thank her for looking after him.

Just like she said, the world needed people like her.

Good people.

Sam stuffed his hands into his pockets, looked up to the surprisingly clear sky, and walked down the street, knowing he was doing his level best to be one, too. Knowing that there the fight would continue, he decided he'd enjoy the walk, before he headed off to wherever he was needed, ready to keep fighting.

Someone had to keep everyone safe.

That's what he had told his son, and Sam was determined to keep his word.

GET EXCLUSIVE ROBERT ENRIGHT MATERIAL

Hey there,

I really hope you enjoyed the book and hopefully, you will want to continue following Sam Pope's war on crime. If so, then why not sign up to my reader group? I send out regular updates, polls and special offers as well as some cool free stuff. Sound good?

Well, if you do sign up to the reader group I'll send you **FREE** copies of **THE RIGHT REASON** and **RAIN-FALL**, two thrilling Sam Pope prequel novellas. (**RRP:** 1.99)

You can get your **FREE** books by signing up at www.robertenright.co.uk

SAM POPE NOVELS

For more information about the Sam Pope series, please visit:

www.robertenright.co.uk

ABOUT THE AUTHOR

Robert lives in Buckinghamshire with his family, writing books and dreaming of getting a dog.

For more information:
www.robertenright.co.uk
robert@robertenright.co.uk

You can also connect with Robert on Social Media:

facebook.com/robenrightauthor

twitter.com/REnright_Author

instagram.com/robenrightauthor

Cover by The Cover Collection

Edited by Emma Mitchell

Proof Read by Martin Buck

Milton Keynes UK
Ingram Content Group UK Ltd.
UKHW041305181124
2926UKWH00008B/24

9 781838 074081